Praise

MW01254637

Tim Norbeck's masterful storytelling, with non-stop twists and turns and heart-pounding episodes of good versus evil, makes *No Time for Mercy* impossible to put down.

Bill Simpson | Retired President & CEO,
Hershey Entertainment and Resorts Company,
and author of *Pivot Point*

Gripping and fast-moving, *No Time for Mercy* highlights a man's conflict between remorse and his pursuit for justice. Set in southwest Florida, the score is settled for victims where the justice system fails.

James Vaules | Retired Special Agent, FBI

Rugged Bart Steele creates his own brand of frontier justice in this captivating page-turner. This is a morality play with a crisp plot, colorful characters and plenty of (deadly) action.

Clark Bell | Veteran journalist, educator and foundation executive

After starting *No Time for Mercy,* I could not stop reading until I finished it. Tim Norbeck has an easy and engaging writing style. His inclusion of interesting bits of history and trivia enhanced the depth of the novel. This is an "I can't put it down" novel.

Robert Oswald | Retired Chairman and CEO of Bosch NA

NO TIME FOR MERCY

TIM NORBECK

Copyright © 2022 by Tim Norbeck

All rights reserved. No part of this publication may be reproduced, distributed, or transmitted in any form or by any means, including photocopying, recording, or other electronic or mechanical methods without the prior written permission of the publisher, except in the case of brief quotations embodied in critical reviews and certain other noncommercial uses permitted by copyright law. For permission requests, write to the publisher at info@whynotbooks.com.

Published by Why Not Books

Paperback ISBN: 978-1-7367266-2-4
E-book ISBN: 978-1-7367266-3-1

Cover and interior design by Tessa Avila
Author photo by Megan DePiero Photography

This is a work of fiction. Names, characters, businesses, places, events, locales, and incidents are either the products of the author's imagination or used in a fictitious manner. Any resemblance to actual persons, living or dead, or actual events is purely coincidental.

Also by Tim Norbeck

Two Minutes
Almost Heaven

To my Aunt Liz

CHAPTER 1

■ How many ten-year-old kids could claim that they killed a grown man? Bart Steele could. And he didn't even use a knife or a gun. But that happened many years before and is a story for another time.

Today, he was sitting glumly in a courtroom with an aching heart while vainly attempting to contain the rage rising within him. The inclement weather outside matched his mood—dark, somber, and foreboding. It had rained earlier, but the Fort Myers sky still looked ominous.

It was late September 2004, and the four-week-long trial had reduced a once robust and energetic man with smiling eyes, a cheerful nature, and sunny disposition into a glowering, sullen, and now almost morose persona. As the large courtroom filled with curious spectators, he sat there ramrod straight, brooding silently. Sallow-faced and with puffy eyes, and more than just a hint of Crown Royal on his breath, Bart Steele was almost a broken man. Then as the judge appeared, the courtroom stirred uneasily as everyone present sensed that the verdict was imminent. Those with skin in the game looked anxiously at the jury. No one had more skin in the game, save the defendant, than Bart. He had lost his beloved daughter Stephanie to this monster, Darrell Martin, who was

1

accused of raping and murdering her. Bart sat rigidly in his seat, his arms and legs nervously fidgeting, as the defendant stood up to hear his fate. Bracing himself for the worst, Bart still held out some hope for a conviction. Beads of sweat broke out on his forehead, and his heart began pounding ferociously.

Judge Patricia Scanlon, seated high on her perch, fixed her attention on the jury foreman. "Has the jury reached a unanimous verdict?" she asked.

"Yes, we have, your honor," foreman Thomas Peters, a balding and bespectacled fifty-something answered. "We find the defendant, Darrell Martin, not guilty."

The defendant might just as well have bludgeoned the aggrieved father as he likely did Stephanie Steele. Gasps of surprise and shock enveloped the scene, and Judge Scanlon quickly banged her gavel down. But to no avail. Martin, not looking at all like he did when he was arrested, signaled his approval with a cavernous smile and a hug for his lawyers. He was going to walk out of the courthouse scot-free, and there was nothing anyone could do about it. There would be no justice on this day for Stephanie Steele.

When Darrell Martin had been arrested and charged with her murder, the accused tall, slender man looked like a bushman with his heavy beard and straggly long hair. Throw in his menacing coal black eyes, and he could have passed as Charles Manson's brother. But, of course, his lawyers changed all that. Here he was in the courtroom now looking like a choirboy in his navy-blue suit, white shirt and tie, and no facial hair. His look of depravity had disappeared, which no doubt had helped to influence the jury.

As the courtroom buzzed with the fervor of a murder trial verdict, Bart sank down in his seat in utter despair and disbelief. But his personal agony and discomfort, as painful and bitter as he had ever experienced before, were about to get much worse.

Bart and Darrell Martin had never made eye contact prior to the trial but looked at each other once when the aggrieved father briefly testified. It was obvious that Darrell's lawyers would not permit their client to take the stand. As the defendant danced his victorious jig after thanking his lawyers, he spotted the dejected father still slumped over in his seat and winked at him. Bart went ballistic. Suddenly his energy was back, and he charged toward his adversary with mayhem on his mind. Out of nowhere a burly law enforcement officer stepped between them, almost as if he had expected the distraught father to make such a move. "I know how you must feel, Mr. Steele. But you can't do it this way." The officer was clearly trying to assuage him while holding him back. The officer did him two favors. One was to save him from an assault charge and the other was to give him an idea.

CHAPTER 2

■ Nightfall came early in Fort Myers that evening. The dark clouds took over the horizon, and a steady rain began to fall. Bart settled down on his couch, exhausted from the trying day, with two fingers of Crown Royal. He sat there in the semi-darkness. He had never been known as a heavy drinker—not even in his college days. That had all changed when his wife, Ginny, died. Stephanie was more of a help to him than he was to her when it came to dealing with the aftermath of her mother's tragic death. Bart started with beer and eventually graduated to drinking at least a couple Crown Royals every night. With Stephanie's urging, he had tapered his habit back to only one drink a night. But now with her gone, there was no one left to intercede. Mourning her loss only added to the problem, and he resumed his prior practice. There was nothing to be upbeat about. He had lost his daughter in the worst way possible. And the bastard had walked free—with impunity, a swagger, and even with that insulting wink. Adding another inch to his drink, Bart pondered over the court officer's words: "You can't do it this way." Adding to his angst was a secret that he didn't want to share with any of his friends. He thought about his spouse of twenty-five years every single day since she had died so tragically on that misty morning fifteen years before.

Virginia, or Ginny, as he called her, was the perfect wife. Now his darling daughter is gone as well. So, one more Crown Royal won't hurt, he rationalized, while pouring another two inches of the golden nectar. This time he added a few ice cubes. Again, his thoughts went back to the officer who had restrained him in the courtroom. *Was he suggesting that I might want to kill the bastard who murdered my daughter, but that I shouldn't simply assault him...at least not on his watch?*

The very thought of him being an executioner resonated. *Why not*, he asked himself. *If not me, who?* He knew the answer to that one. No one. Darrell Martin would probably disappear, and Stephanie's life would never be avenged. At this point, what would he have to lose? He would soon find out the answer to that question.

CHAPTER 3

■ The trial of Stephanie's murderer had been a difficult one for the prosecutor, Silvia Stone, right from the get-go. There was circumstantial evidence, in fact plenty of it, but nothing specific to tie Darrell Martin to the crime. The hardware store's surveillance tape captured him purchasing a few items that were similar to those used in the brutal murder—black duct tape, a shovel, and garbage bags. But they couldn't be tied definitively to those at the crime scene. There had also been small traces of semen in Stephanie's body, but unfortunately, they, too, were inconclusive. It could be Darrell's, but according to the test sample, it statistically could belong to numerous others. And then there was the matter of an eyewitness of sorts. A neighbor of Stephanie's who lived down the hall from her saw a man matching Darrell's general description talking to her from his car the night of her disappearance. The problem was that the witness was in her eighties with very questionable vision. It was a little after dusk, she said, and she thought the man was driving a rather old, dark green car. In fact, Darrell owned a 1987 black Ford Taurus. But the witness had been right about it being old, as her sighting was just two years before the trial. The only reason that Darrell Martin was arrested in the first place was that he had allegedly bragged to his cellmate that he had killed a woman. On the stand during the trial, Darrell's lawyers made the cellmate look like the conniving and lying witness that he was. Mike "the Hammer" Hudson had served time for armed robbery, assault with a deadly weapon, and lesser charges that had first brought him into contact with the defendant. He just wasn't credible, was a poor witness, and probably should never have testified in the first place. Compounding the difficulties for the prosecution was the time period that elapsed between the crime itself and the discovery of Stephanie's nude body, which was partially buried in a vacant lot. Five days tend to compromise a murder scene, and it was difficult for the medical examiner, Russell Corso, to pinpoint the exact time of death.

CHAPTER 4

■ Stephanie Steele had been very close to her father, especially since her mother's death some fifteen years earlier.
At that time, with no siblings to lean on and nary a relative
within a thousand miles, her dad was her rock. In fact, she
attended a local college to be near him. She was majoring in
history and preparing for a teaching career at a high school in
the Fort Myers area.

Since her mother's death, Stephanie and her dad spent an
inordinate amount of time together. Each thought such time
was helping the other, when truthfully, both of them needed
the closeness. In addition to talking and reminiscing about
Ginny, they talked for hours about history, traveled to Boston
and even Mount Rushmore in South Dakota together. Bart
and Stephanie also visited practically every museum in New
York City. She particularly loved the Statue of Liberty and the
Empire State Building. But their most memorable trip together
was the time spent in Washington, D.C., taking in all the sights.
It was within six months of Ginny's death, and both were still
in the recovery phase of that tragedy. They spent two nights at
the Mayflower Hotel, which was an adventure in and of itself
with the venue steeped in its own history. Bart thought that
Stephanie would find it interesting, and they took in a docent's

tour of the hotel's property. The trip had also been planned around Stephanie's eighteenth birthday, which fell on October 7. They visited Arlington National Cemetery, which neither had realized stood on the grounds that had once been owned by General Robert E. Lee's family. Stephanie was eager to see JFK's eternal flame before the two headed for the Smithsonian. Her favorite sight there were the actual ruby-red slippers that Judy Garland had worn while playing Dorothy in the 1939 classic movie, "The Wizard of Oz." The trip had served two important purposes, just as Bart had hoped it would. Their bond, always valued anyway, was strengthened. Arguably as important was the need for them to laugh and enjoy themselves, something that had escaped them since Ginny's death. Both of those objectives were accomplished, and they had flown home feeling better about things.

According to her students, Stephanie was a wonderful and engaging teacher who made United States and world history come alive for them. She had a knack for teaching and a love for it as well. As a result, she was one of the most popular and respected teachers in the entire school. Some of that zeal probably came from Bart, who loved history and the joy of their many trips to historical sites. At age thirty-three, Stephanie had a good life, and she had planned to marry a businessman the following summer. Then suddenly, all the hopes and dreams were dashed, and she was dead—just like her mother. Bart would never forget the sight of Stephanie's lifeless body and began to have bad dreams about why he couldn't have saved her. Consciously, he knew that such a thing was impossible, but his subconscious sleep state didn't seem to appreciate that obvious fact. Bart was clearly a "justice" guy, but he didn't wear it on his sleeve. At least until it all hit home for him. His precious daughter was dead, and the man he held responsible for it wasn't. Her death changed him. Losing a loved one to a murder was different and more difficult than Ginny's death from brain cancer. He had never been an angry man, but he became one after Stephanie's death. The transformation was a dramatic one. He no longer saw issues as grey; they were now either black or white. No more turning the other cheek for Bart Steele. *No parent should ever have to go through this,* he murmured on numerous occasions. There definitely was a pre-Stephanie murder version of Bart and a post one. The post edition would include a dark side that had never manifested itself before her death.

CHAPTER 5

■ Virginia Douglas Steele had been born and raised in Rochester, New York, and graduated from Smith College in Northampton, Massachusetts. An excellent student, she went on to a teaching career that culminated in her desire to become a high school principal. She was a brave and stoic patient who lived almost two years after the diagnosis of a rare brain cancer called GBM—Glioblastoma Multiforma. Such a cancer was a virtual death sentence, and she suffered through surgery, radiation, chemotherapy, and other treatments for a full year and nine months. Ginny had been a very healthy forty-seven-year-old right up until she wasn't. Ginny had experienced headaches and nausea for about two weeks prior to her diagnosis but passed these symptoms off as a mere manifestation of stress. If only that had been true. But, when she fell one night at home and another time needed to have assistance to get off the couch, both her husband and daughter stepped in to insist that she see her physician. A slur in her speech also pointed to something that was out of sorts. Sensing more than a minor problem, Dr. Stephens recommended a neurologist to Ginny. Three days later, after conducting some rudimentary tests, Dr. Hamilton Gurney told Bart and Ginny that he suspected that something was going on in Ginny's brain and that an MRI would be certain to shed more light on it. Within another week, the results of the MRI were available, and the news could not have been worse. Sensing their anguish and abject despair, Dr. Gurney tried to assuage them by mentioning the types of treatments available; he recommended going forward with them. But Bart wasn't buying it.

"What are her prospects for beating this?"

"Well, I won't sugarcoat it for you."

"We don't want you to, Dr. Gurney," interjected a crest-fallen Ginny as she sank lower into her chair.

The neurologist knew from experience there were few positive things he could offer them, but he did his best to hold out some hope.

"There are treatments available, and medicine has made progress in dealing with GBM."

"Like what?" The distraught husband hung onto the hollow words.

Dr. Gurney measured his words and attempted to respond while weighing each word carefully. "The usual treatment is to excise the cancerous tumor, followed by radiation and then chemotherapy. This will take place over several months, and we'll be measuring the progress during that time."

His very resolute and brave but frightened new patient remained slumped in her chair while fighting back the tears. "Doctor, what is my prognosis?"

It was clearly a question he didn't want to answer. "Mr. and Mrs. Steele," he replied as he sat fidgeting with his glasses, obviously uncomfortable. "This is a very difficult disease to control." His countenance grew grimmer with each word.

"How difficult, Doc?"

"I'm afraid that this is the deadliest form of brain cancer, and it is most likely incurable. But with medical advances every day, we will try."

Ginny Steele tried to be stoic upon hearing those words, but her body started shaking, and tears now streamed steadily down her face. Her husband took a deep breath.

"We're going to fight this honey," he declared while holding on tightly to her hand. He tried to convince himself, too, that they would overcome this battle.

The trip home from the doctor's office was somber and silent. One year, nine months and four days, many treatments, very sick days and nights, many tears and much frustration, assertions of love and tenderness later, it was all over. The brave Ginny succumbed to the insidious disease with her husband and daughter by her bedside. Glioblastoma had claimed another innocent victim. Ginny had beaten the odds despite the tragic ending. Only thirty-seven percent survive GBM the first year, and only five percent make it through a second. Dr. Gurney had told them that men are sixty percent more likely to get the disease than women, but that women tend to respond to treatments better than their male coun-terparts. Ginny was just one of those two hundred thousand diagnosed each year. Losing her mother during Stephanie's senior year of high school was devastating, but it was beyond that for Ginny's grieving husband. He couldn't bear the thought of losing his best friend, as he helped his dying wife through that gruesome period. Bart knew that he had to soldier on for his daughter, but it hurt so much. His loving wife was everything to him. They had done practically everything together and shared the same interests. Both enjoyed reading, tennis, dining out with friends, and hanging out at the beach. She was his alter ego, and he was hers.

CHAPTER 6

■ Several weeks had passed since Darrell Martin's acquittal. Bart woke up in a daze one morning. What was an almost full bottle of Crown Royal the prior evening was now reduced to just a few inches. "Hungover" didn't quite describe his condition. Bart was angry and depressed, and he felt like hell. Barely able to get to the bathroom on time, he vomited in steady heaves while sweating profusely. In the past few weeks, he had lost about twelve pounds, attributing the change to his grieving and a poor diet. He had previously been proud of his cast-iron stomach, but now he had been experiencing abdominal pain and had thrown up several times over the past ten days. His back hurt like hell, and he was somewhat lethargic and easily fatigued, but he ascribed it to working out too hard in the gym—another way to clear his head and assuage his grief. Later that afternoon, Bart made his way to an appointment with a gastroenterologist who had been recommended by his family physician. A CT scan and MRI were scheduled, and the requisite bloodwork was performed. Bart Steele stood six feet three inches tall and weighed in at two hundred pounds. He worked out at the gym nearly every night. Why should such a specimen have to be concerned about a few aches and pains? But the mirror didn't lie. Unshaven and with bloodshot eyes, the image reflected back to him was not pretty. His back tightened a bit while he hunched over the sink to shave. Hot showers seemed to revive him, and he bent over, allowing the shower head to direct its magic beads on the sore area on his lower back. He turned up the water temperature, and the relief was almost immediate. Bart was confident that the follow-up visit to Dr. Caldwell's office would be a waste of both of their time.

A breakfast of Grape Nuts, toast, and coffee had made a new man out of him. Most men in Southwest Florida wore shorts—at least to the store or to one's doctor. Not Bart Steele. Almost always, he elected to wear long pants, even with temperatures hovering in the eighty-plus degree range. He thought it was a better look. Khaki trousers with a sharp crease and a baby-blue golf shirt completed the pretty good look for the old Marine.

It took Bart only twenty minutes to reach the doctor's office on the second floor of a new medical building. He had been lucky enough to get both scans and lab work in the same building the previous week. That was one of the nice things about Southwest Florida, he thought—one-stop shopping. Seeking medical attention usually didn't require going to a number of different locations.

"Good afternoon, Mr. Steele. Please fill out these forms and sign them at the bottom, where it is highlighted. If you have your insurance card, I will make a copy and get it right back to you." The receptionist was organized and very pleasant. Bart returned his completed forms to her and then sat in the waiting area. As in most doctors' offices, he thought, there was never a current magazine to bide the time. A nurse finally opened the door and announced his name. Never the worrier, he felt confident as he strode into Dr. Caldwell's office. The gastroenterologist stood up behind his desk and walked over to the door to greet his patient with a handshake.

"Hi, Doc." They made small talk for a few minutes about the weather and golf, and then they got down to business. Dr. Caldwell looked grim, something Bart picked up on right away.

"Mr. Steele, I'm afraid that the news isn't good." Hearing that, Bart sat ramrod straight in his chair and leaned forward.

"The test results show evidence of non–Hodgkin's lymphoma."

There had been two catastrophic events in Bart Steele's life in the past fifteen years, and now he had received news of a crushing third. *I've been through this movie before,* he lamented to himself. He almost didn't care, since he had already lost the two most important people in his life. His mind immediately thought of a Shakespeare line from "Hamlet": "When sorrows come, they come not in single spies, but in battalions." *How true,* he thought.

"How much time do I have, Doc?"

"This isn't necessarily a death sentence, Mr. Steele. With

treatment, eighty percent of patients survive for at least a year, and sixty-five percent live for five years or more." "That's somewhat encouraging," Bart replied, "but how long if I don't bother with the treatment?"

"Hard to say, Mr. Steele, but I strongly advise you begin chemotherapy right away. Without it, the prognosis is not as good. You see, lymphoma is a cancer that begins in infection-fighting cells of the immune system. These cells are in the lymph nodes, spleen, bone marrow, and other parts of your body. Without treatment, you are really rolling the dice here. You are Stage 2 or 3, and to ignore treatment risks that the lymphoma will spread further to your liver and lungs."

"It just snuck up on me, Doc. Should I have noticed something?"

"No, Mr. Steele, that is one of the most difficult mysteries about lymphoma cancer. The early stages are relatively symptom-free, or at least they are mild. You don't know it until you've had it for a while. That's why most cases are diagnosed at a bit later stage, like yours."

"Doc, how many good months do I have? I don't mean the months when I'm flat on my ass."

"Hard to say, Mr. Steele, but with treatment, you'll have a much better prognosis. We'll work with you and set you up with an oncologist to get your treatment started right away." "Thanks, Doc. I'll get back to you when I've digested all of this."

Bart felt lonelier than he ever had as he pulled into his driveway. His previous nadir had been reached after Stephanie's funeral. It couldn't get any worse, he had thought at the time, but it did. *Why should I even bother with any treatment,* he wondered. *I have nothing to live for.* His self-pity was evident as he poured four ounces of Crown Royal over ice. And then he remembered something. "You can't do it this way, Mr. Steele."

"Yes," he exclaimed to the empty walls in his condo. "I can kill the son-of-a-bitch who murdered my daughter." Maybe he did have something to live for after all.

CHAPTER 7

■ There were seven Martins listed in the Fort Myers phonebook. Through the process of elimination, Bart was able to establish Darrell lived at one of the addresses. Bart merely dialed and asked for Darrell by name, hitting the jackpot on his fourth call. Luckily for him, Darrell wasn't at home, and Bart left a phony message with Darrell's mother.

The apartment building was easy to find, but what Bart really hoped for was that the lowlife frequented a bar or tavern. If he did, after a couple of drinks, he would be vulnerable to an attack. There was a bar called the Naked Lady not far from Darrell's building. Bart was sure that his target wouldn't recognize him, but he had grown a mustache in the previous weeks just to be certain. He was equally sure that he would never forget his prey's coal black and evil eyes.

Three nights after his appointment with Dr. Caldwell, Bart drove fifteen minutes to the Naked Lady. It was about eight-thirty on a dark, warm evening. There was a lot of clatter as he walked into the bar, with more than a few patrons looking to get lucky that night. Wearing a Red Sox cap, Bart sauntered up to the only vacant bar stool and sat down. "Red Sox fan, eh?" remarked the seventy-something gentleman seated to his left. In his present ugly mood, Bart was tempted to respond like a smart ass and sarcastically say, "How did you know?" But he resisted that impulse and was glad he did because his seatmate wore a friendly smile and was just trying to make conversation. The man wore a Cubs hat over his thinning grey hair, and he appeared to be a long-time smoker; deep lines were etched in his face—especially in his cheeks and around his pale blue eyes, which gave the habit away.

"I like 'em, but I'm not a big fan."

"Me neither. Curt Flood did the right thing by opening the doors to free agency, but I think it killed baseball for a lot of fans." The old man knew his stuff.

Bart didn't want to get into a long conversation, so he just nodded his head in agreement.

"Charlie Miller here," the man said, sticking out his hand. Bart had to think for a moment. "Doug Parker," he lied as he clasped the outstretched hand.

"Any relation to Andy Parker?"

"Naw."

"Didn't think so."

"You a regular here?" Charlie Miller's new friend asked.

"Yeah, how'd you know?

"Didn't."

"I come in about four times a week to get away from the wife. How 'bout you?'

"First time for me, but I like the ambiance."

"Yeah, people don't bother you. Let me buy you a beer."

"You're the regular," Bart argued, "let me buy you one." After two beers with his new-found friend, it was nine-forty and time to go home. Against his better judgment, Bart reached into his pocket and produced a photograph from the newspaper.

"Ever see this guy in here?"

"Yeah, as a matter of fact, I have. Isn't he the guy who killed that woman? I think his name is Darrell Martin."

Bart played dumb and replied that he thought so, too.

"Why did you save that clipping? Are you looking for him?"

"Not really, but he owes a friend of mine some money, and I just thought I would ask."

"Well, I haven't seen him in a week or so, but he usually comes in on the weekends. Hangs out with a couple of young toughs, if you know what I mean."

"Sure do, Charlie. Hey, it's been nice to talk with you. Hope to see you again."

"Thanks, Doug, no doubt I will. I'm here four nights a week."

Bart slipped off his bar stool and extended his hand to his new acquaintance. After a step, he turned back to him.

"Do me a favor, Charlie, and please don't mention to Darrell or anyone that some guy was asking about him. Hate to see him run off without paying his debt," he added with a smile.

"I don't even know the guy, Doug, and I really don't like the looks of his friends."

"See you soon, I hope. Enjoyed the conversation."

"Me too."

Perhaps it might not be as difficult as I thought, Bart murmured as he exited the bar. He admonished himself for producing the photo of Darrell so quickly. It was important not to sound or appear too eager, but he also knew that he had found a friend who might help him in his search. Of course, Charlie would never know of his real interest in Darrell Martin.

Never a good sleeper, the events of that night made it even more difficult for Bart to settle. He couldn't help but to relive Stephanie's murder but also knew that he had found an informer of sorts. Finally, Bart drifted off in the middle of thinking about different scenarios about how Darrell would die. Imagining how the scoundrel would take his last breath kept him going, but it didn't help him sleep.

CHAPTER 8

■ Over the next two weeks, Bart frequented the Naked Lady four times. Not once did he see his friend Charlie. His eyes scanned the large room each time. There was also no trace of Darrell. It was Tuesday night of the third week when he tried again. Sure enough, there was Charlie sitting on the same bar stool he was on when they first met almost three weeks before. The fellow sitting next to him had no problem moving over a seat. Charlie seemed glad to see him. He still wore that worn and frayed Cubs hat. They exchanged greetings.

"I saw him the other day," Charlie offered spontaneously within a few minutes.

"Saw who?" Bart aka Doug slyly replied.

"That guy who murdered the woman, Darrell Martin."

"Oh, yeah, that one." He feigned a lack of interest in his response.

"Does he still owe your buddy some money?"

"Far as I know."

"I'll bet he'll be here on Saturday," Charlie opined.

"I just might just stop by if I'm in the neighborhood," Bart responded casually.

"I think that dude hangs out with some bad people."

"Think so?" Bart asked.

"Yeah, he was here with those guys I told you about before. Can't help thinkin' they are up to no good. They are loud, crude, and curse a blue streak. The punks had no regard for anyone else, and they were very nasty to the waitresses."

"Well, even being a suspect in a murder case says something about you," Bart acidly replied. They shared a few beers and talked about the growth of the population and traffic in Fort Myers.

"Going to be here Saturday, Doug?" *Thanks for reminding me what my phony name is,* Bart thought to himself. "Yeah, Charlie, I just might make it."

"Great, see you then."

Bart slid off his stool first and headed for the door. There was no "just might make it" on Saturday. The avenger would definitely be there.

At home that night, he poured himself a good two inches of Crown Royal and dropped a few ice cubes into his favorite glass. At least he was getting closer. There was a dark alley adjacent to the Naked Lady that just might come in handy. He had it all planned. Now, all he needed was a vulnerable victim, preferably without his friends. Hopefully the day of reckoning would come on Saturday. Little did Darrell Martin know his future was short. Possibly only a few days.

CHAPTER 9

■ The next afternoon Bart stopped into a local hamburger joint for lunch. No sooner was he chomping into his burger when he heard a disturbance from two booths away. A very big man in his twenties, probably about six feet four inches tall and at least two hundred and eighty pounds seemed to be harassing a young couple sitting nearby. Apparently, the disagreement started because the couple complained the big lug was constantly banging the back of the man's seat. Things were getting ugly, and the huge lout was threatening the guy, who was probably no more than five feet eight and a hundred and forty pounds. It was a mismatch if Bart ever saw one. When the big man sat down next to the girl despite the couple's protests, an angry Bart decided to enter the fray. He stood up, walked over to the booth, and fixed his eyes intently on the bully.

"Don't you think you should pick on someone your own size and leave these people alone?"

"Like you, Grandpa?"

"Yeah, like me."

By then, the manager of the restaurant had been summoned by other customers, and he stood by looking perplexed and frightened. The big man rose from his seat next to the frightened young woman.

"You don't want to mess with me! Grandpa, isn't it time to take your pills?"

"I'll tell you what," Bart said. "Just apologize to this nice young couple, and I'll let it go this time."

Infuriated, the barrel-chested bruiser stood face-to-face with him, so close that Bart could smell the stale tobacco on the man's breath.

"You better stop running your mouth off, you little pissant, or I will wipe up the floor with you!"

Bart fearlessly stood toe-to-toe with his adversary. "I don't start fights, but I do finish them."

Not at all happy with that exchange, the big man pushed Bart back with a thrust of his hand. Bart had expected that move and had positioned his bent right leg a foot back from his left to cushion the blow. Suddenly, Bart also lashed out, fingers extended on his right hand, landing them solidly on the brute's throat. As the victim threw his hands up in defense, Bart stepped forward and followed that move with a vicious karate chop to the bridge of the bully's nose. Sensing his disabled opponent couldn't see or breathe, Bart sent a thunderous right hook into the man's jaw. As the brute staggered back almost unconscious, the sixty-two-year-old former Marine administered the coup-de-grace. Taking the choking man's head in both hands, he pulled it down while simultaneously driving his right knee up quickly. The result was a broken nose, lost teeth, and probably a broken jaw as well. Flat on his back and unconscious, blood poured out of the stranger's mouth and nose. Clearly, it was not Bart's first rodeo. No one in the restaurant could believe what they had just witnessed. Goliath had been taken down in an instant. Bart was no David, but he was considerably smaller than the arrogant bully, who lay in a bloody unconscious heap, his once white T-shirt splattered with his own blood, oozing all the way down to his dirty blue jeans. The young couple, other patrons, and the manager stood there, transfixed, as if in a trance. Everything had happened so fast.

"This should cover the damage," Bart said as he slapped a fifty-dollar bill on the counter in front of the manager.

"Who are you, Mister?"

Ignoring the manager's question, Bart responded, "I suggest you call the police and an ambulance. And then he left with his chest puffed up just a little bit more than when he'd entered. Fighting was never his favorite thing; if there was no way out of one with honor, however, that was different. Then, Bart was all in.

Back at home, he sat down and poured himself a drink. Still a little rattled, his favorite, amber-colored magic juice helped to settle him. Bart smiled at the thought of the huge brute waking up in the hospital with a smashed-in face wondering what truck had run over him. As he drifted off, Bart reminisced about his childhood—friendlier days.

He remembered them fondly, hardscrabble as they were. For some reason, the memories all flooded back as he was trying to fall asleep. Back then, kids played real sports. They were ten or eleven years old when he and Bob, Larry, and Jonathan trudged off to Lincoln Parkway in Buffalo to play some touch football. The parkway was mostly grass but contained some dirt areas with small pebbles. Hitting the ground often resulted in skinned knees and elbows. Soon, some of the touches were too hard, and the game evolved into tackle. They had no helmets or padding, just an old football. There were no prizes for participating. Some other kids often joined them on those Saturday mornings, and, sometimes, things got out of hand. Too tough a tackle usually resulted in a fist fight, but they were all friends in the end. Bloody knees and noses didn't matter. They played until dinner time. Somehow, there were no serious injuries. Bart discovered early that he liked the contact—the harder the better. He seemed to thrive on it more than the other boys. If he carried the ball, he liked to run over people even if he had a clear shot at the makeshift goal lines—usually a couple of sticks. Once the kids all got to know Bart, very few of them were willing to challenge him to fight. Those were the good old days.

Back in those days, the late forties and early fifties, some of the kids would occasionally go on a Friday night hayride.

Sometimes, the girls would join the boys, but Bart was very shy at fourteen and fifteen. One October night in the crispy air, the hayride was stopped by what appeared to be some tough gang members at least a year or two older than Bart and his friends. The gang leader, a tough looking dude in a leather jacket, stepped up to the wagon and began insulting the young girls. Bart's male friends sank lower into the hay hoping to avoid a confrontation.

"Look at all the chicken shits," the lead rowdy maligned and mocked the boys taking refuge in the wagon.

Bart had enough. He stepped out of the cart. "Who made you king?" Even at fifteen, he was a big kid at six feet, one hundred seventy pounds.

Somewhat taken aback by this defiance, the leader backed away for a moment. But sensing that his two fellow gang members were watching him, he moved within a foot of Bart and gave him a shove. It was more of a see-how-tough-I-am shove than a I-mean-business shove. His adversary knew the difference. Suddenly, Bart lashed out with a vicious punch to Mr. Leather Jacket's nose. Blood began pouring out of his beak, and you could hear a pin drop. It was clear to all that if it was a fight the bully wanted, Bart was more than willing to accommodate. To save face, the other two hoodlums grabbed their bloody leader's arm.

"Let's not bother with these chicken shits. They're not worth our time."

Then Bart said something foolish. "How about tomorrow?" he challenged.

"Hey, smartass, don't forget us," one threatened. "We will be looking for you," the other joined in.

"I'm scared," he replied, feeling just a little too cocky. He would regret his brashness.

"C'mon," urged their leader whose nose was still bleeding, "we'll finish this later."

And meet again they did—a week later. This time, Bart was alone and there were five of them. He managed to bloody a few faces and get in some good licks, but the group overpowered him. Thanks to an adult neighbor who happened upon them all, the five ran off and left their victim with cuts on his nose and under his eyes. It could have been much worse. That night, Bart's father, Ed, went out and bought his son some boxing gloves. It was from his father that he learned to get in the first blow and make it count. He was also taught what to do in an unfair fight.

"Son, if you're going to be in a fight," schooled the tough steel worker, "don't dance around. You take it seriously and get him good right then and there." That advice and the boxing lessons held him in good stead for the rest of his life.

Ed Steele and his wife, Gretchen, hoped that Bart might be the first in the family to go to college. For that to happen, their son would have to make it on a scholarship. Ed worked in the open hearth at Bethlehem Steel, and Gretchen did part-time nursing at the General Hospital. Collectively, they could not provide enough family income to send their son to college. Bart was a respectable student, although his ranking in the middle group at a public high school was not going to be enough to secure academic scholarships. His ticket was going to come through his exploits on the athletic stage. He was a good basketball and baseball player, but the two sports themselves would not entitle him to a free ride. But football would. Opposing coaches designed plays away from wherever Bart Steele patrolled. He was a vicious tackler and clearly loved the contact. Coach Malloy also used him as an effective running back, but it was as linebacker where he wreaked the most havoc. Having grown to six feet two and two hundred ten pounds in his junior year, he was lightning fast with a knack for the ball. The opposition feared him. And the college coaches noticed.

By his senior year, five or more scouts would be in the stands for every game. The University of Buffalo was the first to recognize this local phenom, but soon, the bigger schools caught on to the Friday night attraction, and the race was on. Ultimately, Bart chose the University of Pittsburgh, but he could have gone to Michigan, Ohio State, Alabama, Southern Cal, or just about anywhere he wanted. His dad preferred Pittsburgh for him because Ed liked the coach and was promised his son would be an instant starter. Pittsburgh was also less than a four-hour drive from Buffalo. The morning after the bar brawl, a tad hung over, Bart woke up about eight and smiled to himself as he recounted his experience with the big thug in the restaurant. He knew the guy could have bested him in a conventional fight. But, as his father had told him, you do what you have to do. His dad had worked in the steel mill until his mandatory retirement age of sixty-five, after forty-seven years of hard labor in those mills. The old man had succumbed to congestive heart failure and died just three years after his retirement. Gretchen wasn't much luckier. She died from chronic respiratory disease two days after her sixty-sixth birthday. Her lungs just stopped functioning. Ed, who by that time was in the throes of heart disease, flat out gave up when she passed away. He refused his meds, despite the pleadings of his son. Bart buried his parents within three weeks of each other. He knew that his father had worked much harder than he had, and it was difficult for him not to feel guilty about it. Bart had been fortunate enough to retire at age sixty. He had worked as a salesman for a large paper manufacturer and made a very comfortable living. He would never be rich, but that was okay. Money and material things were never that big a deal in the Steele household. Bart was lucky enough to have made some prudent investments, and he could start living a pretty good life at age sixty. But now, of course, there was no one left to live it with him—not his wife, nor his daughter.

CHAPTER 10

■ On Saturday, Bart knew something special might happen. Thinking it might come in handy, he retrieved his snubnose .38 from his closet—a weapon he kept "just in case." *Somebody might die tonight,* he thought. *I probably have less than a year to live but will still outlive that bastard.* It was still pretty hot and muggy for an October evening in Southwest Florida. The Naked Lady was rocking when he arrived at eight. Good old Charlie Miller occupied his usual stool at the bar, just three seats from the end, sandwiched in between two attractive women who appeared to be in their sixties. Bart meandered over to the three; Charlie seemed to light up.

"Say hello to Doris and Kathy," his friend said. He stuck out his hand out of habit and shook hands with all three while removing his baseball cap. "Nice to meet you, ladies."

Doris offered him her seat, as both ladies had stopped by only for a drink before meeting friends for dinner.

"I hope I'm not driving you off," he apologized with a smile.

"Oh, no. We have plans."

"Well, sorry to have interrupted you." Bart apologized to his friend after the ladies had left.

"Nothing to apologize for, Doug." Charlie inched closer to his newly arrived friend. "Your guy is here tonight."

Bart scanned the crowded room but didn't see him.

"There's a pool room in the back, just past the men's room. He's playing with a friend."

"Interesting," Bart replied, pretending not to care that much.

"Yeah, he came in about an hour ago." They drank a beer together and talked about the weather.

"Looked like you were sweet-talking Doris," Bart said with a sly smile.

"She comes in here every once in a while."

"Well, I think she likes you."

"Naw, she knows I'm harmless."

"Don't be so modest."

"I'm an old man, but I wasn't so bad when I was young!" Charlie winked and smiled at his bar mate.

"I'll bet you weren't." By now Bart was growing impatient and wanted a real look at his prey.

"Back in a second," he reassured the old man as he pointed to the men's room.

His first impulse upon eyeing his daughter's killer was to merely confront the bastard, identify himself as the father of the woman he had killed, and then gun him down. But that would be too easy for Darrell. He needed to suffer.

Although Bart had acknowledged the evidence linking Darrell to Stephanie was not totally compelling, he knew in his gut Darrell was the perpetrator. Stephanie and Darrell had dated for a short while. They met on an online dating site, and when Stephanie broke it off, Darrell was not happy. He stalked her every move and tried to call her constantly. He couldn't accept "no" for an answer. *Sometimes you just know,* Bart thought. Instead of acting on that primitive instinct, he watched briefly as Darrell played pool with his friend. Then, he ducked into the bathroom. Bart didn't really have to go but, like most men, he could almost urinate on demand. Blood tests were the perfect example. One could pee just before going to the doctor's or the lab and then unexpectedly be handed the little cup and asked to produce a specimen. "But I just went," wouldn't cut it. So, he stood there, cup in hand over the toilet for a few seconds and, voila, there it was. Not much but enough. It was the same this time as well. He flushed his handiwork and washed his hands, pausing for a moment upon opening the door to get a final glimpse of the man he must murder.

"Did you see him back there?" Charlie was curious when Bart resumed his position at the bar.

"Yeah, he and this other dude were still shooting pool."

"They both look like they are up to no good," Charlie offered.

You're telling me, Bart thought. He just nodded. Bart and Charlie could hear Darrell and his poolmate drinking beer, cursing loudly, and telling crude jokes. Their voices reverberated from the pool room right into the main bar, which had its own din but not enough to drown out their raucous behavior. The snubnose .38 was still in his pocket, and he itched to put it to good use. He decided to wait as long as necessary to see when Darrell left the bar and if he left alone. One way or another, the murderer was going to die; whether it was alone or not would depend on the circumstances. It was now eleven-thirty, and the bar crowd was beginning to thin out. There was still no sign of Darrell leaving the place. Evidently tired of playing pool, he and his companion sat at a small table in the cavernous room and continued to purchase pitchers of beer. Finally, at midnight, Charlie slid off his stool and bade farewell to Bart. Five minutes later, Bart was going to do the same when he noticed Darrell's friend get up and leave. As he walked out within fifteen feet, Bart caught a good look. The man seemed to be in his late twenties, tall, and skinny with a black Fu Manchu mustache. He had an unsavory look about him, with dark foreboding eyes and a nasty scar under his left cheek. *If I have to shoot both of them,* Bart thought, *that would be okay.* Still anchored to his bar stool, he decided to wait another fifteen minutes or so before heading home. Ten minutes later, Darrell made his move. He paid the barmaid and walked unsteadily past the bar and to the exit. For one brief moment, Bart and Darrell's eyes met, but to Bart's considerable relief, there didn't appear to be any recognition on the part of the sleaze. He had that same scraggly look with the beard and long hair and was wearing baggy black jeans and a black T-shirt that bore a skull and crossbones stenciled on it. No longer did he have the look of the choirboy sitting passively in the courtroom. This was the real thing—the real Darrell. Overcoming his strong desire to finish his business right then and there, Bart signaled the bartender for his check and then followed his prey outside. At first, he didn't see him. But as his eyes adjusted to the dark, he searched down the obscure and murky alley, and sure enough, there he was. Something prevented the enraged father from following him and completing the deed, though. Later, as he lay in his bed, Bart wasn't sure why he let the bastard go. There were no witnesses except for the stars above, and his gut told him to do it then, but his heart just wasn't ready to pull it off. He admonished himself for the umpteenth time but knew he would get another chance. The alley behind the bar was dark and contained only an old dumpster. Darrell wouldn't get off so easy the next time. Before leaving, Bart had looked carefully for any signs of surveillance cameras and was relieved not to see any.

Sleep didn't come until three in the morning, but he had wonderful dreams of his beautiful wife and daughter. He missed them both so much; they had been such shining lights in his life. Bart was a tad perplexed when he rose the next morning. Why hadn't he simply run up to Darrell quietly and ended it all right then and there? Someone would have discovered the body the next morning, and no one would be the wiser. Was it that he was afraid to kill a defenseless person? He didn't think so, but he also wasn't sure. While it occurred to him to go to a shooting range for practice, he couldn't afford to take that chance. The police would probably suspect him after the fact and check out the local ranges to see if he had been there. There would be a record, of course, because a shooter must present his driver's license. Besides, he wouldn't be taking care of Darrell from a distance. It would be close and very personal. He would be okay—he knew it. Presented with a similar opportunity again, the Fort Myers area would be rid of one more degenerate. As he fixed his morning oatmeal and coffee, Bart was confident he would be up to the challenging task before him. The alley adjacent to the Naked Lady was wide enough to give him an idea. He would wait until next Saturday to execute it. And, he wouldn't have to worry about anyone in the bar hearing a gunshot. His new plan would necessitate a trip to the hardware store to get some duct tape.

CHAPTER 11

■ It was the middle of the week when Bart appeared for his first chemo treatment. His physician had explained that his Stage 2-3 diagnosis meant his cancer had probably started to spread into surrounding tissue. Without treatment, Bart would likely die within months.

Dr. Stuart Gordon, the medical oncologist, along with Dr. Melissa Perkins, who would administer the chemo, had talked him into receiving the treatment that had the potential to extend his life significantly. Bart's initial reaction was to turn down any treatment because he only had to live long enough to rid the world of Darrell. Any time after that would be gravy. Although not apparent to him then, there would shortly become a reason to gladly extend his life. A very important one.

The chemo fortunately was a low dose, and he tolerated it well, although he did feel a bit nauseous the next day. Saturday didn't come soon enough. When it arrived, he arose early—around seven—and had his usual coffee and oatmeal fix. After his customary shave and shower, the rest of his day was consumed by his thoughts about encountering Darrell in the dark alley. Bart did a dry run on a few nights, checking out the alley for cars or anything else of interest. On those occasions, no one left a car unattended. The alley connected two streets and was only about seventeen feet wide. It would be tight if two cars going in opposite directions attempted to pass each other. Obviously, the alley was built with deliveries and dumpsters in mind.

At eight on Saturday night, Bart left his condo and cranked the ignition of his two-year-old Chevy. He was mostly excited, but he was not without trepidation. Could he do it?

Good old Charlie was occupying his usual spot and had managed to save the seat next to him for Bart—or Doug, as Bart was known to the older man.

"Not here yet, Doug," he stated as his friend sat down.

"Doesn't matter," he lied. He could feel the .38 in his jeans pocket, pressing against his inner thigh. Just before leaving his apartment, he had stared at the photo of his beloved daughter, which occupied a special place next to her mother's photo on his reading table. He could feel the outrage building inside of him and took that anger with him to the Naked Lady.

"Hey, Doug, here he comes," Charlie exclaimed quietly.

Darrell Martin strode into the bar alone and headed directly towards the pool room. Bart turned to catch a glimpse but otherwise did his best to act casual.

"Did he ever pay your friend back?"

"Yeah, apparently he did. I've lost interest in him."

"That's good, Doug. I don't know that I would want to mess with him. He is a skinny looking punk, but I'll bet he carries a knife or worse."

"I wouldn't be surprised, Charlie."

The two bar-stool buddies talked about baseball and politics for well over two hours. Bart nursed a beer for the longest time, since he didn't want to be nauseous—one of the side effects of his chemo. He wanted to be on top of his game. It was almost eleven when Bart excused himself to take a leak. The real reason, of course, was to check up on Darrell. There he was playing pool with what seemed to be a new acquaintance rather than his friend from the week prior. At almost midnight, Charlie and Bart heard a loud argument that seemed to come from the pool room. Suddenly, Darrell's new pool partner bolted from the room while swearing up a blue streak.

"Darrell, you lying bastard! You cheated me, and I will get you back, you son-of-a-bitch!" The bartender came over reluctantly to check on the disturbance.

"Go fuck yourself," was Darrell's reply.

The man charged back into the room, but the burly bartender stepped between them before any blows could be landed.

"You owe me fifty bucks," the man continued as he raised his fist over the stout bartender who restrained him.

"Apparently, you didn't hear me the first time," a seemingly unperturbed Darrell Martin snapped. "Go fuck yourself!"

The bartender was strong, and Darrell's angry opponent realized he was getting nowhere.

"You'll get yours, Darrell. Believe me!" With that he turned and exited the bar.

Charlie nudged Doug. "Looks like that guy meant business. Wouldn't be surprised if he came back."

"Yeah, he seemed really angry, didn't he?" It took Bart several moments to comprehend what a gift had just been handed him.

Charlie left the Naked Lady before midnight, and his vengeful friend was about to do the same. Before Bart could peel himself off the bar stool, he noticed Darrell walk by him on his way out.

Pulling a twenty-dollar bill from his pocket, Bart placed it by the bowl of nuts next to his half-empty beer glass. It would more than cover his tab. He said nothing and scanned the thinning crowd of patrons to be certain no one was watching his or Darrell's departure. A few men were talking football, while others seemed to be engaged in romancing the handful of women who remained. The timing for his exit was perfect. Reaching the street corner in just a few strides, he looked down the alley and saw the bastard trudging slowly just beyond where Bart had parked his Chevy. Walking quickly but silently, he was now just two feet behind his prey.

"Mister, do you have a light?"

"Why the fuck would I give you a light?" Darrell snarled while turning around to face him. It was one of the last words he would ever say. Bart unleashed a thunderous punch with his right fist that caught his unsuspecting target flush in the jaw. The sound of the crunch and the resulting pain in his right hand told him he had been successful. The recipient collapsed like a piece of paper mâché. Bart then dragged Darrell the ten feet to his car and opened the trunk. Grabbing the duct tape, he covered his mouth and bound his hands and feet. Sure enough, there was a switchblade in Darrell's back pocket. Bart removed it and tossed the creep like a rag doll onto a blanket in the trunk.

Bart had a plan and knew what to do next. But first, he looked around carefully to see if anyone had witnessed the scene. Satisfied there wasn't a passerby, he started his car but left the lights off. Slowly, he inched his way in the dark, away from the Naked Lady. Seeing no traffic, he turned right onto the street. By now, he could hear a rumble from the trunk. Darrell had awoken and was kicking his legs, but there was no one to hear him. Twenty minutes later, Bart reached his destination—an abandoned old farm; no one lived within several miles of it. He pulled his Chevy into the gravel driveway, shut off his lights, and proceeded another two hundred feet or so up a hill to the ramshackle farmhouse. A large tree would at least partially conceal the car from the road.

By this time, Darrell Martin was awake and terrified. The trunk opened, and Darrell was yanked out and deposited harshly on the gravel. His muffled cries for help annoyed his captor.

"Listen you good for nothing little piece of shit, shut your mouth or I will blow your head off." As he spat out the words, he menacingly brandished his weapon. Darrell had gotten the message and had the look of stark terror on his face. Bart dragged the man into the vacant farmhouse. The two of them sat together on the floor as Bart waited for dawn, when he would not have to use a light. Finally, daylight arrived, and he couldn't wait for Darrell to actually see him. But there was no recognition.

"You don't know who I am, do you?" His captive shook his head vigorously back and forth.

"You winked at me in the courtroom not so long ago." Still, there was no acknowledgement.

"Listen to me, asshole. I am going to remove the duct tape so you can speak. If you as much as make a single sound, other than to answer my questions, I will shoot you right between the eyes. Understand?" A very frightened Darrell nodded his head vigorously.

Bart was pacing back and forth in front of his captive audience.

"Even if you do yell, no one is within five miles of this place, and there is no one to hear you or help you! Do you under-stand?" Again, the head nodded, causing a trickle of blood to ooze through the duct tape.

"If you yell, you are a dead man." Still, the head nodded as the body trembled. Suddenly, Bart ripped the duct tape from Darrell's mouth, along with almost half of his mustache, too. He winced, and his body quivered, but he said nothing.

"Good boy, Darrell," his abductor mocked him. "You catch on quickly." "Now listen clearly, Darrell, because your life depends on it. Did you murder Stephanie Steele?"

If Darrell was frightened before, it was nothing compared to the sheer and utter terror that engulfed him once he recognized his captor.

"I will splatter your brains on the wall if you don't tell me the truth!" What Bart left out was that either way, Darrell's future would be measured in minutes.

"No, no I didn't," he stammered. "I mean I didn't mean to. It was an accident. She dumped me, and it got out of hand."

"Is that why you raped her?" The enraged father could barely contain his emotions. Bart grabbed the roll of duct tape and applied six inches of it over the murderer's mouth. Darrell Martin hadn't been an honor student, but he sensed what that gesture meant. The blanket was also placed behind Darrell's head.

"Tell you what. I'm going to be more charitable to you than you were to my daughter. I'm going to count off sixty seconds, and then I'm going to fucking blow your head off."

Upon hearing that, Darrell squirmed, and his eyes almost jumped out of his head.

"One, two, three..." Bart almost felt sorry for his victim. Almost. As he counted to sixty out loud, Darrell panicked and shook violently.

"Oh, what the heck," his tormentor said. "Let's go another minute. The count began again, with Bart placing the gun barrel right at Darrell's nose. Expecting the worst, Darrell closed his eyes at the number fifty-nine. But nothing happened. His sense of terror was such that his limp body sagged like a piece of spaghetti. Bart Steele went through the countdown three more times; his daughter's murderer was sobbing like a baby through the duct tape. While he was struggling with himself about actually murdering someone in cold blood, Bart simultaneously enjoyed inflicting fear in this piece of scum. "Playtime is over," he declared, "and it's time to kill you." Then he stuck his hand in his pocket and produced a photo of his beloved daughter.

"Look at this while you die. This is what you took from me, and now, you little bastard, it's time for you!"

He waved the gun barrel in Darrell's face to see him agonize one more time. Then, he placed two thick pillowcases over Darrell's head. BANG! And, just like that, it was all over.

Even without his silencer, it was unlikely anyone heard the shot. Bart was gripped by remorse for a moment but, ambivalently, also relieved that it was over. At last, he had avenged Stephanie's murder.

Bart sat down and attempted to eat a sandwich he had brought with him. When dusk arrived, he removed all the duct tape from Darrell's body. A shallow grave was dug about fifty feet beyond the house and behind two large trees. It might be years, if then, before authorities would discover the body. By then, Bart would have succumbed to his cancer. The connection would never be made.

A first thought after pulling the trigger was to leave the body in the farmhouse. But then, in the unlikely event that he was discovered in the next month or so, Charlie may have told the authorities that his new friend Doug had an interest in Darrell.

With no body and no blood on the farmhouse wall, his disappearance would not be a big thing—perhaps an eventual missing person case, but no one would go to that farmhouse suspecting a murder. And even if someone did, there was no blood or sign of a struggle.

The bloody pillowcases and blanket were deposited in the grave along with the duct tape, and there was no blood on the shovel, so Bart put it back in the trunk. It was as close to a perfect murder as he could devise. Now, he could die. He had avenged the murder of his daughter, and there was nothing left for him to do. Or was there?

He left the farmhouse about seven that night and returned home. The first thing he did was pour a stiff drink. The second was to take a much-needed shower. There was no blood on his body that he could detect, but he reeked of sweat and felt dirty. He had been careful to wear gloves and a disposable jumpsuit, so no blood would be on his clothes. He had left those things in the "grave" as well. Then he washed all of his clothes and even the soles of his shoes—just to be safe.

As he sat and reflected, Bart recalled that on his drive home, he felt proud. He had acted like any other responsible father. The feeling alone of ridding society of a menace should have been exhilarating. But, as he nursed another Crown Royal, he was enervated and suffering pangs of guilt.

I was no better than Darrell, Bart lamented as he thought about the torture that he put the guy through. *He thought he was going to die at least five times. Why don't I feel better about it? I should have just killed him and been done with it.* He thought about one of his father's favorite sayings. "A coward dies a thousand times before his death, but the valiant taste of death but once." Ed had taken it from William Shakespeare's *Julius Caesar,* and it rang true. Hemingway had also said something like that in his *A Farewell to Arms,* but he might have borrowed it from Caesar's creator.

The question before Bart now was whether to return to the Naked Lady. He had grown fond of chatting with Charlie Miller, and he wondered if his new friend would miss him. Would there be a police investigation? Did Darrell have any close friends? Would anyone even know or notice that Darrell had gone missing—or care, for that matter? Would Bart's (aka Doug's) absence arouse any suspicion? Was there surveillance tape at the Naked Lady? Would the police even bother to use it, since no one could point to a specific time for Darrell's disappearance? His parole officer would undoubtedly report him missing if he failed to show up for a regular, scheduled meeting. Even if the authorities could track Bart leaving the saloon shortly after Darrell's departure, what would that prove? No one knew he was pushing up daisies in a grave behind the farmhouse. *No*, the avenging father reasoned, he was free and clear to go back to the Naked Lady and act like nothing had happened. Besides, he would welcome another beer with Charlie and learning if there was any scuttlebutt about the recently deceased Darrell Martin.

"Hi, Charlie," he said on Tuesday night while doffing his Red Sox cap. He wondered when, if ever, his friend had washed the grimy Cubs hat atop of his grey head. But then again, there was something alluring about a crusty old ball cap, and it lent to the old man's mystique. A bar stool was open, and Bart slid in next to his friend. Charlie's old blue eyes lit up. "Didn't think I'd see you."

"Why not? How could I pass up a beer with my buddy?"

"Haven't seen you-know-who yet." *And you never will*, Bart thought to himself. "He paid back my friend, so I no longer give a shit."

"The guy still looks like a prick."

"Can't argue with you there," he agreed, "but I have no interest in him."

Suddenly Charlie remembered something. "I wonder about that angry dude who threatened him?"

"If he does come back, that nasty guy better be ready. He sounded like he meant business." *Clearly,* he thought to himself, *the old man knows nothing about Darrell's disappearance.*

They shared another beer and talked about the red tide that was cluttering up the beaches in Fort Myers and up and down the coast.

"Do you like to swim Charlie?"

"Yeah, but the red tide can make you sick."

"Has it ever affected you?"

"Oh yeah. A couple of times over the years I started coughing and sneezing but nothing really serious. But some people with emphysema and asthma can get bad respiratory problems."

"What the hell is red tide anyway?"

"Do you want the basic 101 or 201?"

"Definitely 101," Bart responded with a laugh.

"Well, there is a marine microorganism called *Karenia brevis* that blooms along the Florida coast," the old man explained, "usually in late summer or early fall. It seems to thrive in the salty coastal waters, and you won't see it grow in fresh-water lakes. Am I talking too much, Doug?"

"You could have been a teacher!"

"Just one more thing, Doug. Two years ago, I was fishing in Sanibel, and I saw a dead grouper on the beach. Had to be at least a hundred and fifty pounds. It was really sad. Red tide kills fish, turtles, and even a dolphin occasionally."

I really like the guy, Bart thought, *but if I asked him for the time, he would probably tell me how to make a watch!*

Finally, at ten-thirty, Bart announced it was past his bedtime. The two shook hands and made tentative plans to meet again on Saturday.

During the short ride home, Bart was pleased there had been no news of Darrell, but part of him wished otherwise. He couldn't explain the feeling. Did he want some kind of credit for what he had done? Bart knew that he could never kill anyone again, no matter how much it was warranted. Or could he? Had he been changed forever?

CHAPTER 12

■ Maybe it was because he himself was relatively close to dying, but for some reason Bart fell asleep thinking about his father's death. The man had given up after losing his wife to a respiratory illness. Bart remembered Ed just lying there in bed, usually drenched in sweat but never complaining. He had pills for the pain but only took them when he couldn't stand the agony anymore. Ed Steele was a tough old buzzard but he no longer wanted to live. Period. Very near the end, he beckoned his son to move in closer to him. Bart took his hand and leaned in. "Don't be a failure like I was. I wanted to be somebody." His voice trailed off.

"Dad," he assured him, "you are somebody."

His father gently shook his head back and forth, indicating his disagreement. Tears rolled down his cheeks.

"I just wanted to be somebody," he repeated.

"You are, Dad. You are." And then the old man was gone. Bart had grieved as he remembered all those times he and his father played football together and how supportive Ed always was to his son. Bart still missed his dad.

It had been different at the end for his mother. She remained the eternal optimist even in the throes of her respiratory disease. Gretchen Steele forgave anyone for almost any trans-gression. One of her favorite sayings was to *do good just for the sheer joy of it.* And she taught her son to never expect some-thing in return when he did someone a favor. "It takes all the goodness out of it," she explained. His mother had been a saint, and, most certainly, the glue that kept the Steele family going. She would never understand—never forgive him—for taking a life, even though she was the most forgiving person he had known.

Bart woke up the next morning at eight, feeling like he had been run over by a tractor. He had probably committed the perfect murder, and the victim deserved to die. So why was he feeling so low? There was nothing in the Fort Myers news-paper about any disappearance of one Darrell Martin. Bart had avenged his daughter's murder and probably saved the life of another woman. So, he had really performed a public service, or so he tried to rationalize.

Two nights later, he met his old buddy at the Naked Lady.

"Hey, Doug, I talked to the police the other day."

"About what. Are you okay?" Bart's interest was piqued.

"They were checking out the disappearance of that guy who we saw playing pool. You know, the mean looking dude who had owed your friend money?"

"You didn't mention that part, did you?"

"No, it wasn't important. But I did tell them about the near fight he had with the other guy."

Bart was very relieved but didn't show it. "Charlie, why do they consider him missing?"

"Oh, apparently his employer reported that he hadn't come to work. And, oh yeah, he had missed a dinner with his mother."

"Probably that other punk he was arguing with," Bart offered. "The police seemed interested in checking that out, and I heard one of the officers ask for surveillance tapes."

"Do they have any here?"

"I think so, Doug."

He didn't want to hear that. Bart might have to come up with a reason for telling Charlie his name was Doug because the police might interview him, too. His friend knew him as Doug, so that might take some explaining. *That wasn't good,* he thought.

"What do you think about the name Bartholomew?" he asked his friend.

"Gotta be honest—not my favorite, Doug."

"Well, that's why I call myself Doug," he explained.

"You mean your name is really Bartholomew? You don't look like a Bartholomew!"

"What the heck is a Bartholomew supposed to look like?" he replied, a little bit annoyed.

"Didn't mean to offend you, Doug." "I prefer Bart," he interrupted.

"You just look like a tough guy to me, and I'm just surprised, that's all."

"No problem, Charlie. I didn't mean to be sensitive. My mother had two miscarriages before she had me, so she thought I was an angel." Bart chuckled, and Charlie reciprocated.

"I'd have used another name too," his friend laughed while nodding his head in approval. "My uncle's name is Marion, and he never liked it."

The two men talked some more about the muggy weather for that time of year, and Bart was careful not to bring up the subject of Darrell Martin again.

On the drive home, he was a lot more concerned than he had been upon entering the Naked Lady.

CHAPTER 13

■ It was a Wednesday morning, and Bart was reading about the North Fort Myers High School football team. The state playoffs loomed, and the Red Knights looked almost invincible. Then an interruption—at about nine-thirty, there was a knock on the door. That was strange. Bart rarely had visitors, unless there was a UPS or FedEx delivery. But he hadn't ordered anything.

He got up from the breakfast table and shuffled to the door. Opening it, he was shocked to see one man in blue with a badge and full gear, and the other man in a suit. The stern guy in the suit spoke up first.

"Good morning. I am Detective Vince Riley, and with me is officer Tom Livingston. You are Bart Steele, are you not?" "Yes, I am officers, would you like some coffee?" Both shook their heads and declined. They entered, and Bart sat in his easy chair, while Riley and Livingston seated themselves on the couch. "Is this about my daughter?" the slightly unnerved host asked.

"Well, sir," the detective began, "we are investigating the possible disappearance of a young man. Do you happen to know him?" he asked while holding up a photo.

"No, I'm sorry I don't, but he does look a little like the SOB who was charged with murdering my daughter." Bart responded as matter-of-factly as he possibly could. He could feel his face changing color. Bart knew from reading books on the subject that if someone was rapidly blinking his eyes, it could be a liar's giveaway. He made certain not to do that.

"Mr. Steele," Riley continued, "have you ever frequented the Naked Lady bar and grill in Fort Myers?"

"Why, yes I have," he replied earnestly.

"Have you ever seen this man there?" The detective again handed him a photo of the missing person.

Bart purposely looked at it for an extra moment or two. "I think I have," Bart nodded his head.

"Do you know Charlie Miller?" Riley persisted.

"Guilty as charged," he laughed, "I usually sit next to him when I'm there."

"Does this man look familiar to you?" This time, the detective showed him a photo of the man who argued on that night with Darrell Martin.

"Again, Detective Riley, I'm not absolutely sure, but I think so."

"In what context?"

"Well, this may be the fellow who seemed to be arguing with that other guy you showed me."

"Your friend Charlie Miller said you both witnessed the argument a week or so ago. Is that right?"

"Yes, I think those were the two. We only really just got a glimpse of them."

"Your friend seemed more certain than you," Riley challenged him.

"That's very possible, detective," he responded. "Charlie is definitely a regular there. I only began going there a couple of weeks ago."

"Makes sense, I guess," the detective nodded in agreement. "Thank you for your time, Mr. Steele. I think that just about does it." Bart accompanied them to the front door and mentioned gratuitously that he was a big supporter of the police.

"Nice to hear Mr. Steele," Mr. Livingston finally broke his silence. "We're always glad to hear that."

The two law enforcement officers disappeared behind the large, solid oak door, and the resident breathed easier. Within ten seconds, however, there was another knock at the door.

Before he could even answer it, Riley unlatched it and peeked in. "Sorry, sir, to bother you again, but we just had one more question. It was a Columbo moment. Bart almost expected him to have on the same ratty and weathered old beige trench coat that actor Peter Falk wore as Lieutenant Columbo in the TV series.

"Please come in," he beckoned them both inside a second time. The three took the same seats they had just vacated a few minutes earlier.

"Do you remember when you left the Naked Lady a week ago last Saturday night?" This time it was the officer who framed the question.

He thought a moment. "I'm guessing that it wasn't terribly late because I never stay that long."

"Could it have been around eleven-thirty-ish?

"Could have been. Why do you ask?"

"Because the surveillance tape has you leaving almost directly after Mr. Martin," Livingston said acidly. "Do you recall that?"

"Not really, officer. I don't really recall whether I left after anyone in particular, but the time would be about right."

"Well, thanks again for your cooperation, Mr. Steele." And for the second, and, hopefully, final time that morning, Bart escorted them to the door.

About three that afternoon, Bart was reclining in his favorite chair. He had not gotten over his encounter with Riley and Livingston. *Do they suspect me? How could they?* He tried to reassure himself. *Darrell will always be a missing person and nothing more than that.* The problem was the police had figured out Bart was the grieving father of a murdered woman. They would be back. Clearly, even though there would never be a body, he certainly did not want to be a suspect. It really didn't matter, he managed to convince himself, since he would probably be dead in another six months or so. He was certain of one thing: He would never again take another life...or so he thought. He was once again reminded that had his mother known of his gruesome deed, she would have disowned him.

Deep down, Bart could rationalize killing Darrell, but torturing him the way he had was unacceptable and out of character. Once he had the bastard under control, he just simply snapped. But until that moment, he never realized that he had a dark side—a very dark side.

Bart knew he would see the police again. And probably sooner rather than later. He wondered if they were certain of the connection and were perhaps watching his daily movements—hoping he might lead them to a body, if, in fact, there was one. How would he explain that he did not positively recognize the very sleazebag who had killed his daughter? What father wouldn't know the identity of every hair on his depraved head? Especially after he had seen him daily for two weeks in court? He had already acknowledged that the photo they showed him had resembled the man charged with her murder but wasn't certain of it. How could he be faulted for that, since Darrell looked very different from the photo in the courtroom?

CHAPTER 14

■ Something caught Bart's attention on TV at the gym one day. The news story interrupted the game he had been watching. Apparently, a man was being accused of shooting and killing a younger man because he didn't want him dating his daughter. Apparently, the teenagers were falling in love with each other and getting serious. What complicated things was that the alleged killer was a white man and the eighteen-year-old victim, Casey Moore, was black.

The case had been going on in criminal court for the past week, but final testimony and the closing arguments were scheduled for the next day. There was something about the case that intrigued Bart. He had always considered himself a person who believed in justice, and the Moore murder reeked of injustice. And he could easily identify with Casey's parents. He lost his daughter to murder, and the Moore's lost their son to a similar act. It was unimaginable.

Bart had to hear the closing arguments. It was a crisp, early December day in Florida, the temperature dipping all the way down to forty-five degrees. Bart, wearing a hat and raincoat, entered the courtroom and sat in the back row. The man being prosecuted was already seated at the defense table, looking spiffy in his well-tailored grey suit. In his forties, he was too old to be a choirboy, but he looked the part. The gist of the case centered around whether the jury would believe the alibi of the accused. His wife swore he was at home at the time of the murder, and no one could place him at the murder scene. He had made derogatory comments about the young man just two nights before the murder, and an elderly witness had testified seeing a late model black Lincoln leaving a parking lot where the crime had been committed. There were legitimate questions.

The accused, Mark Hollister, owned a car very similar to that seen by the witness. But he didn't own a gun nor was one found at the scene. The DA had not been anxious to bring forth the prosecution because of a lack of solid evidence but had done so as a result of pressure from the black community. Bart watched intently as the defendant swaggered to the witness stand. Right off the bat, Bart didn't like him. The man appeared haughty and had a superior air about him. Then, Bart's eyes shifted to the late young man's family, sitting in the second row. He couldn't see much from his vantage point, but he noticed Casey's parents and his younger sister and brother. His eyes landed on the grieving mother, her head bobbing with sobs. Bart smelled injustice coming soon. It was palpable, and he could just sense it. Mark Hollister again denied he was ever in that parking lot on the night of the crime. In fact, he claimed he had not driven his car at all that night. His wife corroborated the entire story. Bart didn't like her either.

As a lunch break became imminent, the eyewitness took the stand. The high-priced defense attorney, dressed impeccably in his navy-blue suit, white shirt, and red tie, sauntered over to the witness. Ten minutes later, the barrister fileted him into minced meat. Apparently, the old man had consumed a few drinks that night, and his eyes weren't that reliable anyway. It was clear to anyone, and especially to Bart Steele, that the credible old man was unfairly rendered almost incompetent by the sleazy defense attorney. The jury wouldn't be out long. On a hunch, putting on his hat and coat and still wearing a mustache, Bart walked to a nearby restaurant before returning to the courthouse.

Sure enough, it wasn't even four o'clock when the news got out that the jury had come to a decision. The result was predictable and left the Moore family deeply grieving. It appeared to Bart that once again, the justice system had failed. He watched closely as the defendant hugged his lawyer and smugly walked out of the courtroom. In the crowded corridor, Bart inched closer to the man who seemed to him to have beaten the rap. He didn't like Hollister's smarmy smile or his wink to his friends. It was too much like Darrell's wink. *Winks or smiles are a sign of getting away with duplicity,* he thought. *I don't like them, and I don't like the defendant.* He waited for the grief-stricken Moore family to finally leave their seats in the courtroom and venture outside. The media attempted to get in their faces for a comment on how awful they felt, but their attorney waived them off. The mother needed help walking, she was sobbing so hard. Bart had that horrible feeling, once again, in the pit of his stomach. Family members sat on the bench directly outside of the courtroom while attempting to comfort the grief-stricken mother. Bart ambled over to them.

"I think the sonofabitch was guilty," he asserted to the father.

"Beyond a shadow of a doubt, as far as I'm concerned," the father replied while hanging his head dejectedly. At that point, Bart leaned into the mourning family members and apologized for what he characterized as a miscarriage of justice. Sensing they would want to grieve alone, he excused himself.

On his drive home, he couldn't strike the image of the sobbing mother from his mind. It wasn't exactly an Emmett Till moment, but it was close. He thought about that sad case so many years ago when the Chicago lad, barely a month after his fourteenth birthday, visited relatives in Mississippi. After patronizing a grocery store with his cousin on August 25, 1955, he was accused of flirting and touching the wife of the grocer. Three days later, a week after Emmett had arrived from Chicago, the body of the African-American boy was found in the Tallahatchie River. He had been beaten, mutilated, and shot in the head. A month later, the grocer and his half-brother stood trial for the murder but were found not guilty by an all-white jury. The following year, in an interview with *Look Magazine,* fully realizing that they were protected by double jeopardy, both confessed their guilt. And to make the injustice sting just a little more, the grocer's wife recanted her testimony that Till had flirted and touched her improperly. The murderers in both evildoings walked away scot-free—like Darrell Martin had. Emmett Till's tragic death occurred in the Jim Crow era of the South. That was the only difference. Casey Moore was killed many years later in Florida. The more Bart thought about it, the more he fumed.

Bart thought about his own experiences with blacks. He had gone with them to grammar school and then to high school. And one turned out to be a very special friend. Josh Johnson was his name, and he was a very accomplished football player and teammate in high school and at Pitt. Like his buddy Bart, Josh got hurt during his sophomore season in college and played sporadically his final two years. It was odd the way the two had met.

Before they had gone to high school together, the two met one Saturday afternoon when they were eleven. Bart and a few friends were playing tackle football in the parkway when Josh and a few of his friends showed up. It ended up being the whites against the blacks. Tackle football, even at age eleven, was rough and tumble, especially without equipment. After almost two hours, Bart took exception to an errant elbow in a pileup and thought that Josh was the perpetrator. He gave him a vigorous push, which was answered by a punch in his face.

By the time the scrap ended with the black kids tugging on Josh while the white kids did the same with Bart, two bloody noses emerged from the pile. It was getting dark, and dinner beckoned. It had been a closely contested game with the black kids victorious at eighty-four to seventy-eight. The two combatants reluctantly shook hands before departing. Bart's father smiled when he saw his son, complete with bloody nose and a puffed eye that was turning black. His mother didn't quite have the same reaction.

"Oh, you poor boy," she exclaimed, applying a cold, wet compress to his swollen face.

"It's nothing, Ma."

"Hope you got in a few good licks yourself," Ed gently remonstrated.

"OK, you men," Gretchen admonished her husband. "All you care about is getting even!"

"What else is there, lovey?" The old man replied with a wink to his son.

"I did, Dad. He was a big black kid who elbowed me while we were playing football. I pushed him, he punched me, and then I punched him back. His nose looks like mine!"

"You didn't fight him because he was black, did you?" his mother asked.

"Heck no, Ma. I fought him because he elbowed me. We even shook hands afterwards."

That's the way things were in Buffalo, and the way things should be anywhere. Blacks and whites going to school with each other, playing with and occasionally fighting each other. But it had nothing to do with race.

CHAPTER 15

■ The night of the Moore courtroom ordeal, Bart had two drinks after preparing dinner. His sadness for the family bordered on despair, an emotion he knew only too well. The sense of injustice, repeated after his own daughter's tragedy, ate at him. He knew they would never get over the loss of their son, just like he would never get over Stephanie. Nonetheless, perhaps thanks to the alcohol and watching a late football game, he slept like a baby. He had just finished his coffee and oatmeal the next morning when he heard a knock on the door. *I wonder if Riley and Livingston are back,* he thought. Sure enough, they were. Wearing sheepish smiles, they reintroduced themselves and were once again led to the living room. This time, Bart was a little nervous.

"Coffee, gentlemen?"

"No thanks, we're good. Just a few more questions for you, Mr. Steele," Detective Riley began.

"Sure."

"Bart, you don't mind if we call you by your first name, do you?"

"Of course not."

"Bart, we are a little puzzled by something. And please accept our sympathy for what happened to your daughter."

"Thank you, both," he replied earnestly.

"We can't figure out why you didn't recognize Darrell Martin when we first showed his photograph to you." Before allowing Bart to answer, Riley continued, "Any grief-stricken father who sat through a trial for two weeks would certainly be able to identify the scumbag who murdered his daughter."

Bart's muscles went taut, and he looked pained. "We understand how difficult this must be for you," Riley said empathetically while leaning forward.

"Thank you. Actually, there is a simple explanation. You showed me a photo where he had a lot of facial hair. I hadn't seen that before. His lawyers had him dressed like a choir boy," he bitterly opined, "and he was clean-shaven in court." But then things got out of hand. The smiles, the gentle demeanor, and friendly sympathy abruptly disappeared. The change was palpable, and the room temperature seemed to plummet. "You know what we think, Mr. Steele?" *So, there it is, now it's Mr. Steele,* Bart thought.

"We think you were stalking Darrell Martin and that you hoped or knew he frequented the Naked Lady." Giving Bart a moment to let that sink in, Riley continued his narrative.

"We think you waited for him at the bar that same night you left right after him. And then you ambushed him in the alley and killed him. Bart, we don't blame you for killing him. We probably would have done the same thing. Just tell us," Riley implored. "I doubt if there is a jury in all of Florida that would convict you. Tell us, and we will help you deal with it."

Bart looked them both in the eyes and still said nothing.

"We can help you," Officer Livingston interjected. It was the old good-cop-bad-cop ploy. Bart wasn't biting.

"I really don't know what you are talking about," the suspect offered.

"C'mon, Bart," the officer again entreated. "We know you did it. We just don't know how." Riley decided to chime in. "It will go a lot easier on you if you just level with me."

"Look, gentlemen," a clearly annoyed Bart said. "Am I sorry that the scumbag has disappeared? No, I'm not. Frankly, I hope someone killed him, and if someone did, I will buy him dinner before he goes to prison! That bastard killed my daughter, but don't come back here and try to blame it on me."

"What do you think happened to him?" they said in unison.

"I don't know, and I certainly don't care. A guy like that probably has a lot of enemies—from gambling or other debts or whatever. All I know is that I haven't done anything to him. But I sure hope that someone else has!"

"I think we're done here," Detective Riley stated as he rose to his feet. "If you have a change of heart, give us a call."

"Detective, I don't know why you don't believe me. I almost hope that the scumbag shows up somewhere, but I won't expect an apology from you."

The door closed behind them, and Bart could hear some whispering but couldn't make out the words. Safely in the car, Livingston was the first to speak.

"I don't think he did it," the police officer opined.

Vince Riley shot back, "I know he did it!" His companion raised his eyebrows with a quizzical look. "Tom, didn't you notice the surveillance tape for that night at the Naked Lady?"

"Yeah, but all we saw was Bart Steele leaving shortly after Darrell Martin. That isn't exactly incriminating."

When they returned to the police station, the detective pulled out the tape machine. He put in the tape and played it in slow motion. "Tom, do you see how his eyes quickly swept the room to see if anyone watched him exit the bar? See right there," he pointed as Bart paused on the tape to look behind him.

"I see it, Vince, but it doesn't necessarily mean that he was checking everyone out."

"No, it doesn't. I just think it looks suspicious. I'll bet he followed him out to the alley and murdered him. Can't say I blame him," he added dryly, "but I want him to fess up about it."

CHAPTER 16

■ That night on TV, Bart watched an interview with the recently exonerated Mark Hollister, of the Casey Moore murder case. He was taken by the man's sheer arrogance. Bart remembered the defendant's smiles to his friends, and the smarmy look of defiance on his face. It reminded him all too much of another defendant who had also walked. He clenched his teeth, bit his lip, and swallowed hard as the unpleasant interview, combined with a bitter personal memory, filled him with resolve.

After the trial, Mark Hollister had returned to his job as sales manager for a publishing company. Very relieved, his staff gathered around him in support, but few mentioned anything about his successful court appearance. Maybe some of them thought that he was very capable of having carried out such a crime.

He smiled nervously as he addressed them all after his perceived ordeal. Some of them were privy to the fact that Casey Moore had dated Mark's daughter. And a few knew that he was quite unhappy about it. After a short discussion, the others departed their boss's office, leaving him alone with his thoughts. He was not one to brood about things, and this recent event would not be an exception. Today, he wore a blue suit with a crisp pink shirt, which would have been a bit too avant-garde for the courtroom. A pink and blue tie brought the ensemble together. At forty-four, he was tall with a slight paunch and looked athletic. He had played some basketball at an Ivy League school and had lived a life of privilege. A slightly ruddy complexion, light blue eyes, and rather bushy brown eyebrows completed that confident look, although he was somewhat concerned about his receding hairline. About a week went by when shortly before noon on a Friday, Hollister's secretary buzzed him and said that a gentleman was on the phone for him and had said it was personal. A tad annoyed with Carolyn for interrupting him, he decided nevertheless to take it. He quickly regretted his decision.

"I saw you kill Casey Moore," the voice on the other end of the line said.

"You must be kidding!" Hollister replied. "I did no such thing!"

"In that case," the voice said calmly, "I'll just go to the police."

"Hey, look mister, whoever you are. They tried me and found me not guilty."

"But you are guilty, and we both know that."

"Listen, I don't know who you are, asshole," Hollister blustered, "but you can't do anything to me. Ever hear of double jeopardy?"

"Yes, I have. But what is your reputation worth? Is it worth ten thousand dollars?'

There was a short pause. "You don't have anything on me," Hollister insisted, starting to sound a little unsettled.

"Oh, but I do. I was there."

"Well, why didn't you come forward at the trial?"

"That's my business," the voice demurred. "I can use the ten grand."

"You're as big a scumbag as you think I am!" the accused responded acidly.

"Not as big as you because I didn't murder anyone. If you want me to avoid going to the police, you will bring ten thousand in one-hundred-dollar bills to Hogan's at ten on Monday night. And you will be alone, because I will be watching."

"Why at ten?"

"That's my business. You be there alone with the money by ten sharp, or everyone will know that you killed Casey Moore."

"How will I recognize you?" an increasingly uncomfortable Mark Hollister asked.

"You won't. I'll find you." A now frightened, perplexed, and shaken sales exec, sweating profusely despite the air conditioning, hung up his office extension. The caller, using a burner disposable cell phone, calmly placed it in his pocket. He was sure of two things. One was that Mark Hollister would be at Hogan's at ten. Two, he would be armed and ready to kill again. Otherwise, the blackmail would continue indefinitely. A man like Hollister simply wouldn't allow that to happen.

CHAPTER 17

■ It was a tough weekend for the accused. For one thing, Angela was still grieving the loss of her boyfriend, and she wasn't entirely certain that her father had nothing to do with his death. For another, Mark Hollister genuinely feared that the caller was a witness to the murder, no doubt a greedy sleaze who would have to be eliminated. Third, his wife, Debra, had her own suspicions about him. She had lied in court about him being at home and had reluctantly bought into his argument that he would be unfairly found guilty if she didn't back his story. Deep down, Debra knew Mark committed the crime. She liked Casey Moore and hated to be in court, but it was the only way she could keep her family together. Mark had emphatically denied it the one time she asked him, but his crimson face betrayed him, and she just knew.

That Friday afternoon after the disturbing call, there was a trip to be made to the bank to secure five thousand in one-hundred-dollar bills. The other five thousand, Mark kept at home in his safe, because that was the kind of guy he was. Now, he would need to at least show it all to his accuser. Once the man shifted his eyes to count the ten grand, Mark would strike with a knife. He wished he still had the gun he had killed

Casey Moore with, but it was now in the river. Just before he had committed the grisly murder, he had tried to buy Casey off with an offer of five thousand, but the boy refused and said that Angela would hear about it. Mark did what he felt he had to do, and he was prepared to do it again.

He had been to Hogan's once before and remembered it was a quiet neighborhood bar. The caller had made a grave mistake choosing that quiet location, he thought, because it would be rather easy to dispose of a greedy blackmailer in such a place. He would show him the money and then slit his throat. The world would be free of one more thug, in fact, Mark would actually be performing a service to the community!

Monday was another difficult day in the office for Mark Hollister. He was fidgety and on edge all day long. The regular sales meeting that he always convened at ten every Monday morning was shorter than usual. The sales manager was not a nice guy to begin with, and his staff noticed that he had an edge to him and was even more irascible than usual. Most of them attributed his behavior to his recent trial. And while they would never tell him, not everyone in his office had agreed with the verdict. The Hogan's meeting that night at ten, however, presented difficulties for Mark. How does one convince his wife that he needed to leave the house at nine on a Monday night? The only thing he could come up with, flimsy excuse that it was, involved going out with friends to a bar to play darts. Debra suspected him of having an affair, and it wouldn't be the first time. But she dutifully went along with his explanation.

Unbeknownst to Mark Hollister, the selection of Hogan's for the rendezvous was not a random choice. Bart had checked it out carefully. On Monday nights, it was quiet with few patrons. It was secluded and had a poorly lit back door area—a perfect site for what he intended to do.

Mark arrived at Hogan's at nine twenty-five and scoped it out. It was cool out, and a gentle breeze was blowing. He was thirty-five minutes early for his encounter with the black-mailer as he walked through the front door. There were two couples sitting at the tables to his left and only three men occupying bar stools. Not much action at a quiet neighborhood bar at about nine thirty on a Monday night. But, of course, that was exactly why Bart had chosen it. Mark sat two stools away from the three men and ordered a beer. Then, he wandered over to the men's restroom to the left and behind the bar. Just behind the restrooms was a back door to the place, which led out to a very dark and quiet alley. There was only one light at the top of the door, and it couldn't have been more than a forty-watter. Clutching his knife in his right pants pocket, Mark stepped out onto the top of the stairway and carefully went down the three concrete steps to the macadam pave-ment. *This is the perfect spot to lure the bastard before I kill him,* was one of his last thoughts.

As soon as his feet hit the ground, however, he heard a sound and turned sharply to his left. At that exact moment, Bart stepped out from beneath the staircase and unleashed a vicious right hook, which caught Hollister flush on the jaw. He staggered back but did not fall. Surprised by his adversary's resiliency, Bart stepped forward to finish the job. But Mark Hollister had other plans. He pulled his knife out and slashed at his attacker, just missing his left forearm.

Bart rushed him and grabbed the man's knife-wielding right wrist with his left hand. They grappled for about ten seconds before tumbling over the bottom step. While going down, a desperate but quick-thinking Bart stuck his fingers in Mark's eyes. His adversary cried out in searing pain as they rolled over several times on the pavement. The rest was easy. Clamping his right hand on Mark's right wrist, still holding the knife, Bart then used both hands to overpower him and steer the weapon inexorably towards Mark's own body. One final roll and thrust, and the knife was deeply embedded in Mark's abdomen. Before Mark could cry out, Bart covered his mouth with his gloved right hand. Fortunately, no one was around to witness the fight. The victor dragged the still-breathing body under the stairwell and placed the satchel containing the money in Mark's hand. Then, he extinguished the light with the help of a rock. He left no fingerprints or DNA, he was sure, since he had the foresight to wear light leather driving gloves. Fortunately, he had not been cut, and there was no bleeding.

The blade had sliced through his long-sleeved shirt but had not penetrated his skin. He thought he was safe but wasn't completely sure.

The big decision for Bart Steele as he carefully guided his car away from Hogan's was whether to call 911. When he left Mark Hollister under the stairwell, the evil man was still breathing—laboriously, but nonetheless, still breathing and had a pulse. It was an easy decision. Bart pulled out his burner cell phone. "I want to report someone under the stairs at Hogan's bar."

"Your name, sir?"

"He looked badly injured," he went on while ignoring the question.

"Sir, I'm sorry, but I need your name," she asked again.

"I suggest that you send an ambulance," he continued, again disregarding her question.

"Sir, please give me ....Click. Bart did the decent thing by reporting the "accident," but he was not going to get further involved.

I wonder if he made it, he asked himself without really caring.

Mark Hollister's death was all over the news the next day. What puzzled the police was the five thousand dollars found at the scene of the crime. It was a cinch that he hadn't stabbed himself, but there were no other prints on the weapon. And it was certain that this was no robbery. Even an idiot could figure that out. So, what was it?

It didn't take authorities long to figure out, once the identification of the victim became known to them. The act had to be in retaliation for the murder of Casey Moore. What else could it be? And since the hush money was on Mark Hollister's person, it pointed to his guilt and perhaps some kind of perverted frontier justice.

Bart just hoped that the Moore family all had alibis because they had already been through enough. The story was in the news for the next several days. It was discovered by the police that Hollister took the five thousand from his bank account. The evidence, what little there was, pointed to the dead man probably being killed by a blackmailer in a payoff gone wrong. So-called insiders suggested to the media that Hollister may have attempted to kill his extorter and keep his money but had the tables turned on him in a violent fight to the end. But such theories, and many of them were advanced by numerous parties, could not explain why the blackmailer didn't merely take the money that he had obviously intended to collect. Was he in too great of a hurry? Did some witness appear out of nowhere and force him to flee without the money? But those explanations didn't hold much water. The parcel of money weighed all of twelve ounces—not a deterrent. Perhaps the killer wanted to shame Hollister. By leaving the money in his hand, it sent a clear message to the public that Mark had indeed killed Casey Moore and had intended to pay off a blackmailer. Maybe the act of disgracing Hollister was more important to his killer than the money. At least that was the way the detectives explained it. As for the grieving Moore family, it turned out that all of them had solid alibis and were never seriously considered as suspects. Much to the chagrin of the two remaining members of the Hollister family, some in the media began referring to his death as the Good Samaritan Murder. Such was the depth that Mark Hollister's sullied reputation had sunk. Bart Steele followed almost religiously the stories surrounding Mark's death and was relieved and gratified that Casey Moore's family was not blamed for it. After turning the knife on Mark during their tussle on the ground, Bart had to make a quick decision about the money. His first thought had been to take the five thousand down to the river to give to the homeless. Then, it quickly occurred to him that if the money was left with the body, the inference would be clear that Hollister had killed Casey Moore after all. And that he tried to pay off a blackmailer. Why that blackmailer had left the money there would still be a mystery, but the main thing accomplished was that Hollister would be exposed for the vile murderer that he really was. Any way one looked at it, mystery was Bart's ally. His decision about the money had to be made on the spot because he heard voices from the front door of the bar as he pulled the body under the stairwell. Apparently, he got it right. And because of his deed, the Moores could prob-ably successfully sue the Hollisters in Civil Court. That was another plus. Not that it would bring Casey back, but at least there would be compensation.

To be totally safe, Bart took the sneakers, gloves, long-sleeved shirt, and trousers that he had worn the night of his encounter with Mark Hollister and deposited them in a dumpster in nearby Cape Coral. Even if found by authorities, they would not be incriminating to him. But why take any chance? Bart Steele had performed an important public service, or so he thought. But he continued to struggle with his new life as a vigilante.

He was a religious man, and he had killed two men. No one would ever know that the count was really three. *Yes, they were scumbags,* he rationalized. *But only God has the right to take a life.* He thought back to the time when he avenged his daughter's brutal murder—just one month before avenging another. As for the third person he had killed, that had occurred many years before and would remain only in the deep recesses of his mind.

CHAPTER 18

■ Bart's treatment on the next day for his cancer somewhat tired him immediately following the medication, but his high energy returned within hours.

He was well aware that he was living on borrowed time but was determined to make the most of it. Having lost his mother, his father, and his wife to illnesses, and his daughter to murder, not to mention his own cancer, any vestige of optimism left soon disappeared. He didn't feel good about his own survival. Sometimes, he thought he would die from the cancer while other times he pondered that he should die. After all, he had killed three people.

He was growing ambivalent about his role as the avenger. A few nights after l'affaire Hollister, Bart sat down with a Crown Royal and the local Fort Myers newspaper. In the Living section, he spotted an article on Nantucket. He had spent two weeks on the island with his Aunt Liz so many years ago, when he was ten. Nantucket is the southernmost settlement in Massachusetts, first settled in 1641, when the island was deeded to Thomas Mayhew of Watertown. Some eighteen years later, Mayhew sold an interest in the island to nine other investors, saving one-tenth for himself. The price? Thirty pounds and two beaver hats. "One for myself," he insisted, "and one for my wife." A pretty good deal back then for the investors, inasmuch as any substantial property there today would be worth millions.

Aunt Liz, Bart's father's sister and a widow, invited him to spend two weeks of the summer at her Bryn Mawr, Pennsylvania, home, followed by two additional weeks in Nantucket. Thinking back on it, he wasn't sure if his parents had wanted to unload him for most of the summer or whether they thought it would be a wonderful new experience for him. Probably a little of both, he thought. Aunt Liz was a beautiful and interesting woman. Knock-down gorgeous in her late forties, she had authored a column for an outdoor sports magazine back when women didn't do that kind of thing. Proficient at hunting, fishing, and riding horses, she also was a huge baseball fan. While in Bryn Mawr, about a thirty-minute drive from Philadelphia's Shibe Park, Aunt Liz took him to a Philadelphia A's doubleheader versus the Chicago White Sox and to see his favorite player, Jackie Robinson, play for the Dodgers against the Phillies.

Bart, at ten, couldn't believe Aunt Liz would stay for every inning of each game. He saw people stirring in their seats around him in the seventh inning, and many left by the eighth. But not Aunt Liz. Knowing of his keen interest, she was so unselfish she stayed until the bitter end of every single game, regardless of the score. *How many people would do that,* he wondered then and still marveled at her endurance and unselfishness all these years later. His Aunt Liz was simply the best.

It was later in that same year that Bart visited his Aunt Liz in Bryn Mawr. Something happened in his hometown that was so unpleasant, he had to work for years to block it out.

CHAPTER 19

■ Buffalo was cold enough that skating was safe from December through March—sometimes even a month before or a month after. On one particular afternoon in 1952, Bart was dropped off by his mother, who believed he would catch a ride back with a friend. It didn't happen that way, as he stayed too late in the day, playing hockey. When the game finally broke up, it was dusk and getting dark, and no one was going his way. Bart hitchhiked home, which he'd done several times before. Only this time, he felt he had made a mistake. Something about the middle-aged man made him wary. Perhaps it was his mustache, maybe his lack of expression, or even his coal black eyes. Whatever it was, Bart felt uneasy about him. Slowly, the man put his right hand on Bart's left thigh, and Bart brushed it away. When they arrived at his stop, across from the cemetery, the man kept driving. At the next street, again Bart spoke up that he wanted to get out.

"Not going to happen, kid," were the man's exact words.

It was lucky for Bart that he had been wearing hand-me-down figure skates as a kid before he was later fitted for his first hockey skates. Bart was a pretty strong kid for his age, and he knew what he had to do. He quietly grabbed one of the skates from his lap between the stanchions, and with both hands, quickly, with all his might, drove the sharp blade protruding from the back all the way into the man's right eye. He connected perfectly, and the blade pierced the eye and went in at least a few inches. The man screamed in pain and threw up his hands, while the car went careening off Delaware Avenue into a tree. If anything, the impact ensured the pedophile's death because the skate blade was driven even further into his brain. No one wore seat belts back then, and it wasn't until the 1960s that American automakers began including seat belts in their vehicles.

The impact threw Bart up against the dashboard, and he bumped his head. But he was in much better shape than the driver. He took one last look at the man before he exited the car and ran home. Blood was gushing from the man's wound, and he wasn't moving. There didn't appear to be any witnesses. On his way home, Bart wiped the bloody blade with some snow and said nothing about the incident to his parents. He didn't read newspapers back then, but the word spread around the neighborhood about the man with the mysterious gash in his eyeball and brain who died in his car seat. Three blocks away, somehow Bart was able to put the experience on hold in his subconscious and never spoke of it to anyone. Every once in a while, the memory of the ugly event would surface in his psyche. Never once did he feel remorse for defending himself in the manner which he did.

CHAPTER 20

■ His breakfast consisted of some toast and coffee that day. Bart didn't feel well enough to have his usual robust feast. The chemo was affecting him this day, and it wasn't a good effect. He began thumbing through the *Fort Myers Beacon Press.* A front-page article immediately caught his attention. "Accused Killer Walks Free" was the headline. Ever the justice seeker, he refilled his coffee mug and read on. Bart could feel his blood simmering as he continued through the article. By the time he had finished it, his ambivalence about being a vigilante had vanished. The article, accompanied by a photo of a smirking Virgil Stassen, explained it all. Apparently, a young woman by the name of Kelly Richards had testified against a gang friend of Virgil's, resulting in a prison sentence. After two years had passed, Stassen tracked the woman down at a neighborhood bar, and they became friendly and drank together. Instead of driving her home, however, he drove to a nearby secluded vacant lot and strangled her to death. Thanks to a few eyewitnesses in the bar, Mr. Stassen was found and arrested by authorities. But that is precisely when things went tragically wrong. The police properly read him his Miranda rights— "You have the right to remain silent. You have the right to an attorney..."At that point, Stassen requested a lawyer but then confessed before the attorney arrived. That was the hitch that set the accused free. In court, the judge suppressed Stassen's confession because it was taken improperly after he had asked for a lawyer, clearly a violation of his Miranda rights. There was nothing anyone could do. Kelly Richards lay dead, and her confessed murderer walked out of court a free man. The article described a frustrated district attorney as saying that "nothing before in a courtroom has ever bothered me so much as this [bleep] walking away from a crime he admitted doing."

Once again, Bart found himself empathizing with parents whom he had never met. He reasoned it must have been so difficult, under any circumstances, to lose Kelly, but to have her murderer walk free because of a technicality in the law was well beyond the pale. He seethed at such a miscarriage of justice. That night Bart fixed himself some hash and peas for dinner and sat down to some local news on television. He didn't eat it all because the chemo left him a little queasy. Sure enough, there was a segment on the Stassen killing of the young Richards woman. Kelly's parents and brother were interviewed briefly, as they came out of the courtroom. Kelly's mother was so distraught she could barely speak, while her father and brother stood by stoically, barely able to say anything themselves. Stassen's lawyer appeared on the screen a moment later, meekly saying he was pleased by the judge's ruling that his client would go free. A smirking defendant appeared next to him but did not speak. *Wise decision,* Bart thought. Upon seeing this charade play out, a very angry Bart turned off the television and fumed. There was only one Stassen listed in the Fort Myers phone book. And he lived at 1219 Taggart Lane. Bart reasoned that the scumbag probably still lived with his parents. Much to his astonishment, Taggart Lane was only two streets south of the Naked Lady. The next morning, Bart decided to use that same burner phone that was impossible to trace. He eagerly dialed the Stassen number. On the third ring, a woman's voice answered. "Hello," he replied in a very friendly manner, "is Virgil there?"

"Whom may I tell him is calling?" She spoke quite formally.

"Paul ah, Paul Miller," he fumbled his answer.

"Just a minute please," she replied politely. A moment later she was back on the phone. "I'm sorry, sir, but he doesn't know a Paul Miller."

"This is the Phillips household, isn't it?" he asked while suddenly regaining his composure.

"No, Paul, it isn't. This is the Stassen home."

"I'm so sorry, Mrs. Stassen, I clearly have the wrong number. Sorry again to bother you."

"That's quite alright," the female voice assured him.

Bart breathed easier upon putting the receiver down and was proud of his quick thinking. Mrs. Stassen probably had no idea what had just occurred, and Bart found out what he needed to know. Virgil indeed lived at 1219 Taggart Lane!

The next day, in mid-afternoon, Bart took a drive to the Stassen house and parked close enough to see the front entrance. He waited a full three hours without seeing anyone enter or leave the structure. Perturbed and rather annoyed, he stuck his hand out the window indicating his intention to pull out onto the street. At that moment, a small, dark-colored sports car honked a warning at him as it darted by. It then pulled into the empty space in front of the light brown stucco bungalow. A young man appearing to be in his mid-twenties and fitting Virgil Stassen's description emerged. He leapt from the car and ran up the pathway towards the house.

Bingo, Bart thought to himself. On a hunch, he decided to stay where he was to see if Virgil had any plans that night. Fifty minutes and some peanut butter crackers later, he saw Virgil descend from the porch of the house and jump into his car. He left with a screech and barreled up Taggart Lane. Bart pulled out immediately and tried to stay within one hundred feet of his adversary. Careful not to arouse suspicion, Bart maintained a safe distance and followed Virgil through several stop signs and traffic lights for about two miles before the small sports car turned into La Hacienda's parking lot on Spirit Avenue. The avenger drove past it, and was going to return home but suddenly changed his mind.

Walking into the establishment, which took up half the block on Spirit Avenue, Bart noticed a long bar straight ahead of him and chose an empty stool nearest the bartender.

"What will it be, Mac?"

"Miller Light if you have it on draft."

"Sure, buddy."

Bart took in the whole room. The bar had at least twenty stools, and there were at least fifteen dinner tables. There appeared to be another room in the back of the restaurant/bar, probably for dining overflow. He put down his beer and ambled past the restrooms to look at the back room. There was a minibar, several small tables, and a large pool table. *My God*, he thought to himself, *do all street punks play pool?*

He didn't see Virgil, so he decided to visit the men's room. Suddenly, the door swung open, almost hitting him in the face. "Sorry, man," the voice apologized, "didn't see you."

"No harm, no foul," Bart replied with a smile.

It was Virgil Stassen. *He's actually a decent young man*, he thought to himself. His prey stood about six feet tall and was a little scrawny at what he estimated to be about one hundred and fifty pounds. Virgil was clean shaven and actually wore a religious silver cross around his neck. Bart thought he noticed a small tattoo above Virgil's right wrist.

When Bart returned to his bar stool, he took a swig of his beer, a handful of peanuts, and mused about his foe. *This is going to be tougher than I thought. I hated Darrell Martin and Mark Hollister, but I'm having trouble disliking this kid. Yes, he did something awful,* he reminded himself, *but this one may be different for me.* He paid his tab and walked to his car, while the old ambivalence soon came back to him. *Who appointed me God?* He asked the same question that his mother would have ventured. His mom would have been so ashamed of him. He knew it; he could feel it. Despite his imagined maternal admonitions, he still felt a responsibility to stand up for others. His father might have been the reason. He remembered one of Ed's favorite quotes but couldn't recall the author: "Strong people stand up for themselves. Stronger people stand up for others." Bart took those words to heart.

The Kelly Richards' family grief became his grief. It was relatively easy for him to kill Darrell Martin. What father wouldn't have done such a deed? Maybe it could have been done in a more humane way, if there was such a term for a murder. Obviously a humane, pre-meditated murder was the epitome of an oxymoron, and he knew that he had gone too far. He hadn't really intended to kill the smarmy Mark Hollister, but Casey Moore's mourning family deserved such revenge. And so does the Richards family. *But I'm having a hard time hating Virgil Stassen.* He wished that he had had a nasty encounter with him at La Hacienda, but he didn't. And his mother had been nice on the phone. The young man had appeared civil and cordial. *But somebody has to mete out justice to him for the Richards family, and I seem to be the only one around who cares.* Back at home, Bart poured himself another drink and thought about his predicament. Later that night as he lay in bed, he convinced himself that perhaps a thorough beating of Virgil Stassen would suffice. But his dark side emerged again to reassure him that the penalty must fit the crime. And a beating doesn't make up for a permanent strangulation and the loss a family will mourn forever over what might have been. With all of these thoughts coursing through his mind, a good sleep was near impossible. The last time he looked at the clock, it was 2:37 in the morning.

He woke up at 8:20 on Friday morning, and his mind relative to Virgil Stassen was made up. Having "kind of" met him and seeing that he seemed to be a decent fellow, he just couldn't find it in his heart to kill him. Maybe he was turning soft, or perhaps the effect of his illness and the chemo used to treat it were influencing his thoughts. He didn't know. But he did recognize that he could not execute Virgil despite knowing the man had committed a heinous crime and deserved to die. It appeared that his vigilante days were behind him.

That night, Bart pulled out the article describing the Kelly Richards' case. He could feel his blood boil once again, but still it wasn't enough to change his mind. The poor young woman deserved real justice, but it would have to come from a higher authority. Bart would, however, administer a bona fide and savage beating to the killer on her behalf. It just wouldn't be to the degree the bastard deserved. He was pretty certain that his killing days were over. Was it because he kind of knew Virgil? *It's a lot easier to kill a stranger than someone you know,* he mused. Mark Hollister and Darrell Martin were strangers. He didn't think he had it in him to kill another human being again.

His plan would be similar to that of Darrell Martin, but without the same grisly ending. One night he would find his prey at La Hacienda, and he would beat him senseless in the parking lot. Much less of a risk than murder, and he might feel a little better about it after it was over. Certainly, his mother would feel better about such a method, although she would disapprove of any violence. The contrast between his mother and father was considerable. Gretchen Steele was a gentle soul while Ed was definitely a give-me-no-quarter-ask-none kind of guy. Bart was his dad's boy!

CHAPTER 21

■ On a whim on Saturday afternoon, Bart decided to go to the movies. He just felt like going and didn't even have a specific movie in mind. There was a relatively new theater in South Fort Myers, a huge building that housed sixteen smaller theaters for different films, much like the other such buildings that had cropped up near almost any large population center in America. One of the nice things about going to a matinee was there might be only five people or so in the audience at two in the afternoon, and you could basically take almost any seat in the house. The discounted price was an added attraction.

He decided on a new Clint Eastwood film, bought his ticket, but passed on the popcorn and other goodies offered at the concession stand, and then entered Theater 7. There were eight people in the seats, all old guys with grey hair like him. After the movie, which all of them seemed to enjoy, he walked toward the lobby and decided to visit the men's room. As he sidled up to one of the several urinals, he noticed that he was alone. Taking the closest one, he unzipped his fly and took care of business. As he was finishing up, he noticed the presence of another man who had just come in and taken the urinal farthest away from him. He couldn't believe his eyes! Bart quickly glanced at the bottom of the four stalls behind him but didn't see any activity. As he walked past Virgil Stassen, he impulsively and almost instantaneously placed his right hand behind his foe's head and violently shoved it into the concrete wall just above the ceramic urinal. Virgil groaned and began to slump to the floor. Bart stepped in, propped him up a bit, and slammed his head, face first, again into the wall. Still, no one else had come into the room. Quickly, Bart grabbed the fallen and bleeding man and pulled him into one of the stalls and locked the door behind them. Bart positioned the unconscious man across the toilet bowl and applied the coup de grace. Tensing his arms and cupping his hands for maximum effect, and with Virgil's bloody head held between Bart's knees, he vigorously brought those hands together against Virgil's ears. His victim would live but would undoubtedly have a serious hearing problem for the rest of his life. As a final measure, he kicked the motionless victim in the ribs. This gory scenario all took less than two minutes. As a final indignity, Bart placed Virgil's head over the toilet bowl and put the seat down over it.

Opening the stall door, he didn't see anyone else and quickly headed out the closest exit. When he got to the lobby, he pretended to be blowing his nose, just in case there were surveillance cameras. Only a young couple with their drinks and popcorn walked by him. As casually as possible, he walked to his car, again holding a handkerchief up to his face.

It would be twenty minutes before Virgil would be found and another fifteen before the ambulance arrived. Bart got home by five, very shaken by the experience. He had no idea that he would run into Virgil like that, and he had acted entirely on impulse. It was a vicious deed, but he had done it for the family of Kelly Richards. Part of him thought about killing the defenseless Stassen in the bathroom stall, but he couldn't quite bring himself to do it. Besides, his victim would probably feel the effects of the attack for many years to come. He would live, but he would bear the emotional and physical scars forever.

Over a turkey sandwich and a beer, Bart was somewhat proud of himself for avenging a brutal murder, but he also had concerns. He hadn't had the opportunity to plan the deed and thus, may have made some incriminating mistakes. While none came immediately to mind, it had happened so quickly. Fortunately, the urinal had flushed automatically and had no lever to push. That was a lucky break because he never would have thought about it. Otherwise, the police could have lifted his prints and he might have been in trouble. Once in the stall, Bart did have the wherewithal to use a piece of toilet paper to place the seat over Virgil's head, but that action had been more about hygiene. But what about any surveillance tapes? Since he had walked into the theater without knowing what would happen later, he didn't use his handkerchief for disguise. If somehow the authorities were to suspect him of anything, he might have to admit that he was in the theater. But, so what? They had nothing on him. Darrell Martin's disappearance would never be traced to him, nor could Mark Hollister's death.

Finishing his sandwich, he dripped a little mayonnaise on the inside of his knee. He wiped it clean with a napkin, but then he saw it—a few drops of blood had coagulated on his blue jeans, the result of straddling Virgil between his legs while placing his head in the toilet. He started to sweat profusely and literally tore the pants from his body. *What if the police come right now?* he worried. But sanity took over, and he realized such a thing was impossible—at least for now. *Hell,* he mused, *they probably haven't even identified him at the hospital yet. Unless, of course, he had carried a wallet.* Bart looked carefully at the jeans but didn't notice any other blood stains. The tip of his left shoe had what looked like a possible remnant. He knew he had to get rid of the jeans and shoe. "Now," he said out loud to himself. Taking some scissors out, he carefully cut out the blood stain. Then, he placed the small two-by-three-inch scrap in one plastic bag, both shoes in another, and his cut-up blue jeans in a third container. He was tired and wanted to get rid of the evidence the following morning but knew that he couldn't afford to be lazy or reckless. Driving up Route 41, he spotted a Walmart on his right and pulled into the crowded parking area. The time was six forty-two in the evening. He casually dropped the jean's patch and shoes into a garbage bin right outside the store. People were too intent on buying something to even notice his movements. He left the blue jeans in his car for another stop. A chain drug store was on his right going home, so he pulled in and dropped the plastic bag in the refuse container outside the front door. Probably more careful than he needed to be, he pulled a wide-brimmed hat down over his ears just in case there was a surveillance camera. Bart arrived home at about seven twenty-five and pulled out the bottle of his favorite Crown Royal and a glass of ice. Sometimes, he liked to pour the golden nectar over a few cubes and just sip it. Other times he liked it with water. Tonight, it was straight over ice.

"The Gladiator" was one of Bart's favorite movies, and he noticed it was showing on TV at eight that night. That gave him over a half hour to watch a Super Bowl rerun, and he eagerly sat down with a bowl of potato chips. At eight, he switched stations to "The Gladiator," a film he had seen at least four times. He knew the story line by heart—a once powerful general is forced to become a common gladiator because the emperor is murdered by his son who seizes the throne. Reduced to slavery, Maximus, played by Russell Crowe, rises through the gladiator ranks and avenges the murders of his family and his emperor. The film was greeted with acclaim from the critics and received five Academy Awards—including Best Picture and Best Actor for Crowe. "The Gladiator" is probably high on the movie list of macho men, and Bart Steele was definitely one of them. He also liked the film for its justice theme, which certainly rang true for him as well. Bart had taken his daughter, Stephanie, to the movie when it first came out in 2000. After watching it together, they went to a late dinner and talked about it. He couldn't remember exactly when it was that his father had instilled in him the need to stand up for others. He surmised that it was probably in his early teens because there were instances where he stepped up—just like the quote that Ed had cited so many times. Bart enjoyed watching the movie for at least the fifth time and then went to bed feeling a bit guilty about roughing up Virgil Stassen. But that emotion was secondary to his satisfaction in knowing that he had somewhat atoned for the gruesome death of Kelly Richards.

After a restful Sunday spent watching golf on TV, Bart knew a Monday cancer treatment loomed on his horizon. He was seeing Dr. Gordon twice a month, and his chemo was having only a mild deleterious effect on him. He got a little tired and nauseated within an hour or so afterwards, but the feeling passed by dinnertime. This time was no different, but Bart did take a nap after the treatment. He was still in a confused state of mind about his beating of Virgil Stassen when he woke up. *How can I feel any remorse over hurting a scumbag who had brutally killed an innocent young woman?* Perhaps it was because he hadn't known Kelly Richards. He didn't know Casey Moore either, but he didn't intend to kill Mark Hollister.

Before Monday's dinner, he sat down and read through the local newspaper and spotted a more up-to-date report on Virgil Stassen. Apparently, the victim did not remember the exact details of his beating, nor did he know if there was more than one assailant. He did remember seeing a movie with a friend and going into the bathroom. That was the extent of his memory about the incident. There was a photo of Virgil's now grotesque face, and at the end of the article, a police phone number that any witness could call and report details. Seeing the photo filled Bart with remorse. He hadn't given the defenseless man a chance. That was not the way he was raised. A sneak attack such as the one he perpetrated on his adversary, however loathsome he may be, was not an honorable act. He remembered his now deceased Uncle Pete's stories about fighting the Nazis in World War II. Pete had fought in Europe and had been a member of the 101st Airborne Division, which had fought so bravely at Bastogne in the famous Battle of the Bulge. Bart remembered fondly the stories told by his uncle and how often the old man had used the term "honorable" to describe many of them. He never went into the brutal specifics and mostly talked about the guys in his unit. The Steeles seemed to all be about honor and standing up for others.

Bart's father was contributing to the war effort as a steelworker, so he was not summoned for duty. Pete, however, was selling cleaning supplies, so he was tapped for service in January of 1942. He was going to enlist the day after Pearl Harbor, but their father was ailing and their mother needed him home. The 101st Airborne Division, which Pete joined, was also known as the "Screaming Eagles." It was a specialized light infantry division of the U.S. Army that trained for air assault operations.

Many people didn't realize that the Battle of the Bulge in Belgium was the largest battle fought by Americans in WWII. More than one hundred thousand Americans were killed, wounded, or went missing of the over half million who fought there. Pete Steele was one of the survivors. It was named the Battle of the Bulge because the enemy German troops formed a bulge—or wedge—around the area of the Ardennes Forest in initially pushing through the American defense lines. Against all odds and pushed to the absolute limit, the 101st wouldn't budge and managed to hold its ground, and in so doing, changed the course of the war. On one of the rare occasions when Pete would talk specifically about his time in the war, he told his brother Ed and nephew about an incident early in that Ardennes conflict. He had encountered four German soldiers on patrol in the forest and ducked behind a tree. Using the element of surprise, Pete stepped out and mowed down three of them with his M1 Garand, the primary U.S. Army rifle of the day. The fourth German, who looked to be only about fourteen or fifteen years old, held his gun pointed at Pete but didn't fire. The impasse probably lasted for all of two seconds, Pete said, but it seemed like an eternity. The boy finally dropped his rifle and ran back into the woods. Uncle Pete just could not bring himself to shoot an unarmed enemy soldier in the back. He did what he considered was the honorable thing to do and let him escape. Undoubtedly, Pete explained, the boy would not have gotten out of there alive if others in the 101st had been present at the time. But he just could not kill a defenseless young German soldier. He often wondered after the war if the young man had survived, and if he later had children of his own.

After killing the three Germans, Pete walked over to them to be certain they were dead. They were. He collected their German Lugers and trudged back to camp to join his 101st colleagues. When Pete died in 1986, one of the captured Lugers was found in his effects. Bart's cousin, Pete Jr., probably still had the souvenir. There was one other notable footnote surrounding the Battle of the Bulge, one which gave rise to unbearable anger and anguish for the American troops. In the very early days of the famous battle, one hundred American artillery spotters were meeting together for a briefing in Malmedy, a town about forty-four miles north of Bastogne, when they were captured and held captive. A German Gestapo unit then machine-gunned them all to death. This brutal and cold-blooded execution of POWs only seemed to instill even more resolve in the Americans. It was obviously a tragic story which only served to reinforce Bart's strong sense of justice. When Bart went to bed that Monday night after thinking about his Uncle Pete and how brave and honorable he had been, he was ashamed of himself. Would he have done what Pete did and let the young German soldier flee? Based on his cowardly action in attacking a defenseless Virgil Stassen, probably not. In order to get any sleep at all that night, he had to remind himself over and over again that Virgil deserved what he got—and he was lucky to be left alive.

CHAPTER 22

■ It was Thursday of the following week when the doorbell rang. "Who the hell would be at my door at ten in the morning?" Bart wondered aloud. It was Officer Tom Livingston and Detective Vince Riley.

"Remember us?" the detective asked, his voice dripping with sarcasm. Bart was tempted to respond in kind but thought better of it.

"Hi, gentlemen," he greeted them warmly, faking it all the way. "C'mon in. How about a cup of coffee?

Officer Livingston started to demur, but Riley interrupted.

"Sure, we could use one."

The law enforcement officers followed him into the kitchen and sat down at the small table. Once the coffee was ready, they moved into the living room—or great room, as so many Floridians described them. There was a slight pregnant pause, which Vince Riley filled.

"So, Doug, what have you been up to?"

At first Bart didn't get it and looked quizzically at the detective.

"Well," Riley added, "we just wondered what Doug Parker has been up to in the past six weeks since we last saw you."

It took a moment, but then Bart got it. Obviously, the two had a more thorough conversation with his friend at the Naked Lady, Charlie Miller.

"Oh that," he laughed, trying hard to sound like it didn't matter. "I don't know about you gentlemen, but I didn't want to use my real name with a total stranger in a seedy bar." Detective Riley grimaced upon hearing that response.

"Not sure that we do, Doug. What were you doing in a seedy bar anyway?"

Bart could feel the heat rising under his collar. He really was getting to detest this smarmy detective but couldn't afford to have Riley sense it.

"I was feeling really low that night after my daughter was murdered."

Showing no empathy, the aggressive detective pressed forward. "Is that why you showed Charlie Miller the photo of Darrell Martin the first night you met him?"

There was too long a pause before he answered. "Yes, I admit it. I had hoped to see what kind of a bastard would do that to my daughter."

Vince Riley put down his coffee cup and leaned in, fully expecting a confession. "I don't blame you, Mr. Steele. I might have done the same thing. Is that when you decided to kill him?"

At this point Bart was perplexed. He knew all about the good-cop-bad-cop routine but was surprised to see both in the same person. Clearly, after all the past animosity and sarcasm, Riley had changed tactics. Even Officer Livingston seemed a little surprised by his partner's conversation. But the junior member knew his place, and he merely sat and observed.

"I did go to the Naked Lady hoping to see the bastard," he acknowledged, "but I didn't go with the intent to kill him."

"Who would blame you if you had?"

"Look," Bart said with his eyes fixed on Riley. "I hated the SOB, but killing him wouldn't bring back my daughter."

"No, but it would give you satisfaction and maybe a sense of justice." Using his first name again, the once combative detective continued his line of questioning. "Bart, in your situation, Tom and I probably would have done the very same thing. If a scumbag murdered either one of our daughters and then walked, we would want him dead."

Bart knew that Riley was groping for something—anything—to incriminate him. He also knew, or was pretty darn sure, that Darrell's body had not been found. Not wanting to provoke the detective into resuming his bad-cop schtick, he parsed his words carefully. He looked them both directly in their eyes.

"I understand that both of you are doing your jobs, and I appreciate that. I have to assume that Darrell Martin is still missing. Otherwise, you wouldn't be here. I know that you are both trying to help me. I know that you think that I murdered him and that you can understand if I had done just that. I hate Darrell Martin. I hate what he did to my daughter. And I hope that the guy he argued with in the Naked Lady killed him. He deserved it. But I didn't do it."

Riley looked especially perturbed, although Livingston continued to maintain the same placid gaze.

"We want to help you, Bart. If you just admit what all three of us know you did, we will be your allies on this. No jury will be tough on you if you come clean now. But if we get proof later on, it won't go well for you." With that the detective rose from his seat, indicating that the meeting was over.

"One last thing," the host interjected. Riley sat down again.

"Why do you both assume that Martin is dead? He could have run off somewhere to avoid paying a debt. Why are you so sure?"

"Bart," Vince Riley responded, "my twenty-two years in law enforcement tell me. My instincts tell me. Livingston and I ran down the other suspect several weeks ago. You know, the guy who you and Charlie saw at the Naked Lady that night—the one who argued with Darrell Martin and threatened him? The same night that you were seen leaving the bar shortly after Darrell? And then, no one ever saw him again."

"Yeah, I remember," Bart sheepishly agreed.

"He is a two-bit hood," Riley said boldly, "but he's not a killer."

"How can you tell?"

"Years of experience on the force, plus the punk has no record of violence. And," the detective added disdainfully, "he had an alibi. Something I might add," he said defiantly to his host, "you don't."

Bart sensed that it was best to leave it at that. As the officers got to the front door, he offered his hand to them. Dourly, Vince Riley declared that they would meet again. And then they were gone. He knew that the body of Darrell Martin would never be found. And he would be long gone in a grave himself by the time it ever was! But still, an uneasiness enveloped him. Bart wondered if they suspected him in Mark Hollister's death? Or the beating of Virgil Stassen? *They didn't bring it up,* he thought. *I wonder why?* He would hear from his police friends again.

CHAPTER 23

■ Ever since his diagnosis of cancer after the death of his daughter, he had really shunned his friends. He didn't want their pity, nor did he feel comfortable talking with anyone about either. But he missed those breakfasts and the tennis games. Bart wasn't an accomplished player, never having taken up the game until his early forties. By sheer energy and athleticism, however, he managed to be competitive, even with the few who had played high school tennis. Recognizing the mental agony their friend was experiencing, the men held a spot open for him. But they never pressured him about it.

Within a few days after Riley and Livingston's visit, Bart was contemplating his not so bright future over a dinner of leftovers. He was drinking too much, and the result left him with an uncustomary ring of flab around his midsection. The guys also met one night a week for a restaurant dinner, kind of a guys' night out type of thing. The effect of poor eating habits left him with some extra weight. But too much booze, bad food, and little to no exercise was a recipe for an expanding gut and poor health. Then again, he knew his days were probably limited.

Bart decided to call his best friend, Ken Clark. Like his ailing compadre, Ken was in his early sixties. He was not a football player but had played tennis in high school and college and was an accomplished doubles player. More importantly, Ken was a good guy and a loyal friend. In the past few months, he had called Bart regularly to check on him and to schedule a tennis game or perhaps a breakfast or dinner. Like Bart, he too had a daughter. But Kathy was married with a family of her own and living about as far away from her parents as was possible in the continental United States. Not by design, but because her husband held a job in Seattle.

"So great to hear from you, Bart!" he exclaimed when he picked up the receiver.

"Ken, is it too late for an old reprobate to come back to your tennis group?"

"Are you kidding me, Bart, we would love to have you. In fact, I have an opening tomorrow morning at nine-thirty. Mike Hansen can't make it."

"Terrific! It's been months, and I have missed you and the guys. But I must warn you, I am out of shape."

"Bart, you always hold up your end, that's for sure," his friend reassured him.

It was 9:05 the next morning, and the eager but paunchy athlete was dressed and ready to go to their tennis club. Jack DeMarco was the first old friend he saw. Jack sold paper for a living, was a solid guy, and a good tennis player. One by one, the other six ambled into the lounge, and everyone greeted Bart warmly.

"Please have patience with me," he pleaded. "I'm rusty, fat, and getting too old." They all guffawed almost in unison. Of the eight players that day, Bart was probably somewhere near the bottom talent-wise, but his competitive days on the grid-iron and natural instincts gave him an edge that few others in his group possessed. Ken played with Bart, and they won the first set 6–2. But the cancer patient wilted badly in the eighty-eight-degree morning, and they barely hung on in the second set 7–5. The trifecta of not having played in the past two months, the heat, and the effects of the chemo left Bart with little energy at the finish.

Six of the eight guys, including best friend Ken Clark, remained for some iced tea, a beer or two, and some laughs. Bart hadn't enjoyed the camaraderie in too long a time, and he realized at that moment just how much he had missed it and them. He told Ken he would like to go back to his old regular status if that was possible; they were able to be flexible because they had the option of adding one or two of the teaching pros to the group, if necessary.

On the way home, Bart felt better mentally than he had in at least a year. But his physical being had been neglected and was feeling the effects. The guys were getting together for dinner the next night, and he was in. The Crown Royal went down especially easy that night. But boy, was he tired, and his back hurt. He tried to nap in the early afternoon but to no avail. As he drifted off to sleep shortly before eleven, it was the first night in a long time he hadn't thought about being an avenger. Five of them met for dinner the next night at Girardi's, a favorite Italian haunt of theirs, and Bart felt like a new man. He had forgotten how much he had missed the guys and the friendly banter. Sitting back in his chair in the midst of them, he thought what a great shock it would be for them to know they were dining with a serial killer. *Yes,* he thought to himself, *I am a serial killer.* The FBI defines a serial killer as someone who has killed two or more people in separate events. By that definition, someone could gun down twenty-five people in a school or mall shooting and not qualify as a serial killer. *Technically,* Bart thought, *I'm not really a serial killer because I didn't intend to kill Mark Hollister. He tried to kill me,* he reasoned, *and it was an accident. And the incident when I was ten didn't really count.*

Since 1900, about three thousand American serial killers have been identified. Collectively, these monsters have ended the lives of almost ten thousand people. Experts claim that about one-third of the killers did so for the enjoyment, meaning that they killed for the mere thrill of it all or the lust or for the power they held over their victims.

Greediness finished second as about thirty percent did it for financial reward. Fortunately, Bart didn't qualify for that undistinguishable cluster either. Where he probably belonged was in the eighteen percent who killed out of anger. Anger and revenge had motivated him to kill Darrell Martin. Sympathy and compassion for the Moore family prompted him to seek revenge on Mark Hollister.

To probably no one's surprise, a firearm was the preferred murder weapon for forty-two percent of serial killers. Some six percent favored poison while two percent actually used axes. Some rumors over the years suggested that serial killing was primarily a white man's sport. But actual figures belie that. About fifty-two percent were white, forty percent black, and seven percent Hispanic. Many serial killers experienced childhood trauma or an early separation from their mothers. Often, they are loners who fear any relationship. The infamous Jeffrey Dahmer, the killer who dismembered and partially ate seventeen boys and young men, explained his bizarre behavior by saying he didn't hate his victims but wanted to "keep them with me." Gerald Stano, the killer of at least twenty-two unsuspecting women, compared each act to "stepping on a cockroach." By killing them, he "owned" them.

Serial killers tended to prey on the most marginalized members of society. That was generally their schtick. It was the modus operandi of the most prolific serial killer of them all, Samuel Little. The former boxer confessed to at least ninety-three killings between 1995 and 2005. His victims were usually prostitutes, drug addicts, and homeless women—those who stirred up little news or interest.

CHAPTER 24

■ Christmas had come and gone, and the news was super good for Bart early in the new year. Bart's cancer, bad as it was, seemed to be in remission. His medical oncologist, Stuart Gordon, MD, had reviewed all the test and blood results. After a series of scans and more blood tests, it appeared that his cancer seemed to be gone. Dr. Gordon carefully explained that while Bart seemed to be in remission, there was always the chance that microscopic cancer cells still remained in his body even after his successful treatments.

"The chemo worked its magic," the physician stated somewhat triumphantly, but cautioned against overconfidence. "These cells are not really detectable or even visible through our imaging equipment, but if they do exist, and they might," he cautioned, "there could be a return of the cancer."

They sat and talked some more while Bart processed the information. At first, he was excited and then—not so much. But he did recognize that he had received a huge break, at least for the moment.

That evening, he called his friend Ken with the good news. He wasn't about to hex himself by claiming that he had beaten cancer. Bart had seen an ad on TV in which a cancer survivor had exclaimed, "I beat cancer!" He truly hoped that the person had but thought such a proclamation was not only premature but foolishly arrogant as well. *Only God cures cancer,* he thought to himself. *If I am lucky enough to avoid a recurrence, I will never brag about it. But I will be grateful.*

Ken was ecstatic upon hearing Bart's news.

"That's great, buddy, just great!"

"I don't want to get too excited, Ken, but it is obviously good news." Then he explained the ramifications and that the cancer cells could return.

"I've been praying for you ever since the diagnosis, and I won't stop now," he reminded his friend.

It was then in the conversation when he almost did it. He came ever so close to doing it, but thank goodness his brain kicked in. Simply put, Ken could never know about his other persona—that of a serial killer. For a lot of reasons, one being it would make Ken some kind of accomplice or accessory, or someone aiding and abetting a criminal who committed a crime. Bart would never put his friend in such jeopardy. A lawyer friend straightened him out the next day. Having knowledge of a crime is not punishable, he told him, unless someone is directly asked about it during a criminal investigation and refuses to cooperate. But it didn't matter. Bart knew that he couldn't share his felonious behavior with anyone. It was time to move on from his recent life as an avenger and enjoy tennis, dinner, and the camaraderie with his friends.

His health was now good, due to some likely miracle from God, but he couldn't afford to get too excited about it. *You don't beat cancer,* he said over and over to himself, *you get a reprieve, hopefully for the rest of your life.* Cancer experts might disagree with his judgment, but it didn't matter. That was how he felt about it, and that was that.

After two games the following week, Bart felt like he was getting back in shape and was pleased that he was no longer huffing and puffing on the court. Chatting with his buddies after the match also gave him a mental lift.

While walking to his car in the grocery store parking lot later one of those afternoons, he noticed a woman drop her grocery bags. Fruits and vegetables were scattered around and under her car. He moved quickly to her side and offered help. She seemed flustered and was attempting to reach a grapefruit that had rolled under the vehicle. Her back was towards him.

"Here, let me help you," he offered as he got down on his knees and saw two grapefruits, several tomatoes, and some lettuce just out of his grasp.

"That's sweet of you, but don't get your shirt dirty." Ignoring her comment, he crawled under the car to retrieve the elusive produce. He gathered the five items and crawled out, triumphantly handing the groceries over.

"You are so kind," she thanked him, "but look at your tennis shirt. It's all dirty!"

"Oh, that's okay," he insisted. The grime said otherwise. He had managed to get some oil and some reddish and brown substance on his white polo. He looked closer at her and was taken by her breathtaking beauty. She stood about five feet six with grey hair cut in a pageboy style. Perhaps it was because many older women preferred to color their hair, Bart generally did not find grey hair very appealing on a woman. Maybe it had something to do with women in their seventies or eighties going with the natural look. But whatever the reason, for him, grey hair on women was generally a turnoff. Not on this fair lady, however. She had a firm jaw, almost perfect teeth, and a pert nose. As they exchanged the dropped groceries, he noticed she was not wearing a wedding ring. Normally, he never noticed such details, but something about this lady made him look. Her enchanting green eyes drew him in. They stood and gazed at each other for an awkward moment.

"Well, thanks again," she said with a smile. But he didn't want to walk away and end the encounter.

"By any chance," he stammered, "would you consider having coffee, or aahh, a lunch sometime with a guy you just met who has oil on his shirt?" Now she smiled broadly.

"Do you have a name?" she asked with a devilish grin.

"Oh, I'm sorry," as his face turned crimson from embarrassment. "I'm Bart Steele, and I live about a mile away."

"Hi, Bart Steele. I'm Sally West." He noted the impish look on her face when she responded.

"What would work best for you, Sally, coffee or lunch?" He was still clearly flustered and began shifting his feet. She noticed but went along with the flow.

"Either is fine, Bart, although lunch might be more fun!"

"How about next Monday at noon at Leonardo's?"

"Oh, geez, I'm sorry. I have an appointment then."

Just as Bart was sensing a brush off, and looking more uncomfortable by the moment, she weighed in again.

"But I could do Tuesday if that works for you?"

Now he was back in the game! "Sounds good to me," he said with a momentarily lost confidence returning to his voice.

As she got into her car, he began to walk away. She lowered the window. "Don't you want to know how to reach me?" she grinned.

He ambled over to her car door, now feeling totally humiliated. "I'm sorry. I'm not so good at this."

She wrote down her cell phone number and handed it to him.

"No problem," Sally said with a smile. "See you next Tuesday at twelve noon."

His enthusiasm upon meeting such a pretty woman was somewhat deadened by his almost botched attempt to arrange a lunch date. *What an idiot I am,* he admonished himself over and over again during the drive home. *She must think that I came down with yesterday's rain! That I am a real dork.* But the bottom line was that they did establish an actual meeting. He reasoned that she couldn't have thought he was that bad. After all, she didn't say "no." But he froze. Bart was badly out of practice, and he knew it.

While he was married to his soulmate, Ginny, he didn't even bother to look at other women. And since her tragic death, he had barely dated at all. Just a few times, in fact, but he just couldn't get into the process. He missed Ginny, and there was no one who could take her place. But a wonderful feeling engulfed him now after his chance encounter with Sally West, and he didn't feel guilty about it. He just knew that Ginny would approve of whatever, if anything, might happen. He put his groceries away and poured himself a Crown Royal. For some reason, he put the glass aside and had coffee instead.

CHAPTER 25

■ On the other side of town in the law offices of Gold, Mellman, and Spence, there was a conference going on among the partners on how to offer the best defense for their client Frank Bender. Bender had been charged with murdering his wife, Kathy, but her body was never found. There was plenty of circumstantial evidence, however, and it all pointed to Bender's guilt. For example, there were detectable droplets of his blood discovered on the kitchen floor, thanks to the chemical agent Luminal. Since 1937, the Luminol reagent has been used to detect blood stains—even after several years. There had been an effort to remove the stains with bleach, but applying Luminol to the suspected area resulted in a blue glow. Tiny particles of blood could cling to a number of surfaces for years without anyone suspecting it. This was detected only a few days after Kathy Henry Bender's disappearance. Frank Bender had also told a business associate that "he had no use" for his wife. Furthermore, he had participated in several affairs over the past few years. It was a neighbor, not the husband, who reported Kathy missing. And Frank Bender had taken out a one-million-dollar life insurance policy on Kathy just five months before she disappeared. These were the issues facing Jeffrey Gold, the lead defense attorney.

Kathy Bender's car was found on a deserted street along with her cellphone, purse, and keys. But her purse had been stripped of its contents. Of course, the defense would vigorously argue that the crime scene resembled that of a robbery and possibly a murder. There were no footprints found around the car, as it was parked on a dry macadam surface. At first the prosecutor showed little interest in pursuing the case against Frank Bender, but the circumstantial evidence kept piling up. And her parents, friends, and brother continued to pressure the DA's office. Frank Bender insisted he had nothing to do with her disappearance and would never do anything to harm his wife, the "mother of my two children." He did not really require an alibi because of the absence of a body. No one knew what, if anything, had happened to Kathy Bender or when it could have occurred.

It was a hot, muggy Monday in mid-March, even for Southwest Florida, and the courtroom in Fort Myers was packed to the gills. This trial was garnering much public attention and notoriety, and the media was making the most of it. It was not an easy case for the prosecution. Far from it. There was no body. Under English common law, which had been adopted by the United States in its infancy, a dead body was required to prove a murder.

In the 1900s, the law began to change in both countries. In a case in England in 1954, the court found that circumstantial evidence was enough to establish the matter of death despite the absence of a body. The United States followed suit in a 1960 California case, Scott v. California, where the court also found that circumstantial evidence was enough. The court had said, "Circumstantial evidence, when sufficient to exclude every other reasonable hypothesis, may prove the death of a missing person, the existence of a homicide, and the guilt of the accused." While it was—and still is—true that the absence of an actual body makes a murder prosecution extremely difficult, no longer was there a hard-and-fast rule that there had to be a body for a murder conviction.

Since Kathy Bender's body was never found, the conviction of her husband, Frank, was going to be the most difficult case that District Attorney Floyd Sherman had ever handled. Sherman was a tough and resolute prosecutor, but he faced many challenges ahead. But things were not so rosy for the defense either. Jeffrey Gold would have to overcome some pretty significant obstacles himself. For one thing, the circumstantial evidence was not very compelling if taken fact by fact, but the sum total of them pointed to Bender's guilt. And then there was the matter of the defendant himself. Frank Bender was far from the perfect client. Short, squat, and a slightly balding man, probably in his early fifties, his dark beady eyes added to his sinister look. A scar over his left eye did not help to soften his appearance, and it was an easy decision for Gold not to put him on the stand to testify. Despite dressing in a sharp new brown suit, blue shirt, and patterned brown and blue necktie, Bender was the perfect example of putting lipstick on a pig, giving it a purse, and calling it Monique. It was still a pig.

That Monday morning, Prosecutor Floyd Sherman went to great lengths to lay out all of the circumstantial evidence against Frank Bender for the jury. The DA was nattily dressed in a dark suit, white shirt, and light blue tie. Probably in his early sixties, his hair was grey, and he wore it short, just as he had years ago in the Marine Corps. He had a hawkish nose, bright blue eyes, and a determined look on a long and narrow face. Initially he had been reluctant to bring the case to court but had been heavily "leaned on" by the family of the missing woman. The media also got caught up in the wave of sensationalism and helped to create the public demand for it. Sherman thought Frank Bender guilty but was concerned that without a body, he would not be able to convince a jury of it. Sherman called two women as witnesses who testified to Bender's lack of fidelity to his wife. He also called the co-worker who had heard the defendant complain that "he had no use for his wife." That detail might not have resonated so much with the jury had it not occurred just two days before her disappearance. Seven women on the twelve-member jury were wives themselves, a fact not overlooked by Sherman. He also pointed out that the defendant had not filed a missing person report with the police. In questioning the forensic expert, he hit hard on the blood stains on the kitchen counter and floor, which he pointed out had been cleaned up by Bender. The Luminol, of course, revealed them. "They had been married for twenty-three years," the DA told the jury, "and Mr. Bender had not previously bought life insurance on her. Five months before she disappeared," he continued, "somehow, he just happened to get the idea to purchase it. You fill in the blanks," he said emphatically as he looked the jurors squarely in their eyes.

The weakness in the case still loomed rather large. No body.

By the time the cross-examination of the witnesses by the defense was concluded, and the prosecution had completed its arguments, it was 3:20 in the afternoon, and Judge Hastings called for an adjournment. "We will resume at ten tomorrow morning."

CHAPTER 26

■ That Monday night Bart was absorbed in his thoughts about his lunch date with Sally West the next day. He was not aware of the drama across town involving the scurrilous Frank Bender. But eventually he would be.

It took at least thirty minutes for Bart to completely decide what to wear. And then, after he had made the final decision, he changed his attire again. The khakis were a given; what was presenting the problem was his choice of shirt. His first choice had been a pink golf shirt. What better way to show a woman that he was comfortable with himself? But he didn't think he looked good in pink, even though he liked the color. Then he tried on a red one but quickly rejected it as making too big a statement. He loved yellow but reasoned that no one really looked good in that color. Finally, he decided on a pale-blue golf shirt. *Good grief,* he chuckled to himself, *is this what women go through to find the right outfit?* Although he had a big enough torso to comfortably accommodate a large shirt, Bart always preferred the snug fit of a medium. It made him feel stronger, he reasoned, but he often took flak for it from his friends, especially his tennis buddies. "I dress for my comfort, assholes, not yours!" were his testy words. Having finally decided on his wardrobe for the next day, he wandered into the TV room and watched a little tennis on the Tennis Channel. He was excited about his meeting with Sally but apprehensive as well. *What is the worst that can happen,* he asked himself, as he always did when facing a situation he couldn't control. *She doesn't like me, and we have a nice lunch—that's it,* he tried to convince himself. But Bart Steele was a competitor. She had to like him, or he will have failed. Even if he ended up not particularly liking her, it was important that she like him. Wasn't that how the real male ego worked? He didn't sleep well that night.

Not so far away lay Sally West, also thinking about her lunch date. Her husband had died of a heart attack two days after his fifty-sixth birthday, which turned her into a widow for the past four years. She missed the intimacies of marriage and being able to depend on someone else. Sally's friends, both married and divorced, rallied around her and kept her in their social circle—at least for the first few years. She didn't blame them for not continuing the indulgence indefinitely. They all had their own lives, filled with their own children and grandchildren. She understood that and maintained a close relationship with Carol Mooney, a divorcee and a friend with similar interests. They would dine out occasionally, go to art shows, and play tennis. But her dance card, so to speak, was not close to being filled. Sally had gone on a few dates over the past three years, but the men seemed "a tad full of them-selves," as she put it. Carol agreed. Neither one considered it worth their while to go out just in order to go out. But there was something in Bart that Sally found appealing. He seemed earnest and had a sense of humor. Both qualities she considered attractive, and they had manifested themselves in only the few minutes during the short time they had met. Bart did have her attention, at least for another day!

CHAPTER 27

■ It was ten sharp in Judge Hastings' courtroom when the bailiff made his announcement. "All rise. This court is in session, the Honorable Norwood Hastings presiding."

The judge sat high on his throne, his silver hair almost shining. He was a tall, thin, African American man, standing a full six feet four with high prominent cheekbones. Somehow, one got the immediate feeling that Hastings was in full control and not someone you would want to cross. Perhaps it was his flashing eyes, maybe his harsh demeanor, but whatever it was, he commanded respect by his mere presence. Now it was the defense's turn to present its closing argument. Jeffrey Gold rose slowly from his seat at the defendant's table and walked rather deliberately to the jury box. Almost too handsome, he cut a very patrician figure with his prematurely white hair. He wore his closing-arguments power suit. The navy-blue suit, crisp white shirt, and yellow-and-blue-striped tie gave him an elegant and confident appearance, all enhanced by his perfect posture. Jeffery Gold stood six feet tall but seemed taller. He looked like he could have played Cary Grant in a movie, sans the dimpled chin. Great teeth, a narrow but strong nose, and blazing green eyes completed the look. The defense would be all about him and not his sluggish and uninspiring client Frank Bender. And that, of course, was exactly the point.

Scanning his eyes back and forth, Gold looked all of the jurors in the eye. "You all deserve," he began, "our tremendous respect and admiration for giving of your time to a most serious case. A man's life hinges on your ability and willingness to process the information that has been provided to you and come to the right conclusion. We thank you for this important service," he concluded.

What the prosecutor undoubtedly considered pandering, others in the courtroom thought adroit. This man clearly resonated with people. That is precisely why he was considered the best defense attorney in Southwest Florida. And he wasn't finished with his comments.

"The prosecution has presented to this court a ragtag case involving no actual evidence whatsoever and wants you to believe a few meaningless occurrences. Everyone in this room is concerned about the whereabouts of Kathy Henry Bender, including her husband, Frank—especially her husband, Frank! The members of the prosecution presented you, the jury, with a puzzle. And they want you to fill in the last few pieces of that puzzle because they haven't got the faintest idea of what, if anything, happened to Kathy or what might have prompted her to leave."

The courtroom buzzed after this remark, and members of the Henry family shifted uneasily and unhappily in their gallery seats.

Gold continued to ridicule the blood samples found in the Bender kitchen. "Of course, they were his," he asserted. "He cut his hand while slicing a tomato! The prosecutor went to great lengths to accuse my client of using a cleansing agent to clean up the mess. Of course, he did," he explained. "Wouldn't you all have done the same?" As for the life insurance policy taken out five months before his wife disappeared, if he did that with a later crime in mind, why wouldn't there be a body so he could collect the funds right then and there? It will take five to seven years to collect on a missing person. If anyone were guilty of such a crime for money, that person wouldn't go the missing person route."

Point by point, Jeffrey Gold demolished the prosecution's case. Bender's I-have-no-use-for-my-wife comment was greatly diminished in importance through cross-examination. The attorney suggested that such a remark was one that every husband or wife had probably made at one time or another during their married lives. Gold dealt with the accusation of several affairs with the claim that Kathy Bender did not want to have sex with her husband, and that he made a few bad choices instead of remaining celibate. But he said it in such a way as to insinuate that she was not a good wife.

He didn't say it directly, but he implied it in a very smooth and non-offensive manner. The defense counsel explained that his client hadn't reported his wife as missing because several times in the past during their marriage, Kathy had gone away for a few days—something the prosecutor later challenged as a statement without foundation.

Clearly, this was far from Jeffrey Gold's first rodeo. And then Gold somehow made the biggest mistake of his illustrious legal career. On a whim—and a great lawyer usually knows better than to act on a whim—he could have lost the case right then and there. Fortunately for him and his client Frank Bender, no one seemed to notice. "Who knows," he paused, "maybe Kathy Bender will walk in that courtroom door right now. We just don't know." With that comment, everyone's eyes shifted from Jeffrey Gold to the door. Everyone, that is, except for one person. Frank Bender didn't look because he knew full well there was no way Kathy was going to walk through that door, now or ever. And that was because, of course, her undiscovered body lay undisturbed three feet under the ground near a small, shady tree. When the defense counsel saw that his client didn't look at the door, he knew two things: one, that Bender killed his wife; and the other, that he almost made a monumental mistake. Jeffrey Gold would never make such a courtroom error again. He was so relieved no one else saw. But unbeknownst to him, someone else did.

Taking a deep breath, he sauntered back to the jury box, for his final remarks. These would be the most important he would speak during the entire trial. Again, he stood ramrod straight and looked into the jurors' eyes to be certain that they were listening attentively to him.

"You have an immense responsibility," Gold reminded them. "Justice depends on it. Our system of justice depends on the credo that a man is presumed innocent until proven guilty. My client, Frank Bender, has been accused of a terrible, terrible crime. But you have sat through all of the testimony regarding this case, and you heard the prosecution's attempt to make something out of nothing. We all hope and pray that Kathy Bender will turn up and be well. We wish her and her family Godspeed. But there is not one scintilla of tangible evidence that ties my client to any crime. A man is presumed innocent until proven guilty. They have no case against Frank Bender! And the prosecution has not convinced anyone that there was a crime. They have not and cannot prove that there has been one. The burden of proof is on them. As you all know, because you have taken your responsibilities so seriously, it is incumbent on the prosecution to prove my client Frank Bender guilty beyond a reasonable doubt. They haven't even come close to that standard."

He moved away from the jury box and then suddenly turned back to face the jurors. "Thank you again for your service on this jury. You have all been very attentive." One did not need a degree in jurisprudence to recognize that Jeffrey Gold had resonated with the jury. Just how much would be determined later.

It was twelve minutes past two when Judge Hastings announced there would be a thirty-minute break before the prosecution made its closing argument.

"We will reconvene at two forty-five." At precisely that time, Floyd Sherman's name was called to make his final comments. He stood in front of the jury box confidently.

"Thank you all for your service during this trial," he said earnestly. "We have the defendant's blood spatter in his home. He was carrying on two separate affairs, had conveniently taken out a million-dollar life insurance policy on his wife after twenty-three years of marriage and just five months before she disappeared, and he had uttered to an office associate that he had no use for his wife. Those remarks were made just two days before her disappearance, and he had not even reported her missing. What that adds up to," he said firmly, "is murder."

He took a deep breath and continued. "Her car is then found by the side of the road in a desolate area that she would never visit. Frank Bender's hands are all over this crime. There are just too many incriminating circumstances and coincidences to reach any other verdict but murder. Thank you for your attention, and again, thank you for your service."

Judge Hastings then gave his final instructions to the jury. Among them were to isolate themselves from inappropriate influence until they came in the next morning to begin their deliberations. But, of course, almost all jurors violate those instructions.

CHAPTER 28

■ About five miles away, a different drama had been playing out. Bart had walked into Leonardo's five minutes early at 11:55, but Sally was already occupying a booth. Upon seeing her, he took her hand and kissed it. He really didn't know why he did that. It was just an impulse.

"You look terrific," he exclaimed.

"You're not so bad yourself," was her riposte. She was already sipping on a lemonade. And he was somewhat flustered that she had beaten him there.

"Sorry, I'm a little late. But I am a little early," he smiled.

"My father always told me," Sally continued on, "that one should always be early to any meeting. I'm one of those, if-I'm-late-send-flowers kind of girl!" He laughed.

"How refreshing. Your father is a wise man."

"Was a wise man. He died last year at eighty-eight."

"He must have had a nice life."

"He did, thanks."

Bart couldn't take his eyes off her. She was absolutely beautiful in her yellow sleeveless golf shirt—the same yellow he had rejected for himself, reasoning that no one would look good in it. Her white Bermuda shorts were just the perfect length, not too short but not too long either. "I wasn't sure that you would recognize me, at least without an oil slick on my shirt." She smiled. Just as they were looking at the menus, a tall and thin form appeared by their table. It was a tennis friend of Bart's.

"So, now I see why you blew me off for lunch today."

"Sally West," Bart interrupted, "I want you to meet Les Crane, who used to be a good friend of mine." All three laughed.

"Can you blame me, Les?"

"No, not at all. I went to the gym instead."

"I can tell by the smell," Bart guffawed. "Thanks, friend. I do look a little ratty in this old shirt and shorts."

"Nothing little about it!"

Sally was clearly enjoying the tete-a-tete between the two good friends.

"I'd ask you to sit down with us, but I'm afraid that you might!" Bart declared.

"Nice to meet you, Sally," Les announced as he started to back away from the table.

"You, too," she acknowledged.

Suddenly, Bart beckoned his friend back. "Les," he said with a big grin, "you should know that the seventies just called, and they want their clothes back!"

"Bart, just don't play too close to the net tomorrow, something fast might be coming your way."

"Bring it on, buddy," Bart retorted with a smile.

Sally had clearly enjoyed the friendly banter between them.

During their lunch, they spoke more like old friends rather than two people on their first date. She got him to open up first. After a quiet discussion of his childhood, he told her about Ginny and what a great marriage they had enjoyed together right up until the bitter and sad end. When he spoke in a hushed voice about the death of his daughter, Sally reached across the table and took his hand in hers and caressed it. He was very moved by her gesture, not in a sexual way, but with her empathy.

"That must be so difficult for you," she tried to assuage his grief. Tears formed in his eyes.

"Yes, it's hard, but you have to go on. A lot of bad things have happened to a lot of good people, but somehow, they found the spiritual energy, faith, and strength to move on. It's one day at a time for me, but the pain subsides a tiny bit with each passing day. Please tell me about your life," he said with a lump in his throat.

"Well, I'm not sure that it's very interesting or entertaining for that matter."

"It is to me," he responded earnestly. She was taken by his four words and the obvious sincerity behind them.

"Well, I was born in Seneca Falls, New York. Does that mean anything to you?"

"As a matter of fact, it does," he responded.

"What exactly?"

"Well, it was the home of Elizabeth Cady Stanton when they held the first women's rights convention in 1847."

"Wow," she exclaimed, "I'm really impressed."

"Now I have a question for you!" he interjected. "What was the first country to give women the right to vote?" She paused for a moment before shaking her head side to side. "Well, it was New Zealand in 1893." He was on a roll.

"What was the first state to grant women the right to vote?" Again, she indicated that she didn't know. "Wyoming in 1869," he triumphantly declared. Clearly, he demonstrated his women's rights bona fides, and she was impressed.

"I can't believe that you know all that—that any man does. I would love to talk more about this next time we get together."

"Whenever you want," he nodded his head approvingly. *Wow, she must like me,* he thought.

Returning to their pre-Seneca-Falls remarks, she began, "Well, anyway, we moved to Bryn Mawr when my sister and I were young."

His eyebrows arched upon hearing this, and his entire face broke out in a huge grin.

"Did I touch a nerve?" she asked, noticing his reaction.

"Keep going. We can come back to it."

"Well, anyway, I went four years to Smith College in Massachusetts and married right out of school. My husband was from Boston, and we were married for almost thirty-four years before he died of a heart attack four years ago. It was just two days after his fifty-sixth birthday. Fortunately, my daughter was grown by then."

"That must have been tough for both of you, especially when he was only fifty-six."

"Believe it or not, that wasn't as tough for me as something he had done two years before." She took a sip of her lemonade to aid her dry throat.

"I don't know why I'm telling you this, Bart, because I hardly know you." He leaned in toward her, sensing her distress. "He had an affair with a younger woman that lasted for almost three years." Her face was grim, and she was fighting back tears. Now it was his turn to take her hand. She continued.

"Sam confessed to me about two months before he died. I suspect that he told me only because he was so consumed with guilt, and not because it was the right thing to do." Sally now had an edge to her voice and was clearly perturbed. He stroked her hand and tried to soothe her.

"The guilt probably contributed to his early heart attack," Bart observed.

"You know, I thought of that. It probably did."

He didn't want to appear too forward and so, he released her hand.

"You are very easy to talk to, Bart Steele," she murmured, "but I'm sorry I had to say all of that."

"Things happen for a reason, Sally, and maybe you just needed to get that off your chest."

To his great surprise, she clutched his hand again for just a little too long. It made him feel important. Neither of them wanted dessert, but there were silent signs they didn't want the lunch to end either. They talked about tennis and the Bryn Mawr connection for another twenty minutes or so and then decided to meet on Friday to hit balls together. They walked to her car and continued their conversation. And then he had a decision to make—to kiss or not to kiss her? That decision was taken out of his hands when she leaned forward and gave him a peck on the cheek. It really wasn't a forward and aggressive move, but it was a positive nevertheless.

"You're a very nice man, Bart, and I'll look forward to Friday morning." And then she drove away.

He had totally enjoyed their lunch and time together. Bart Steele was very taken by Sally West and couldn't think of anything he didn't like about her. She was beautiful, athletic, had a nice trim body, and was so easy to talk with. He was gratified and excited that she had actually made the first move. While he had stood there twisting in the wind and wondering what to do, she took control of the situation and kissed him. It would hardly constitute a passionate kiss, far from it. But it was a kiss. She liked him, no doubt about it.

A very happy and contented man poured himself a drink that night. His body had basically atrophied, almost all of it, before he met Sally West. There had been no excitement in his life for too long, but all that now had the strong possibility of changing.

CHAPTER 29

■ Wednesday morning in Fort Myers was unusually muggy. Members of the jury filed into the courthouse to begin their deliberations in the Frank Bender murder case. They were then escorted to a private room where they would begin discussions until a verdict was reached. The first business to be conducted was to elect a jury foreperson. When the seven women and five men sat down at the rather long rectangular table, Harriet Means was the first to speak. "I would like to suggest that Rosemary Pettit, who is sitting to my immediate left, be the foreperson of this jury. She was a legal secretary and has been on several juries." A few men grumbled quietly, probably an indication that they preferred a man in that position. But Rosemary easily won the vote, and she would preside over the jury deliberations. She immediately called on Brian Porter, a grey-haired gentleman appearing to look in his sixties.

"I think that Bender guy is a scumbag and guilty as sin." A few heads nodded in agreement.

Sara Sanchez was next to speak. "I think that he is guilty because he wouldn't testify."

At this point, Ms. Means interjected again. "Because of Rosemary's experience, perhaps she can address Sara's comment and fill us all in on other pertinent matters."

Rosemary Pettit scanned the jury members to gauge their degree of interest. Most of the heads nodded affirmatively, so she proceeded. "I am aware of some studies that back up Sara's comments. While Judge Hastings did instruct us not to infer guilt because the defendant didn't testify, many jurors tend to believe it anyway. But we should try," she implored the others, "not to prejudge Mr. Bender just because he didn't testify." Then, she shared other things she had learned in other trials. "Generally speaking, opening statements by the prosecutor and the defense attorney can be very effective as long as they don't over-promise." She added, "Prosecutors in most cases have a better idea about how they are performing than defense lawyers. If the prosecutor presented well in his or her closing argument, the juries tended to look more favorably on the prosecution. But there may be a simple explanation for that. The last events or remarks are better remembered. Of course, the opposite of that can also be true. If the prosecutor stumbled or was ineffective in their closing, you might look more favorably on the defense." Rosemary Pettit may have been considered a bit pedantic to some, but most of the jurors seemed to appreciate the information.

The jury deliberated until noon, when its members took a boxed-lunch break. During their lunches of turkey, beef, and chicken salad sandwiches, potato chips, and pretzels, and small containers of fruit, and cold and hot drinks, the jurors relaxed a bit and most engaged in somewhat stilted conversation. At this point, they were hesitant to talk about any aspect of the case they were now involved in.

After their slow start, the jurors tended to get along quite well, thanks in part to Pettit's leadership, although the women tended to sit together, apart from the men. They had made considerable progress in a little over two hours and had already taken several votes. The first round of informal polling found six jurors in favor of conviction and six against. Only one woman voted for the defense. Key points made by all but one of the men that seemed to resonate with one of the seven women was that while no one liked Frank Bender, the matter of his actual guilt was not established by the prosecution. In fact, all of those who voted in favor of the defense and Bender, actually expressed their belief that the defendant was guilty of the crime. But as one of them said, "He's probably guilty, but a person is presumed innocent until proven guilty. But there is nothing to tie him to the crime. Nothing!"

The second vote went 8-4 against conviction. Now, all five men, including Brian Porter, supported the defense, while two more women switched their votes. The two seemed to feel more relieved that the men felt he was guilty but honestly didn't believe the prosecution had proven its case. Several groups of two or three continued side discussions about the case, and no longer were the women and men split up. Clearly, Rosemary Pettit was the right person to lead the jury. "Well," the foreperson reminded them, "the last vote was 8-4 for acquittal."

Nancy Helms raised her hand. "As you know, I have been one of the holdouts. It's hard to let someone off when you just know deep in your heart that he's guilty. But I am now ready to change my vote and acquit the bastard." Her face turned crimson, and she immediately apologized to her eleven colleagues for her language. "But he is," she added with a smile.

Molly Warren raised her hand. "I, too, have been a holdout but agree with Nancy that there is just not enough evidence to convict this guilty son-of-a-bitch." She also grinned. Now it was a 10-2 vote for acquittal. But two jurors, Debbie Plant and Alice Newcombe, didn't want to budge.

Debbie was the first of the two dissidents to state her case. "You know he's guilty; we've all agreed on that. Can't we delve deeper into the evidence and find something that we can hang him with?"

Alice emphatically agreed. "We just can't let him walk. His murdered wife deserves better than this. We all deserve better than this!"

At this point, Wally Baker, a fifty-five-year-old welder, wanted to be heard. "I can't disagree with anything that has been said here," he offered, "but we have a responsibility to do the right thing. In my heart of hearts, I know the bastard is guilty—and I'm not going to apologize for using the word. He is a rotten bastard, and I would kill him myself if I was his wife's brother. But I'm not, and we have to see that justice is done according to the law. In my view, unfortunately and sadly, the prosecution has not proven his guilt. The slime bag is presumed innocent until he has been proven guilty." Perhaps it was his passion in saying that he would kill the defendant himself, were he the brother of the missing woman. Maybe it was something else he said. But the bottom line was that he was the catalyst in helping the jury to reach a final verdict.

It was 2:13 in the afternoon when Rosemary Pettit took the vote, and this time it was unanimous. The jury foreperson notified the clerk who then informed the judge. Deliberations took officially four hours and thirteen minutes, but in reality, much less time than that. Word quickly spread to the interested parties and the media. The jury in the Frank Bender case had reached a verdict.

Bart had enjoyed a nice day, thinking about Sally West, and was eagerly awaiting their planned tennis game on Friday morning. He was looking forward to playing with the guys that morning, too. But this was different, Sally had captivated him. It was something that transcended her beauty. It was not a question about her looks, and she was even well-endowed, although that wasn't it either. Sally was a real find, and to think that he had accidently met her in a parking lot. There was no woman in the entire five years since Ginny died who even sparked the slightest interest in him. But Sally seemed to be the entire package. Smart, kind, athletic, passionate, and caring. And she was incredibly attractive to boot! He wondered if she felt the same way or at least if she was thinking about him too. She really mattered to him—even though they had just met, and he only had lunch with her. Perhaps it was that particular time in his life when he genuinely needed someone. Whatever it was, he couldn't bear the thought of losing Sally. He knew it sounded pretty silly; he barely knew her. When he came home from his errands, Bart had a light lunch, relaxed, and read the newspaper. At the same time, Judge Hastings' courtroom was about to come to order. Media and spectators rushed in to get a seat. Observers didn't know what to make of the early verdict. While conventional wisdom says that a quick verdict generally indicates sympathy for the defense and an acquittal, it can also go the other way. For example, it could simply have meant that the jurors were overwhelmed with a recognition of the defendant's guilt. In other words, no one really knew for sure.

Members of the jury filed into the courtroom, and the judge gazed out at the assembled crowd. His eyes rested just for a moment on the family of Kathy Bender. The verdict slip was handed to him by the bailiff. He looked at it but without any sign of emotion. Judge Hastings then asked Foreperson Rosemary Pettit if the jury had reached a verdict.

"Yes, we have, your Honor."

"And what is your verdict?"

At that point, the hair on defendant Frank Bender's neck stood up as it did for his attorney.

"We the jury, find the defendant not guilty."

A stunned silence gripped the courtroom. Members of Kathy Bender's family were shocked, and some slumped forward, crying in their seats in disbelief. Members of the media dashed out of the courtroom no doubt to call in their stories. Frank Bender, now a free man, hugged Jeffrey Gold who was almost equally relieved. Most of those in the courtroom were surprised by the verdict, having come to believe Bender's guilt. If not by the evidence, they were struck by his cavalier appearance and attitude when listening to the case against him. It was clear he had very few friends. No doubt well over ninety percent of the courtroom observers thought him guilty. But here he was a free man. Guttersnipe that he was, Frank Bender wasn't smart enough to keep his elation to himself. When the TV reporters fell all over themselves to get a word from the newly acquitted defendant, he was more than eager to accommodate them. As they were leaving the scene, Gold could be seen solemnly chatting with his victorious client. Being the good attorney that he was, undoubtedly, he was most likely advising him to be humble about the verdict and to hold back any rhetoric. But, of course, Bender wasn't buying any of it. Gold tried vainly to prevent him from speaking, but the arrogant defendant stepped forward anyway in front of the cameras outside of the building. A reporter yelled out the question, "So, what are you going to do now that a jury has found you innocent?"

Incredibly, the base and despicable Bender disregarded his attorney's advice and uttered words that he would later regret, words that would come back to haunt him. "I guess I should say that I'm going to Disneyworld," he brashly shouted out in glee, "but I love Fort Myers' beaches, and that's where I'm heading." His comments drew only disdain from those close enough to hear them. Fortunately for the aggrieved family of Kathy Henry Bender, no one heard his live remarks. But all would hear them later that night on the news shows and for several days later. One person in particular who was not aware of the case, would soon see those insensitive words on television.

To his credit, defense attorney Jeffrey Gold immediately recognized the gravity of his client's words and behavior and attempted to rectify the situation. He quickly stepped forward and attempted to mitigate the obvious damage. "What Mr. Bender really means is that while he is understandably happy about his acquittal, he feels badly for his wife and her family, and he hopes that she turns up soon and is well." Gold knew after his own blunder in court that his client was guilty because he was the only person, he thought, who hadn't looked at the door when Gold foolishly suggested that Kathy Bender might actually come through it. The distinguished defense counsel didn't like his client, but he knew that he had to act in court like he did. Because the jury would be watching. But now, Frank Bender was acting so egregiously that he had to step in. After all, to a certain extent, an attorney's client can and often does reflect on him. He hoped that he had stepped in on time, but he knew that networks would play up Bender's brazenly disdainful and near contemptuous words. Gold's attempted disclaimer or recantation, he feared, would not see the light of day. His prescience was proven that night and on television for the next several days.

Bart Steele prepared his usual makeshift dinner that Wednesday night and turned on the local news. He was appalled by Frank Bender's insensitive remarks despite not knowing anything about the case. Then he saw Kathy Bender's brother go into some detail about it and became livid. After reading about the case in the old newspapers he had recently discarded in his recycle bin in the garage, his old vigilante feelings, dormant for a few weeks, rekindled in full. The next morning, Bart arrived at the tennis courts, and part of him was hoping that Les Crane might not make it. But sure enough, there he was.

"Hey, lookee here," Les said looking up from his seat, "lover boy Bart Steele is in the building." The five other tennis players who were there early all smiled and applauded as Bart walked by, his face turning crimson. "Seriously guys," Les opined, "Bart's girlfriend is a real doll and someone way too good for him!"

When they went on to the courts, Les approached Bart to say Sally seemed like a great gal and that Les was happy for Bart. During the matches, Bart did see a few high-velocity volleys from Les directed his way. But he handled them with relative ease and even whistled an overhead a tad too close to his friend. All eight buddies decided to stay for lunch instead of going out for dinner that night. There were a number of inquiries about Bart's new "girlfriend," but all were sincere and in good fun.

"Honestly, guys, she isn't my girlfriend. I've only had one lunch with her, but she is a dynamite woman and a looker too." Les poked his head forward and nodded enthusiastically. They all good-naturedly kidded Bart about Sally, but the conversation soon shifted to the Frank Bender case. Everyone thought he was guilty.

CHAPTER 30

■ Sure enough, the newly exonerated Frank Bender did just what he said he would do and went to the beach in Fort Myers the very next day. He was photographed frolicking in the water, seemingly without a care in the world. His attorney had strongly advised him to lay low and stay out of the public eye—at least for a few days immediately following the trial. But Frank was a free man now and out of control. Several people on the beach recognized him from the extensive publicity the trial had generated and pointed him out to other puzzled onlookers. But no one came up to him to engage in conversation. He would be known as "the murderer who walked." But he didn't seem to care.

CHAPTER 31

■ Both Bart and Sally were ten minutes early for their tennis game on Friday. The outdoor club had nine Har-Tru clay courts, and all were regularly used until the magic hour of eleven each morning. Many Floridian tennis players managed to convince themselves that it was much cooler playing at eight or nine. Bart didn't care much either way, figuring that the time didn't really matter when the temperature hovered near ninety degrees with an equally stifling humidity and little breeze. They would have the court from nine-thirty to eleven. Sally was dressed in a matching blue-green skirt and tank top. "Hi," he greeted her, as he leaned in for a casual hug.

"I was hoping it wouldn't rain," she said with a quick look at the threatening sky. They both began hitting balls to each other from the service lines and eventually moved back to their respective base lines. She had good form and strong strokes and it was clear that she had played more than a little tennis in her time. After a while, they took a short break and sat down on the bench and drank some water.

"You have definitely played some tennis," he complimented.

"I did play some in college, and my father used to play with my sister and me."

They went back to the court and played a competitive set which he won 6-4. In the lounge, they both had lemonades, but it was too early for lunch.

"By any chance, are you free for dinner tomorrow?" he asked.

"I am not only available, but I would love to have dinner."

He would pick her up on Saturday night at six. It was a typically hot and humid early April day in Fort Myers. Bart began his Saturday by reading his local newspaper over coffee and oatmeal. There were photos of Frank Bender on the beach along with a news story on how Kathy Bender's family was handling both her disappearance and her husband's acquittal. There was no closure for any of them, and they were angry and in mourning. The more he read about it, the more Bart assumed Bender's guilt. He decided to go to the beach to see if the creep might be there. Between the TV coverage and the newspaper reports and photos, he was certain that he could identify him were he to see the jerk. Bart spent an hour on the beach without any success, until he ambled over to a vendor selling hotdogs. When the man in front of him turned to carry his drink away, Bart couldn't believe it. There he was. He was sure of it. Demolishing his own hotdog and washing it down quickly with an iced tea, he followed Frank Bender to his towel and decided to stick around. Within ten minutes, the paunchy murderer got up and walked to the edge of the water. Then he ran in about ten feet and kept chugging along until he was up to his neck. Not a strong swimmer, Bender enjoyed the ocean but was averse to going in over his head. He stood there in water just past his chest, about eighty feet from shore. By the time he returned and toweled off, Bart Steele was gone.

CHAPTER 32

■ Three weeks and four more dates with Sally came and went before it happened. A jogger ten miles away was running with her dog when the canine left the path and started digging at something. The jogger walked over and saw what she suspected to be a makeshift grave near a shady tree. Perhaps it was nothing, but she got an eerie feeling. She couldn't really see anything, nor did she wish to, but she stopped and called the police on her cell phone. Amy Stephens was her name, a nineteen-year-old junior at the community college. The police asked her to stay despite her uneasiness, so that she could answer any questions. It took the authorities less than a half hour to arrive and unearth the decomposing body. At that point, the only thing they knew for sure was that it was the body of a middle-aged woman. Her arms and legs had been bound with duct tape, and there was a plastic bag over her head. Forensics took over, and her DNA eventually led to her identification as Kathy Henry Bender. The crime was easy to establish, but the only evidence was the duct tape and the plastic bag. The victim had been fully clothed, and there was no sign of any sexual assault. The cause of death appeared to be blunt force trauma to the back of her head.

This news, of course, led to a firestorm of protest and crit-
icism of the police, the jury, and even the judge. The prior
evidence against Frank Bender had all been circumstantial,
but the discovery of her body just served to galvanize public
opinion against him. People were howling for Bender's scalp,
but he had already been tried for murder and had been found
innocent. Kathy Bender's family now demanded justice and
directed their venom toward her husband. The term "double
jeopardy" began to appear in all the news reports relating to
the discovery of her body. Legal experts were called upon to
explain the term. Simply put, it meant that no one, even the
arrogant and probably guilty Frank Bender, could be prosecuted more than once for the same crime. Upon the discovery
of Kathy's body, little evidence was obtained. And none that
pointed to Frank Bender's guilt. The bottom line regarding
the defendant was that he was found not guilty in a criminal
proceeding and, therefore, he could not be tried again for
that same crime. What members of the public who followed
the case had difficulty accepting was that the development
of new evidence that might point to Bender's guilt could not
justify another trial. He was a free man, and there was nothing
anyone could do about it. Members of the Henry family could
rally around the dead woman all they wanted and could bring
a civil action against her husband, but he could not be found
guilty in a criminal court. The genesis of double jeopardy

went all the way back in history to the days of 355 B.C. Athens, Greece. Such protection was recognized early on by the courts in the western world, and the concept has withstood the test of time ever since.

People in coffee shops and restaurants in the Fort Myers area were almost obsessed with the Bender case, and conversations about it were as frequent as those regarding the weather or anything else. Not an inherently wise man, and foolishly defiant, Frank Bender did eventually listen to Jeffrey Gold's advice to lay very low since the discovery of his wife's body. He even avoided the beach. Attorney Gold told him in no uncertain terms that the body would trigger a new public contempt for the defendant.

For several weeks, Bender worried that the evidence might be tied to him even though he had been circumspect in handling his dead wife's body. He had worn gloves the entire time and had disposed of them and the shovel in a deep lake. The instrument used in the blunt force trauma that had rendered her lifeless had been a small baseball bat, which he later burned. His attorney had already advised him that he could not be retried for the murder, even if new evidence pointed to his guilt. This, he found, was not that comforting. He worried that his two daughters, twenty-one-year-old Ellen and twenty-two-year-old Sara, might turn on him. During the trial, they had supported him, as so many children of one murdered parent often do. When presented with the possibility of losing both parents, it was easier to rationalize the potentially guilty actions of the accused. But the unearthing of their mother might change that dynamic.

CHAPTER 33

■ Meanwhile, the relationship between Bart and Sally was growing stronger and more intense. They had both agreed to take it slowly and see where it led them. He thought he was in love, but she wasn't there yet. She did clearly adore him and looked forward to every time she was with him. While Bart had no family members to introduce Sally to, she did have a thirty-year-old daughter and had reached the point where she was eager to have them meet. It was in mid-May when her daughter, Ann, came down from Providence, Rhode Island, to visit for a week. The winter had been especially cold in New England, so Ann was happy to see her mother and enjoy some warm weather. Ann was a tennis player like her mom, so they all decided to meet at the tennis club on Saturday morning and then stay for lunch. Ann was a blond beauty, pretty much like her mom. She wore her hair in a bob, and her facial features were almost perfect. A pert nose, white and straight teeth, and full lips gave her the look of a model. Ann also stood straight with the posture of a dancer.

The week came and went, and Bart saw Ann with Sally three more times. Ann was so much more than a pretty face. They both shared a love of history and Mark Twain's humor, and Ann also dabbled in writing poetry, which fascinated Bart.

There seemed to be little doubt that the two liked each other, which greatly pleased Sally. After Ann had returned home to Rhode Island, the couple went out to dinner, and over drinks, decided to take the relationship to the next level. Bart was excited but also apprehensive. What if he couldn't perform?

After a sumptuous steak dinner on this Saturday evening and the drive home, the magic moment arrived. Sally took his hand and strolled to her bedroom. He thought for a moment that he might need another drink. After some gentle caressing on top of the bed, she pulled the sheets and blanket aside and disrobed. The sight of her naked body deeply aroused him, and he took his clothes off while he held a steady gaze into her eyes. While the actual act itself lasted for only a few minutes, they remained silent on the now-moist and tousled sheets and held each other close.

"I'm quite a bit out of practice," he murmured, but she placed two fingers over his lips.

"It was wonderful, Bart, and everything I hoped it would be."

"I was afraid you would be disappointed in me."

"Not a chance," she assured him. She asked him if he wanted to spend the night, and he responded affirmatively with a passionate kiss.

"Do I sense that you might want to go again?" she asked mischievously. And so, the passion continued.

He woke up the next morning to the smell of bacon and eggs, and he eagerly jumped into his clothes and headed for the kitchen. Sally stood over the stove, and he went behind her and kissed the back of her neck before embracing her around the shoulders. It had been a wonderful night, which was clearly going to extend into the next day. He was happier than he had ever been in the past fifteen years. They drank coffee and munched on toast as they thumbed through the Sunday newspaper. There was considerable coverage about Kathy Bender's now-apparent murder and the recent discovery of her body. The news greatly upset Sally, and she expressed her scorn for Frank Bender.

"You know he did it. I thought he was guilty as soon as we all knew she was missing. And now the dirty bastard walks free!" For some reason, Bart didn't tell Sally that he had seen the slime bag on the beach a few weeks before. He almost blurted it out, but something inside of him told him to hold back.

She kept on. "Can't they get him if the tape can be traced to him?"

"Unfortunately, no. He is free and clear because of double jeopardy. And, get this," he added angrily, "now he is eligible to collect on her life insurance because they found the body. The only thing the poor Henry family can do is to sue Frank in civil court, and that will be of little consolation to them."

"Do you want to hear something insidiously ironic?" Without waiting for an answer, she continued, "Can you imagine the Henrys winning in civil court, the very same blood money that Bender collected on the death of their own daughter?"

He contemplated the concept of such a thing. "I can't even bear the thought of it, although I would love to see him pay reparations to them."

CHAPTER 34

■ Public opinion polls expressed on television and in the news-papers were almost in unanimous agreement that Frank Bender needed to pay some kind of penalty for the heinous crime.

Not so far away, that same subject of numerous conver-sations was contemplating his future. Clearly with the public opinion so strongly against him, he had no alternative than to move away. But he convinced himself it would look bad for him to choose that particular time to leave the area. Everyone would think him guilty. But then again, everybody already did. While he never believed his life was in danger, Frank did stay out of the public eye and away from the Fort Myers beaches for another week. The police had contacted him after Kathy's body was found, but they made no effort to hold him or charge him. He correctly surmised that they had absolutely nothing in the way of evidence to tie him to the crime. And even if they did, there was nothing they could do about it. Smiling broadly at the thought of their powerlessness, the remorseless criminal began thinking about how he might spend the life insurance money. Perhaps a villa in Italy, maybe a luxurious home in Colorado. *Why not both,* he thought to himself. *I don't want to be too anxious to collect the money,* he reminded himself, *but I don't want to stay here a day more than necessary.* His warped and demented mind should have been focused on other things. He decided to remain in town indefinitely, or at least until the insurance money came in. It was precisely at that time when an obscure column written by a young and unknown cub reporter for the *Fort Myers News Observer* appeared. Jesse Lytle was the writer's name, and he had just recently celebrated his twentieth birthday. He had also been in Judge Norwood Hastings' courtroom on the same day that defense attorney Jeffrey Gold made his huge blunder during his closing argument—his gaffe about Kathy Bender coming through the door, when everyone directed their attention to it except for the defendant. Jesse Lytle was sitting in the gallery that day, and his eyes just happened to be fixed on Frank Bender and his every move. Just like attorney Gold, Jesse also learned from that interaction that the defendant had to have committed the crime. Why else would he not have turned his head to the door, as everyone else did? Lytle wrote about the trial in general and asked the question: "Why had Bender not looked at the door like everyone else? Could it be that he knew full well why it wasn't worth the bother? She was dead, and he knew it. And he knew it because he did it." The *News Observer* didn't have a large readership, but one subscriber in particular, Sally West, read the column and fumed. She showed it to Bart over dinner.

"This proves his guilt," he shouted out, shaking in anger. "Can you imagine the poor Henry family?"

"And Kathy Bender," she reminded him.

"The rotten scumbag walks while they bury their daughter."
"And don't forget the million-dollar insurance money," she added. "Want to watch an old Alfred Hitchcock movie?" she yelled from the TV room.

They had just had dinner, and Bart was helping himself to some cookies in the kitchen. "Sure. Which one?"

"'Dial M for Murder.' The one with Ray Milland and Grace Kelly."

"Haven't seen it in years. I think that was the first of three films she did with Hitchcock."

"Couldn't tell you, dear." It was the first time she ever called him that, and he liked it.

"I was a teenager when it came out. Apparently, Hitchcock originally wanted Cary Grant and Deborah Kerr for the roles, but Grant didn't want to play a villain, and Kerr was busy making another movie."

"Well, Mr. Steele, aren't you the fountain of information?" she cooed.

"Not really. I always liked the Hitchcock movies."

"Anything else you remember about 'Dial M' before it comes on?"

"Olivia deHavilland—remember her from 'Gone with the Wind?'"

"Sure."

"Well, even before Hitchcock wanted Kerr, he offered the role to her, but she wanted too much money."

168

They both settled in and enjoyed the film over popcorn and lemonade. When it had ended, she had two observations. "Bart, did you notice that almost everything in the movie was indoors? I wonder why?"

"Well, it was originally a Broadway play, so that's probably why it all—or most of it anyway— took place indoors."

"Makes sense," she acquiesced, "but I also noticed something else that I bet you didn't see."

"I'll bet you a roll in the hay!"

"Typical man's response," she pretended to admonish him. "Seriously, Grace Kelly's dress went first from very bright red and got progressively darker as the film evolved."

"That, I must admit, I didn't notice. What I did notice, however, was how pretty Grace Kelly was—although she can't hold a candle to you."

Sally snuggled closer and kissed him. And, after the movie, they talked again about the Kathy Bender murder and Jesse Lytle's newspaper column. They stayed together again that night, but over breakfast the next day, he told her about his health situation. He assured her that it was under control, but it worried her then, and she would continue to be concerned about it.

CHAPTER 35

■ Bart was still very upset about the killing of Kathy Bender, especially after her body was found. The avenger role had changed considerably for him in the past few months. It was one thing to kill someone when you only had six months or so to live; it was quite another to kill when you might be held responsible and spend time in prison. Bart had been compelled to avenge Stephanie's murder, regardless of whether he had cancer. It just had to be done. The only thing he regretted was the extra time he took to pull the trigger. Losing a daughter the way he did gave him an empathy that he had never before experienced. He surmised that sometimes you have to lose someone very special and dear to you in order to understand someone else's grief. He was not necessarily proud of what he did to Darrell Martin and Mark Hollister, but he wasn't going to lose sleep over them either. As far as he was concerned, the world now contained two fewer scumbags. But what about Frank Bender?

Someone had to make things right for the Henry family, and no one else was in sight. Bart decided to take the matter into his own hands, but he was undecided about how, when, or even where to do it. The contrast between the grieving Henry family and the smug and smarmy Frank Bender made the decision an easy one. He would avenge the Henrys, but he had to be more careful now than he had been in the past. Now, thanks to a favorable health prognosis, he did have something to lose. He also now had Sally West. This avenger would have to be very circumspect and would only end Frank Bender's life if the perfect situation presented itself. It was a Wednesday morning when he left his house and headed to the beach. Given the right opportunity, Bart was mentally ready to do the deed. The idea came to him on Tuesday night, and he predicted it wouldn't be that hard to execute. It was about eighty-two degrees when he arrived at the shore. His eyes scanned the beachfront. There was no sign of his prey. Having seen him before near a vendor while the snack bar area was being renovated, he wandered over there for a look. It was a little after eleven. Still no Frank Bender. He worried for a moment that perhaps he had left town and hoped that wasn't the case. Bart would come back on Saturday and hope for the best. The best, of course, would be that Bender would be there and was alone. If so, he would be dead before sunset. With Bart and Sally spending so much time together, he would have to conjure up or devise some believable excuse for him to go to the beach without her. He thought about telling her about his plans for all of a nanosecond but realized that no woman in the entire world would understand either his motivation to do it or forgive him for such a savage act. *Perhaps, God forbid, if Ann had been taken from Sally the way Stephanie was taken from me, then she might understand.* But he understood that for anyone to truly understand vengeance, they had to undergo something immensely personal. And he wouldn't wish that on anybody.

At dinner on Thursday night, Bart told Sally that an old college buddy was in town, and they agreed to meet at the beach on Saturday. She was fine with the arrangement, so he was home free. He stayed overnight with her and watched a movie on TV. Friday was a slow day for him, and he thought several times about returning to the beach then instead of Saturday. Call it intuition or a hunch, he had a distinct feeling that the lowlife would show up over the weekend. Bart arrived a little before eleven in the morning. He first tried the snack bar, which had just reopened, but there was a long line, and Bender wasn't in it. And then he spotted him.

He was alone, wearing an orange bathing suit and stretched out on a towel. After ten minutes—which seemed more like thirty—Bender abruptly got up from the sand and headed to the water. Springing into action, Bart quickly shed his sandals and shirt and left them along with a towel on a fence post. Then, he followed his quarry to the water line but was careful to lag at least forty feet behind him and to his left. It was then that he donned his snorkeling gear.

Keep going, keep going, Bart silently urged him on. Bender walked rapidly forward, indicating his intention to venture out into the deeper water. As the avenger followed, he stayed out of visual range of his target. Soon, Frank Bender was up to his chest in the water. Bart continued out further, until the water reached to his lower neck. He was now ten feet behind his prey and about thirty feet to his left. It didn't really matter if Bender saw him or not; they were just two guys frolicking in the water. In fact, it looked for a moment as if Bender had looked Bart's way. But no matter. As he moved closer to his objective, Bart paddled around in the water trying to look harmless. He looked toward the beach to see if anyone was watching. The lifeguard was at least two hundred feet away, and his eyes seemed to be focused on a pretty young woman. Now, Bart was only ten feet behind Bender, still slightly to his left. Bender was facing the beach and jumping up and down with the waves at the moment Bart struck. Moving in quickly behind him, fueled by adrenaline, Bart applied a headlock and sat down quickly. Totally surprised by this overt aggression, Frank Bender sank with him like a stone. He tried to fight back, but underwater and straining for breath, the result was predictable. It would only be a matter of time. The drowning man was wildly flailing his arms, but the bubbles were the only evidence of the life-and-death struggle going on four feet below the surface. Soon, Frank Bender's lashing arms went still, and the bubbles ceased. While continuing to hold him under the water, Bart stood for a moment and surveyed the immediate area. No one was within one hundred feet of them, and those on the beach appeared unaware of the combat that had just taken place. Lowering himself once again into the cool water, Bart swam another sixty feet or so further out, still wearing his snorkel, all the time dragging Bender's lifeless body with him. Then, he let go of the corpse and swam underwater at an angle away from the body and toward the beach. When he had traveled what seemed like eighty feet or so, he surfaced and looked back. The dead man's head was bobbing between the small waves and then disappeared from view. Bart hadn't realized, and would learn later, that a cadaver in the water begins to sink as the air in its lungs is replaced by water. But it will float better in salt water because it is denser than fresh water. Acting as nonchalantly as possible, Bart began trudging through the water and back to the beach. When he reached the shoreline and the hot sand, he snuck another look. From his distance and vantage, he could see that the head had reappeared and resembled a large cork floating harmlessly in the water.

Mission accomplished. He took only a minute to dry himself, slipped into his sandals, and made a beeline for his car. As far as he knew, no one at the beach that day had a clue what grisly crime had just been committed, or that Bart Steele had even been there. But he was mistaken.

CHAPTER 36

■ On his drive home from his encounter at the beach, Bart was very careful to observe all of the traffic laws. He was a good driver anyway but would be especially circumspect early that afternoon. He had just rid the world of one more thug and hoped that the vengeful act would bring some kind of closure to the Henry family. Based on his own experiences, he knew that it would help but would never serve to totally fill the void. The Henrys, and the Moores before them, recognized this with undoubtedly countless unfortunate others. Just like Bart, they would never get over it.

He fixed himself a sandwich, reached for the Crown Royal, even though it was still early afternoon, and then rejected it, instead opting for iced tea. Thanks in part to his new relationship with Sally, he knew he needed to cut back on the booze. Most importantly, he wanted to do it anyway. He sat back in his easy chair and visualized the scene at the beach once Frank Bender surfaced. How long would it take? Had someone already discovered his body? *Hopefully,* he thought, *no children would have to witness it.* Or did Frank Bender float out in the Gulf of Mexico with the current? *Perhaps he'll never show up at all?* Worst of all, Bart knew he couldn't share his feelings with anyone, not even Sally. Especially Sally. He would be sure to watch the Saturday night news. One thing was for certain. If a body washed up on the Fort Myers beach, it would be big news. Perhaps not so huge in New York or Chicago, but this was staid little old Fort Myers. Also inescapable: There was no way the media would downplay the incident and avoid alarming the people. Just the opposite. While he wasn't what one might consider a captious critic of the media, he was just being realistic.

That's what they did. It sold newspapers and gained TV viewers. Eleven o'clock could not come soon enough for him. He had already called Sally to fill her in on some of his day, not all of it obviously, but most of it. His friend hadn't shown up, he fibbed, so he just went for a swim. Sally had spent the day shopping for a new refrigerator. The news came on and the lead story was about a robbery and killing in the Summit section of Fort Myers. He knew no one had discovered Bender's body yet because anyone would understand that the drowning would be the first attraction. As the media adage goes: If it bleeds, it leads! Part of him was disappointed because he wanted the Henry family to know that the bastard had died. As careful as he had been, however, rarely was there such a thing as a perfect crime. He may have come close, but it might still be possible to hold him responsible. How, he couldn't imagine, but it could happen. So, his thoughts that night about finding Frank Bender were ambivalent. Maybe the vile and despicable man was floating towards New Orleans or even Houston, Texas. If that were the case, he would never be identified, even if found.

CHAPTER 37

■ Bart went to bed after the sports report but couldn't sleep. He returned to his TV to see a midnight movie. The next day, Sunday, he had promised to spend with Sally. It was about two in the afternoon. They had been together starting with the ten o'clock church services. She looked up from her magazine and asked him if everything was okay. "You seem otherwise occupied, Bart. Is anything the matter?"

"No, hon," he lied. Just a little tired from the beach yesterday, and I watched a late movie last night." He had previously told her about his cancer and his miraculous remission, but she always expressed her concern when he showed signs of fatigue. Bart had enough "machismo" in him that he never wanted to tip his hand, as he put it. He wasn't about to exhibit weakness to anyone, especially Sally. No question about it, and like him or not, he was his father's son. Just like Ed, he was a stand-up guy, tough and unyielding. Most people with such a personality were also hard-headed, and he wasn't about to break that mold.

The Bender story was all over the evening news. Part of him was actually relieved. Both Sally and Bart leaned forward to hear every word, but obviously for different reasons. As the local news anchor described it, a man was fished out of five feet of water on the Fort Myers beach that very afternoon. Police did not know the identification of the man nor were they sure of how he died. It appeared to be a routine drowning, but the coroner and medical examiner were working on the body at the time of the telecast. "No one knows," the reporter continued, "exactly how long the body had been in the water." That part of the story wasn't exactly true because Bart could have told them it had been there since about eleven-thirty the previous morning. By the eleven o'clock news later that night, the body had not been positively identified, although speculation was it was Frank Bender. Sally nudged him and asked, "You were at that beach, Bart, did you see anything?"

"Nothing out of the ordinary," he responded.

"It's got to be pretty hard to drown at a public beach."

"Maybe he had too much to drink." During Bender's death struggle, Bart was careful not to apply too much pressure on his headlock. If it could be determined by the medical examiner that the victim was choked before drowning, then it was a matter of murder and not a mere accident. He was confident that his arm would not have left marks on the dead man's neck. But sleep, nonetheless, did not come easily for him that night.

CHAPTER 38

■ Monday was pretty much a nondescript day for Bart, with the exception of an important visit to Dr. Stuart Gordon. The oncologist seemed to hold Bart's fate in his hands. An MRI taken a few days before his appointment revealed that his cancer was still in remission.

"As I've said before, Mr. Steele, I don't want you to get too overconfident. While the MRI doesn't reveal any overt sign of cancer, there could still be some microscopic cancer cells in your system."

"I'm feeling like my old self, Doc. So that should count for something, right?"

"Absolutely. You should be very happy with the MRI results."

As he left the oncologist's office, he was very upbeat but wished that these physicians could be more positive. *I guess they have to cover themselves if something goes south,* Bart rationalized, *and they spend every day with very sick patients. No wonder they don't smile very much.* He called Sally with the good news and was very grateful. Now that she was becoming a big part of his life, his health really mattered to him.

It was Tuesday morning at about ten when he heard a firm knock on the front door. "Now, who the hell can that be?" he murmured while tidying up the kitchen. He opened the door and saw two familiar faces.

"Good morning, Mr. Steele," they both said in unison.

"Gentlemen," he greeted them with an outstretched hand. "I wasn't expecting to see you again."

"I'll bet you weren't," Detective Riley countered with a sardonic smile.

"Coffee?"

"No thanks."

"So, to what do I owe the honor of this visit?" Bart asked, his voice dripping in sarcasm as he motioned for them to sit down.

"Well, it seems that wherever you happen to be, someone either dies or goes missing."

He looked quizzically at Riley. "Not sure what you mean by that detective."

"You were at the Naked Lady shortly before Darrell Martin disappeared or was killed. You may have also been at a bar called Hogan's when a guy by the name of Mark Hollister was terminated. And now, we want to ask you where you were late Saturday morning?"

"I was at the beach."

"Good answer. We know you were. Do you want to know how we knew that?"

"You guys seem to know everything. Yes, I would like to know how you knew I was at the beach."

"You're a celebrity, Bart. Did you see the newspaper this morning?" the detective said mockingly.

"No, I haven't."

"Well, there's a photo of you at the snack bar taken exactly at 11:02 Saturday morning."

"I don't want to seem rude Detective Riley, but so what? And why would anyone want to take my photo?

"Beats me," Riley laughed, "but apparently it just reopened that day, and you were lucky enough to be there."

"But, as it turns out, it was also the same day that a fellow by the name of Frank Bender went swimming and ended up dead."

"What could that possibly have to do with me?"

"You seem to show up places where people die," Riley went on.

At this point, newly promoted police Sergeant Livingston interjected. "Mr. Steele, we are beginning to think that you or someone else may be involved in some recent vigilante-type killings."

Bart's body stiffened, but he had to work hard not to show any emotion.

Livingston continued. "As you know, a man by the name of Mark Hollister was murdered a little more than a month ago at a place called Hogan's. Both Vince and I wondered if you have ever been there?" Without waiting for a response, the sergeant forged on. "We also would like to know if you have been to the movies recently?"

Now, despite trying so hard to appear cavalier about these accusations, Bart was clearly feeling the heat. But he kept reminding himself that they were on a fishing expedition and were just trying to throw him off guard.

"No and yes would be my answers to your two questions. I was at the movies about a month ago, I think, but I've never been to Hogan's.

"Do you remember the name of the movie?"

"Yeah, I think it was called "Blood Work." Gentlemen, I beseech you, where are you going with this? Do you honestly think I'm a killer?"

"Mr. Steele," Detective Riley replied as he took over the interrogation, "we think that such a thing is very possible. A man by the name of Virgil Stassen was brutally assaulted at the very same movie theater you attended on the very same day. And you know something else, Mr. Steele?" he asked rhetorically. "The attack was just about the same time that you were viewed on the surveillance tape leaving the theater." Riley stopped his harangue and looked closely at his suspect, hoping for some sign of guilt. Sweating, shifting uneasily in his seat, or the look of fear would all be tip-offs indicating culpability. Bart was cool enough not to succumb to those tell-tale hints. But he had to struggle to contain himself. "Excuse me, gentlemen, but I don't know, nor have I ever met, any of those men you mentioned. Why on earth," he continued while attempting to sound as sincere as possible, "would I suddenly resort to violence when I have lived such a placid life? Outside of a little mayhem on the football field," he said with a nervous laugh, "I am a very peaceful man."

"Yes, we know all about your football career at Pitt," Livingston intervened. "We are big football fans."

Now, Bart had real proof that they were looking closely at him, and the thought of it was unsettling. "Your thinking that I killed anyone is preposterous."

Detective Riley jumped back into the fray. "Is it? We find it interesting that these events have all occurred since you murdered Darrell Martin—not that he didn't deserve it."

Not taking the bait, Bart didn't mind showing his disdain at the remark. "I did not murder Mr. Martin—or anyone else for that matter," he said firmly. He leaned forward on his seat, placing an elbow on each knee. "Please don't accuse me of something that hasn't even happened. Have you found him? If not, how do you know if anyone murdered him, much less me?"

"We don't have proof of that, but we think that we are dealing with vengeance killings here. All four victims were unsavory types who had literally gotten away with murder. They had it coming to them, Bart, especially the punk who killed your daughter. But no one has the right to take matters into their own hands," he said emphatically. "Not even a grieving father. Having said that, Bart, I wouldn't blame you if you had killed them all."

"And you and Officer Livingston have concluded that I must be the vengeance killer?"

"Actually, it is now Sergeant Livingston. He was promoted two weeks ago. But yes, we think the evidence points to you."

"Congratulations, sergeant," the flustered suspect said with conviction, "but you are both barking up the wrong tree and losing valuable time as well. And one other thing," he pointed his fingers toward them. "How do you know that this Binder, Bender guy, or whatever his name is, was murdered? The television and newspaper reports suggest that he drowned."

"Well, it's a theory now," the aggravated detective spit out, "but there were people on the beach who were taking photos and one guy filming the beach scene. We might actually see what happened to Mr. Bender." Upon saying this, Riley couldn't help smiling.

"Not that this hasn't been enjoyable," Bart announced sarcastically, "but I'm sure we all have better things to do with our time." Detective Riley stood immediately, followed by his compatriot and headed to the door. "I have a feeling that we will be meeting again."

"Gentlemen," he addressed the two law enforcement officers, "I know that you are just doing your jobs, and I appreciate that. But you have the wrong man." He wanted to end their encounter on a positive note. When the officers had left, Bart sat down heavily in his easy chair, took several deep breaths, and predictably thought about the beach and Frank Bender. Were there really people with cameras out there, as Riley said, or was he just trying to get a rise out of me? Would there be suspicious marks on his neck? Was it even possible that some camera could capture his countenance from that distance? Bart hadn't seen any camera when he followed Bender into the water, but then again, he wasn't really looking. And he was somewhat surprised that Bender's identity had already been established. When he observed him getting up from his towel on the beach to head for a swim, he hadn't seen a duffel bag or any other items besides a football jersey and sandals. But it was also true that he wasn't really focused on the towel. As it turned out, at the end of that Saturday afternoon, beach attendants had noticed a sole towel left on the sand in the midst of people in chairs watching the sunset. The large red-and-white beach towel, sandals, car keys, and a Tampa Bay Buccaneers football jersey were easy to spot. One of the attendants turned the jersey over and saw the name BENDER in large block letters. Obviously, it must have been a Tampa Bay football fan who had gone into the water but hadn't returned to get his items. A limited search didn't reveal anything out of the ordinary, so the articles were put away in the lost and found section of the beach hut. It was only when the body of Frank Bender was discovered the next day that the items became relevant. Word leaked out that the murderer who walked found himself a watery grave.

CHAPTER 39

◼ Intermittently that Tuesday night after the Livingston and Riley visit, Bart thought about possible evidence that would link him to the violence he inflicted on the four men. He also thought he was silly to worry because there couldn't be any, since he had been so careful. Bart begged off dinner with Sally that night, too absorbed with such concerns. His tennis game with his friends on Thursday couldn't come too soon. Riley had gotten into his head, just exactly what the seasoned detective had intended to do. Bart was more concerned about being caught than he was remorseful for the deed he had done. But protecting one's ass tends to do that to a person. Sally was worried about Bart. He hadn't seemed the same since that Saturday when he went alone to the beach. She didn't know of the surprise visit by the authorities on Tuesday morning, and he was in no mood or position to tell her about it.

Detective Riley was personally on the case, a fact that annoyed Bart. *The bastard's not going to let up on me if it's his case,* he reasoned accurately. But the medical examiner had told Riley directly that he was ninety-five percent sure Bender's death came as a result of drowning. There was a slight redness on the neck area in front, but the body had probably been in the water for more than twenty-four hours.

Some fish or other object in the Gulf could have rubbed against his neck, or it could have been merely a manifestation of the decomposition of a body that had been in water for over a day. The official ruling, much to Riley's dismay, was death by accidental drowning. Bart Steele was definitely off the hook for that one. That night the much-relieved suspect dined with Sally, and they spent the night together. She didn't know why Bart was his old self, but she took comfort in knowing that all seemed well.

CHAPTER 40

■ About seventeen hundred miles north of Fort Myers in the town of Golden Valley, Minnesota, Billy Ray Dirks had a big problem. In a seldom visited lovers' lane some six years earlier, the now thirty-three-year-old reprobate had murdered a couple in their parked car and dumped their bodies in nearby Lake Minnetonka. Sneaking up on them late one summer evening on a moonless night, Billy Ray executed them with a .22 pistol through the open windows. It was not a random shooting. Patty Post had been his girlfriend for over two years, and he thought that he owned her. The other victim, the driver of the car, Peter McFadin, had only been going out with Patty for two weeks. She had broken up with Dirks three months before her death, but he did not accept it. He had openly stalked her for that entire time and had even threatened her.

There was no actual evidence at the scene, other than traces of the victim's blood, nor had the bodies been discovered, but Billy Ray was clearly more than a person of interest in their disappearance. Patty and Peter's car had been found by police the very next morning, but there was no sign of their where-abouts. Patty's family strongly suspected that Billy Ray Dirks had to be involved in what clearly appeared to be a crime. He lived with his mother, and she provided him with a perfect alibi. His mother, Bonnie, insisted to authorities, however, that her son had spent the entire evening with her watching television and that he had retired before her. Both mother and son readily identified the programs and movie they had allegedly viewed together. With that seemingly ironclad alibi and no bodies, the possible suspect was not tried despite peoples' suspicions. Billy Ray had suspected that the couple might drive to Lovers' Lane having followed them there on the Saturday before he accomplished his dirty deed. He put their bodies in black garbage bags to minimize any blood flow left in the car and tried to clean up any blood spatter he could readily identify, as quickly as he could. His original plan had been to bury them, but he got a different scheme when he spotted a beat-up old rowboat nearby. Such a thing was not that unusual to see around the shoreline. The boat had been placed on several cinder blocks to keep it off of the ground, and it was secured to a makeshift post with several yards of rope. Making as little noise as possible, and using his pocketknife, he cut the rope and tied a cinder block to each of the bodies in hopes that it would help to sink them deep into the bottom of the lake. No bodies, no crime, he figured. The moonless night was both a help and a hindrance to his malevolence. On one hand, the darkness covered his deed and allowed him to move about without being seen. But the black night prevented Billy Ray from seeing if the rowboat was seaworthy. Fortunately, the oars had been left lying in the bottom of the boat. As he rowed out some five hundred feet to unload his cargo, he could only hope that the small craft would not take on water. It did not. When he reached his destination, he gently lowered each body over the gunwale. He knew that a noise around a silent lake can be picked up rather easily. It was just after midnight, and there were no lights surrounding the lake. Everyone must have been in bed. He carefully made his way back to the shore but was about one hundred feet away from where he had embarked. Then, he made his way to his car and drove home very carefully so as not to draw unwanted attention to himself. His mother was still up, as she usually was late into every night, and he explained to her that she had to give him an alibi.

"Trust me, Mom," he beseeched her, "I didn't do anything wrong I swear to you. But you have to back me up." The two of them went over the TV shows she had watched in his absence just to be certain that their stories fit each other's version. But the problem for Billy Ray was that now, the bodies had been found after six years spent on the bottom of Lake Minnetonka. His first reaction was to feel assured that so many years had passed that any attempt at identifying the bodies would be fruitless. He was wrong about that. Bodies decompose at different rates and in different climes. Incredibly, Patty and Peter's bodies were almost intact. How was that possible? Lake Minnetonka is the ninth largest lake in a state famous for great bodies of water, and there are some very deep places in it. Most importantly, the water was incredibly cold. One of the very deepest parts of the lake was only five hundred feet or so from the shore, with summer homes dotting the landscape.

CHAPTER 41

■ The eventual discovery of the murdered victims was nothing short of a miracle. It never should have happened. And it never would have had it not been for the persistence of Agnes and Tom Wilson. For years, they had known that their daughter had drowned in the lake. Sara Wilson had gone swimming one summer day with friends three years before. Unfortunately, they all realized too late that she had submerged without ever surfacing. Search and rescue teams were called in and futile efforts were made to drag the area with grappling hooks. Sometimes these efforts are successful, but success is usually attributable to good luck. In the Wilson's case, no one could find their daughter's body. Even knowing that she had drowned did not come close to giving them closure. There was a need for them to see her body or at least her remains. A friend mentioned to them that they had recently read of new advancements in underwater search-and-recovery efforts and that it might be possible to recover her body even three years later. At first, they thought it was impossible, but they deeply yearned for closure. And they would soon have it. But there would be another dividend as well. The sonar device sent pulses of sound waves through the water. The pulses detected not one body but a total of three. Two were packaged, as the experts described the scene, but the third was found in the conventional position. According to recovery experts, a dead body sinks through the water starting with its chest facing down and parallel to the surface. At the time that the feet hit the bottom, however, the knees then buckle, which causes the body to turn over onto its back. The arms are outstretched, which adds to the ghastly scene. That was exactly how Sara Wilson was found, and there was actually little decomposition of her body. Recovery experts said some bodies maintain their shape for many years, depending on their resting place. If they reside in deep and cold places, like the bottom of a frigid lake, the decay slows considerably. The search-and-recovery specialists performed their magic, and the Wilsons could finally bury the body of their beloved Sara.

During the discovery of Sara Wilson, salvage experts saw two other forms on the floor of Lake Minnetonka. If they were human bodies, they surmised, they must have been the victims of murder. No arms were outstretched. Clearly, they had been "packaged." Just like the body of Sara Wilson, those of Patty Post and Peter McFadin were easily recognizable, despite having been under the surface for six years. It was easy for the medical examiner to establish the cause of death for both victims. Unlike Sara's fate, the bullet wounds made the cause of death obvious for the couple. Dental records were used to officially confirm their identities.

The act of drowning is usually both silent and swift. As experts explained to the Wilsons, a person fighting to avoid suffocating in water rather quickly exhibits what is known as the "instinctive drowning response." In it, the victim struggles to keep his or her nose and mouth above the water with arms outstretched in the effort to stay alive. That reaction also renders them unable to wave or yell for help. "That would explain," the specialists told the Wilsons, "why your daughter was unable to scream for help and why her friends didn't know that she was in trouble." They explained that survival efforts could only be sustained for thirty or perhaps up to sixty seconds before the person silently slips below the surface. They explained that the five stages of drowning were surprise, involuntary breath holding, hypoxic convulsion, unconsciousness, and, finally, clinical death. If the three bodies had moved to or been deposited in warmer or shallow water, they would have decayed rapidly and resulted in the putrefaction of their flesh. That process produces gases, especially in the chest and stomach area, which in turn inflates a corpse like a balloon. Fortunately for the Wilsons, Posts, and McFadins, the bodies were found almost intact on the chilly floor of Lake Minnetonka. All the Wilsons knew was that they were comforted that they finally had some closure about their daughter's fate.

CHAPTER 42

■ With the recovery of Post and McFadin, the heat was suddenly on Billy Ray Dirks. Their bodies had been discovered, proof they were indeed dead. Definitely, this was a case of murder. Billy Ray's mother had her suspicions all along and was deeply disappointed in her son—but, blood is thicker than water. She wouldn't think about recanting her version of the alibi. Of course, her son was with her that night and even preceded her in going to bed. But it was obvious: Billy Ray must have done it. The law might not have enough of a case to try him, but everybody in the area knew. People in Southwest Florida did not. The police called Billy Ray into the station in an attempt to break him down and have him come clean, but he continued to assert his innocence. No one was buying it, but there was little they could do unless new evidence emerged. One detective on the case told Billy Ray the hangman was waiting for him when he slipped up. That may have been a mistake on the lawman's part because the threat scared the sleazebag into taking action. He explained to his mother that the law would never leave him alone unless they caught the real murderer. His only recourse, he insisted to the only person on earth who loved him, was to leave Minnesota for good—with one caveat. He would fake his own death, for her sake as well as his own. Bonnie would have to aid him if he were to successfully pull it off. Billy Ray would also have to commit a few more minor crimes in doing so, but they would pale in comparison to the evil deed he was responsible for six years ago.

His plan was really straightforward. He would make it appear that he had been murdered—by the same people or person who'd executed Patty Post and Peter McFadin. If Billy Ray could create doubt, perhaps his mother might benefit and be less scorned for giving birth to him. And he would be free from further harassment. It might be a longshot, but he had little choice in the matter. The police might yet come up with some evidence to tie him to the gruesome crimes. He had made sure to throw the .22 caliber instrument of murder into another lake on his way home that dark night. After, of course, wiping it clean of his fingerprints—just to be extra careful. There had also been an attempt to file off the ID number on the weapon, but with limited success. While it was unlikely that the police could ever tie Billy Ray to the murder scene, he was under pressure and needed a plan to get the heat off of him.

Billy Ray decided to stage his own murder scene. He had already received death threats and had reported them to his attorney and the police. All that would fit nicely into his scheme. It would be necessary to purchase a medium-sized knife with a serrated edge. That part was easy, and he made sure to wear a fake mustache and a floppy hat for the security cameras. The most difficult part of the overall scheme was to draw some of his own blood. He would need that at the scene of the fake crime as well as shoes that were not his size. Billy Ray remembered years before cutting himself accidentally while slicing tomatoes. The blade went into the flap of skin between his lower thumb and forefinger. It didn't hurt much, but it bled a lot. So, he did it again, this time on purpose. He checked everything out the night before he executed his plan. Sure enough, a rowboat was approximately in the same place. There was no one in that secluded spot where he had killed Patty and Peter. This time, however, there was a visible moon. The success of it all would depend to a great extent on his loving mother. She would have to furnish transportation from the lake and then to a seedy bar so that he could steal a few license plates and a car that was serviceable enough to get him to Florida. Bonnie Dirks would also have to continue lying for her son.

It was about ten the next night when his mother followed him to the seldom used lover's lane. The moon was barely visible. He drove his beat-up 1987 Chevy, which he would subsequently leave near the lake. While she waited for him with her lights off, Billy Ray began staging the scene, careful to wear rubber gloves. He sat in the passenger's seat and thrust the knife towards an invisible driver, making sure to cut into the fabric and even to nick the steering wheel. Then, he dipped the serrated knife into the baggie holding his blood and wiped the handle clean. Being very careful to preserve the blood supply, he dropped the knife on the floor and spilled a little blood spatter on the driver's seat and the console. His next step was to traverse the thirty-five feet or so through the grass and hard ground down to the sandy turf, in which he left his footprints leading to ten or more feet to the water. Once in the lake, he walked another thirty feet north, until he spotted the huge rock that extended into the water. Billy Ray climbed on it and carefully made his way onto a big log, which enabled him to navigate without leaving any trace in the soft sand. It was important that he leave no exit prints. When he reached his car, he changed into much larger shoes and clumped his way back to the water's edge, making sure to walk near the footprints he had left while wearing his regular shoes. He knew it was much more difficult to leave discernible prints on the grass and harder ground, but he had no doubt that the forensics people would see them. It was obviously much easier to leave them on the ten-foot trek of sand. Near the water, Billy Ray sprinkled what was left from the blood pouch on the seat and gunwale of the rowboat and tugged it ahead into the water. Once he had waded out some five feet or so, he stopped suddenly. There was a noise, and he feared that he was not alone. He could almost hear his heart pounding. Fortunately for him, it was just a couple of birds. While still in the water, he steered the small vessel about twenty-five feet south and then pushed it back up onto the sand. Then, he trudged back near his car, walking as heavily as possible in order to leave visible footprints. Stepping out of the big shoes, he tiptoed to his car and waved to his mother, parked just behind him. The entire operation had taken him less than thirty minutes. He didn't want to spend any more time there than necessary, but he also recognized the high stakes. A small mistake could mess up his plan and so, prudence would be the best course to follow at all costs. It was nearly ten-thirty when he flashed the thumbs-up to his loyal and devoted mother. Leaving the keys to the Chevy in the ignition and the doors unlocked, he jumped into his mother's car and reminded her to drive very slowly, so as not to attract attention or leave any tire tracks. On the way to Topsys, a seedy bar about three miles away, Billy Ray noticed a dumpster by several closed stores. Bonnie Dirks drove into the lot, and he surreptitiously dropped off the larger shoes that he had worn at the scene. He made sure he was still wearing his rubber gloves. Then they were on the way to the bar. His mother dropped him off near the entrance to Topsys and pulled out of sight around the corner to wait for him, just in case the car theft didn't go well. He had just managed to unscrew a Nebraska license plate from a late model Cadillac when two men emerged from the bar. Billy Ray quickly ducked behind a parked Oldsmobile. They were laughing loudly and didn't see him. Soon they drove away. After managing to filch Nebraska and Wisconsin license plates, he ambled over to inspect the ten cars remaining in the lot. A dark grey Toyota, probably eight or nine years old, caught his eye. Utilizing a skill that he learned while working at Tony's Garage, he was able to hot-wire it in less than a minute and pulled out of the parking lot. Upon hitting the street, he flashed his lights twice to his mother. A few blocks later he noticed another rubbish container and got rid of the gloves.

They would meet at her house in twenty minutes. "Mom, I'm so sorry to involve you in all of this," he began once they were safe in her living room. "If I didn't leave and stage that scene, the cops would hound us forever. There would be no peace for either of us. Somehow, they think that I killed that poor couple, and they will never leave us alone. With my death, maybe we can both find some peace."

"Tell me again, Billy Ray, that you didn't kill that couple."

"I didn't, Mom, honest."

"I just couldn't live with myself if I thought that you did it."

"Mom, I would never lie to you about something this important."

"I wish you didn't have that darned skull and crossbones tattoo on your neck. I never, ever liked it. It's just not you." He really didn't care what she thought.

And then he gave her a big hug. He changed out of his wet shoes and pulled out his duffel bag. In it was ten thousand dollars—her life savings, which she had given him. Billy Ray had sworn to return it somehow, but she knew that was just another one of his empty promises. She attributed her son's downfall to losing her husband, the boy's father, back when Billy Ray was only thirteen. It had been downhill from there. Luckily for the fleeing felon, the Toyota's gas tank had probably been filled on the owner's way to Topsys. That was a break. Before kissing his mother one last time, he replaced the Minnesota plate on the Toyota with the one from Nebraska. He had always wanted to visit Nebraska, he snickered. Just as Billy Ray was pulling away from the curb, he remembered something important. Racing up the steps to the back door, he breathlessly reminded his mother to give the police the latest threatening letter that he had "received" just days before. Carelessly, he had left it on his dresser. As he had told his mother, it had been placed in their mailbox in a simple white envelope and without a stamp. It had taken him almost a full day to prepare it, collecting huge block letters from three newspapers in order to complete it. He was going to tell his mother of its real genesis but decided against it. He didn't want to worry her, but, this way, she wouldn't have to play-act again when she explained it to the police.

CHAPTER 43

■ The note read: "IT IS NOW YOUR TURN TO DIE. WE KILLED THEM AND NOW WE ARE GOING TO KILL YOU. PREPARE TO DIE BILLY RAY! WE ARE NOT FOOLING AROUND."

Early the next morning, Bonnie Dirks called the police to report that her son was missing. She followed the script precisely. Officers looked around the premises. Luckily for Billy Ray, he had placed his wet shoes in his new vehicle. They came up with nothing. The block-lettered warning note they considered suspicious and rather amateurish. Two of the three officers thought that Bonnie's son may have prepared it himself, and they scoured the house hoping to find the remnants of torn up newspapers. But Billy Ray had thought of that too, merely placing them in a plastic grocery bag in the backseat of the Toyota.

The third officer to examine the note gave it some credence. Yet, they were very much aware of the thirty-three-year old's probable and likely connection to the Post and McFadin murders. Bonnie's role in providing her son with a rock-solid alibi did not endear her to law enforcement officials or the public. In short, the Dirks' credibility was close to nil. No one really seemed to care whether Billy Ray was missing or, for that matter, murdered. But they continued to do their jobs.

Acting on a tip from a couple of teenagers who had seen an abandoned car in the area, the three officers decided to go out to the same area where McFadin had left his car near the lake years ago.

"Well, lookee here, Sarge," Officer Hamilton exclaimed to his partner. He had seen what appeared to be an abandoned 1987 Chevy.

"Park here, Jack," Sergeant Sam Gifford commanded. "We don't want to contaminate the area. It may be nothing, but it also might be a crime scene." Guns drawn, they were circumspect with every step.

"I see what looks like blood, Sarge, and a knife as well." Seeing no one around, they holstered their weapons and put on some latex gloves. It was ten minutes later that the forensic investigators arrived. There didn't appear to be any tire prints near the vehicle or in the immediate area. The ground was too hard and there hadn't been rain in over a week. Small traces of blood were discovered in the front seat along with the serrated bloody knife. "It looks like there was a struggle in the front seat," one of the investigators opined. The footprints on the sand were easily visible and plaster of Paris casts were immediately made of them. Two different tracks led to the water, but there was no sign of any coming back. That really puzzled those at the scene until Sergeant Gifford yelled to them from about twenty-five feet away.

"Look here, there are some exit tracks, and a rowboat."

Hustling over to him, it was clear that someone had come out of the water. But only one person. The tracks seemed to match one of the two sets of prints leading into the water some twenty-five feet away. And then there was the matter of what looked like blood splatter in the rowboat. Samples were taken for further DNA examination. The yellow crime scene tapes went up, and people were assigned to survey the area. At first glance, it appeared that two people had entered the water, probably in the rowboat, but only one had exited. Where was the other person? Was the body dumped in the lake? It appeared that way, although Detective Scott Hardy, who had just joined the busy scene, was not so easily convinced. He was a chiseled veteran of twenty-two years on the force and a skeptic by nature. Hardy had sharp facial features and a natural scowl. All the investigators knew that the car had belonged to Billy Ray Dirks. His mother had given his description to them along with the make of the car. Knowing of the Post and McFadin case and Dirks' likely involvement in it gave the hardened detective reason to pause.

"The scene looks a little staged to me. For all we know, he may be halfway to California by now." He continued to look around the premises for some telltale sign of a prepared scene, but everything he saw seemed to add up despite his bias. "If Billy Ray Dirks faked his own death, he's smarter than I think he is. Let's keep looking," he urged them. "We need to check all the blood samples," a forensic specialist by the name of Chuck asserted. "If they are all identical, at least we'll have some idea of what may have happened."

On the way home, two of the forensic investigators stopped by the Dirks' residence. Bonnie had been told by her son to expect that, and to also anticipate providing a DNA sample for Billy Ray, perhaps his hairbrush or toothbrush. Officers took both to the lab. Three days later, Detective Hardy personally delivered the news to Bonnie Dirks. Predictably, she said she needed to sit down and then began sobbing. Hardy noticed that despite her wailing, there were no real tears. She dabbed at her eyes, but this clearly wasn't the first rodeo for the battle-tested detective. He wasn't buying her act but didn't admit that to her and instead tried to comfort her. So tempted to berate her, he felt sorry for her for being the mother of such a scumbag. Scott Hardy now just knew in his gut not only that Billy Ray Dirks had faked his death and staged the scene, but also that his mother was in on it. She likely was manipulated by her son, but she had to be involved in his disappearance. The detective also knew for certain that the dirty bastard must have killed the innocent couple six years before, and he vowed to find him and bring him to justice.

CHAPTER 44

■ Billy Ray Dirks smiled to himself as he sat in his modest apartment in Fort Myers. Keeping one thousand dollars for himself, he had already opened a savings account under the assumed name of Frank Short. He was confident the police might think Billy Ray Dirks lay dead at the bottom of Lake Minnetonka, but it really didn't matter. No one would know where to look for him anyway, and not even his mother knew of his whereabouts. When he ran out of money, he would simply either steal it or hope to get a bartending job. The heat was off, and life was okay for Billy Ray. A couple of almost full ashtrays littered the two small tables, competing with the smell of stale beer. Empty cans were strewn around the small space, but he only cared about the TV set, which was operable.

A week later in Golden Valley, Minnesota, unbeknownst to Billy Ray, the forensic investigation of the possible crime scene involving his 1987 Chevy, the rowboat, and footprints was settled. Or, unsettled was probably a more appropriate term for the case status. There was no actual crime, but one may have occurred. All of the blood stains or droplets did in fact belong to Billy Ray. His mother's DNA helped to confirm that. There were more stains found in the car, on the knife, on the seat and gunwale of the rowboat, and a speck on a small rock on the sand near the vessel. The forensics people scoured his car, both inside and out, for fingerprints but only Billy Ray's were found.

His prints had been entered into the national data bank six years before, when he was a suspect in the Post and McFadin disappearance. In short, most of the investigators deemed the scene staged and considered that Mr. Dirks was probably a fugitive and quite alive and living somewhere else. It would be considered a cold case, but not one that anyone really wanted to pursue. There remained an interest, however, in apprehending him for further questioning relative to the brutal slayings of Post and McFadin. When he slipped town, which most of the villagers increasingly believed, Billy Ray had shifted the scorn of the townspeople to Bonnie Dirks. Almost seventy-three-years old and in poor health, probably due to depression and a lifetime of smoking, she died two weeks after she saw Billy Ray for the last time. During those two weeks, he had two reasons for not contacting her. The first was an obvious one: The police would probably be tapping her phone in the hope of tracking him down. He also really didn't care about speaking with her again. She bore him, raised him, and turned over her life savings for her son. There wasn't anything else she could do for him. Billy Ray was a scumbag's scumbag and a user. People like that seldom seem to get what they deserve, at least that was the general feeling of Golden Valley residents.

CHAPTER 45

■ Meanwhile, things couldn't get much better for the relationship between Sally and Bart. They were connecting on every level, and Sally's daughter, Ann, adored Bart. All three loved old movies, good books, and going to museums.

One early afternoon after a tennis game, Sally and Bart were lounging around enjoying sandwiches and iced tea.

Out of the clear blue, Sally began. "Bart, did you see 'It's a Wonderful Life?'"

"The Frank Capra movie starring Jimmy Stewart?"

"Yes, that one. Many people in Seneca Falls insist that it was our town that inspired the name of Bedford Falls."

"That's kind of neat," he responded. "I don't know of anybody who doesn't like that movie."

"Do you remember the high school prom scene where the floor opens, and the kids fall in the pool below?"

"Who wouldn't?"

"Well, that was filmed at Beverly Hills High School. The gym is still there," she said, "and still used!"

"I thought it was a winter Christmas movie filmed in New York."

"Bedford Falls was a fictional name and was supposedly a combination of Seneca Falls and Bedford Hills, but the entire film was shot in Encino, California, at the RKO Encino Ranch. Apparently, they built the set for Bedford Falls in two months, and it covered four acres. It had a Main Street, seventy-five stores, a factory, and a large ranch."

"Why do you know so much about the movie?" he chided her.

"Don't get me started," she replied. "Everyone from Seneca Falls is proud of having our town play a part in the film. In fact," she boasted, "we even have an It's a Wonderful Life museum and festival every year! If I'm not totally boring you," she said playfully nudging his forearm, "I can tell you more."

"Go on, pray tell," he chuckled.

"Don't say I didn't warn you!"

"Remember the drug store scene when the pharmacist, Mr. Gower, slapped young George on the ear? You know, the one where Gower got drunk after hearing that his son had died in the war?"

Bart nodded his head in affirmation.

"Well, the boy who played the part of young George," she continued, "said that the actor who assumed the role of Mr. Gower actually was inebriated when he did that and apologized after he drew the actual blood from his ear."

"You are a wealth of information!" Bart chuckled.

They chatted about local happenings while finishing their lunch, and then headed to Sally's house. Their lovemaking, while initially very intense and frequent, slacked off after a few weeks just as it did for most couples. But they still enjoyed their physical relationship, snuggling and closeness on a regular basis. They were both readers, interested in politics, and liked to keep physically active. Tennis was a good outlet for their energies along with frequent visits to the gym. Bart lost his growing paunch and was in his best shape in at least fifteen years. He had recently paid a visit to Dr. Gordon, and the news was still positive. There was no sign of the cancer in his MRI, but the venerable physician cautioned him again that it was always possible for it to rear its ugly head again. Bart was in the best place that he had been since the loss of his wife and daughter. By now, he was pretty sure that he was in love with Sally but waited to tell her until he was quite certain it would be reciprocated. It was probably the competitive-man thing again, which had helped to shape him. But it was easy for him to imagine spending the rest of his life with her.

In fact, he was at the point where he didn't want to think about his life without her. She wasn't quite at that stage yet, but unless there were some uncharted impediments ahead, it was not a difficult thought for her to embrace. Sally West would never forget her husband's betrayal, but that would not be an obstacle for her to move on with Bart. Theirs was a satisfying and loving relationship but an unfathomable challenge for them loomed ahead on the horizon. It would shake their relationship to the core.

CHAPTER 46

■ It was a few days later when Bart heard a knock on his door. Everyone with the exception of Sergeant Livingston and Detective Vince Riley used the doorbell, so Bart knew who to expect when he opened the door. This time, however, he was in a jovial mood. They seemed to be as well, and they sat down together in his living room. Riley began. "Look, Bart," he said earnestly, "we know that we have been unduly tough on you in our past meetings."

That expression, and put as sincerely as Riley articulated it, briefly unnerved the host. "Thanks, detective. I know that you were just doing your jobs."

"Please call us Vince and Tom," he requested. "We're actually here on a social call."

Bart wanted to believe it, but his antennae were still up.

"You doing okay, Bart?" Livingston asked.

"Yeah, thanks. I've recently met a wonderful woman. While I'll never get over the murder of my daughter," he added, "I no longer think of it every minute of every day."

"I don't think that we showed you enough respect when we first met you, Bart," the detective seemed to apologize. Bart started to reply, but Riley stuck his finger up to shush him. "You were going through a horrible time after the death of your daughter, and we were too focused on finding what had happened to her killer instead of understanding your grief. You were pretty nice to us that day, Bart, far nicer than I ever would have been in your shoes."

The host got up and brought in a bowl of potato chips and a few sodas. Their discussion went on for another twenty minutes while the law enforcement officers maintained their friendly tone.

"Did you ever find Darrell Martin?" he asked.

"No, we didn't, and I'm not sure that I give a shit about it," Riley answered. "As you know, there was a guy by the name of Mark Hollister," he went on to say, "who was killed. But he was a scumbag like Martin."

"And then that guy, Virgil Stassen got beat up in a movie theater," Sergeant Livingston broke into the conversation. "He was also a thug. And now the Frank Bender case that we had leaned on you for. All bad people, and we thought we had a vigilante on our hands. But nothing has happened recently."

"And Bart," Riley followed his partner's comments, "some of the guys down at the station were actually glad that they got what they deserved. We still don't know about Martin," he admitted, "and some of us are through caring." As they got up to leave, Riley had one last thing to say. "I don't know if you had anything to do with one of these cases or even all of them, and don't you dare quote me on this—but if you did, I can't blame you."

Bart shook their hands firmly and was very surprised but pleased by the pleasant encounter. He walked them to the door. Pausing for a moment, Riley then offered something that puzzled him. "If you ever need us for anything, give us a call." And then he gave Bart both of their cards.

Bart stood there in the doorway totally dumbfounded after they left. Did they know something? Could they have found a body? Was it possible that he left evidence of his violent struggle with Hollister or Bender? What about Virgil Stassen? He almost wished Livingston and Riley hadn't appeared at his door, but something also made him feel good about the visit. *Do the police actually ever do this, or were they just trying to set me up?* he wondered. He didn't know it then, but he would someday ask for their help.

CHAPTER 47

■ Holly Shannon, an attractive tawny blond who had celebrated her twenty-fourth birthday just a week before, jumped out of bed early and was eager to get ready for work. She waitressed at Flo's Diner in North Fort Myers and was in an especially good mood that day. She and her boyfriend had talked two nights before about the possibility of getting engaged. Her work colleague, Mary Nix, was going to join her that night after work for a few drinks to celebrate. It would be the last night of Holly's short life. The two friends arrived in their separate cars at Dixon's about nine thirty. They had laughed and planned for an engagement that hadn't even happened yet, but they were excited with anticipation. At about ten twenty, their girls' night out complete, they left the bar together and headed for their cars. Mary was the lucky one. She was able to leave her vehicle in the parking lot, but Holly had to walk one street over from Dixon's. It was a dark night, the moon barely visible. The only thing that illuminated the area were a few dingy streetlights at the corner. Unfortunately, Holly had to park halfway down the block. She was nervous and now wished she had taken up Mary's offer to drive her to her car. Anxious and filled with trepidation, she almost ran the last five or more steps to her 1991 Ford Taurus and fumbled with her keys as she sought out the keyhole. At that precise moment, a figure jumped out from behind a tree and cupped his gloved hand over her mouth while holding a sharp knife to her throat.

"Make a sound, and I will slit your throat," he threatened. Hitting her over the head with the thick handle of the knife and rendering her unconscious, he pushed her inside her car over to the passenger side. Then, he drove away silently to a secluded park that he had previously picked out for just this occasion. After putting on a condom, he brutally raped her, slit her throat and then pushed her behind a clump of bushes. The last thing that Holly would see in her twenty-four-year-old life was a small tattoo of a skull and crossbones below his left ear.

Driving very close to Dixon's to retrieve his own car, the savage thug left Holly's Ford almost in the same place he had kidnapped her. While seated at the bar, he had seen the two attractive women drinking at a small table near him, and he noticed them leaving alone. Walking casually out of the bar, he watched them say goodbye to each other. It was at that moment that he hatched his plan. To avoid suspicion, he stayed on the other side of the street during most of his walk, and then he saw one woman had parked with the driver's door at the curb. That way it made it easier for him to cross over and surprise her from behind the tree.Her body was discovered by a jogger at six forty five the next morning, and the police arrived at seven. The scene revealed nothing in evidence other than the partially clad young woman with dried blood almost covering up the gaping wound in her neck. Subsequent forensics would confirm she had been raped and was the victim of a barbarous crime.

Holly's friend Mary Nix had contacted the police after her friend had failed to show up for work the next day at Flo's. She retraced their steps the previous night for them, which led to the discovery of her car just a few spaces from where she had originally parked it. But only the murderer knew that unimportant detail. Her purse had been dumped at the passenger's side of the Taurus, and the wallet still held her credit cards but no money.

"It wasn't enough for the creep to rape and kill this poor girl," an officer at the scene lamented. "The bastard had to rob her as well," he said bitterly.

Law enforcement officials agreed that the person who assaulted her had most likely seen her in the bar. Surveillance tapes were grainy at best and didn't include a good likeness of anyone sitting at the bar or at one of the tables. The police were at loggerheads.

The media did what it does best, and that was to scare every single woman within ten miles of Dixon's. In fact, business at the bar tailed off considerably for the month following the crime. Poor Mary Nix found it difficult to even go to work. The authorities had told her what she already knew: She was very lucky to be alive and that having parked her car in the parking lot undoubtedly saved her life. She knew that and such knowl-edge only served to make her feel guilty. What really bothered her was knowing that if her friend had accepted her offer to drive her to her Taurus, Holly would still be alive. Mary Nix would need counseling to aid her in dealing with the horrible memories and guilt. Of course, she would never forget it. People in her position never do. Meanwhile the psychotic perpetrator of this heinous crime followed the news stories. He had killed the poor girl and had added insult to injury by robbing her of twenty-seven dollars. "Beer money," he called it. There was no sign of contrition, not for Billy Ray Dirks. But there never was for psychopaths.

CHAPTER 48

■ Bart and Sally were now almost at the point where they were living together. Most of their time was spent at Sally's house, which was larger than Bart's dwelling, but occasionally they stayed overnight at the condo. Ann had recently moved with her husband and two children to Hartford, Connecticut, so Sally planned to visit her.

"Why don't you come with me?" she begged. It was early in the summer, and they could easily drive there. Sally offered to drive her BMW, but he preferred to take the trip in his trusty Toyota. They left on a Wednesday morning before the sun came up to ease the traffic burden. It took ten hours to get to their overnight stop in Columbia, South Carolina. and passed what seemed to be thousands of South of the Border signs advertising three hundred and fifty acres of restaurants, gas stations, a video arcade, motel, mini-golf, and a fireworks store. They began seeing the Pedro mascot signs at the Georgia–South Carolina state line and continued to view them until they reached Virginia. There were one hundred seventy-five of them in all, and what seemed amusing at first began to bug Bart.

"For crying out loud, if I see one more of those...." Sally agreed and laughed heartily!

They spent the first night in Columbia totally exhausted and had dinner before going to bed at a motel right off of I-95. The decision to go for it and drive another twelve hours to Hartford the next day depended on how well they slept. Arising at six, they quickly showered and packed up the car and hit the road at six-thirty. They were determined to be at the Ann and Alfred Barkley house by dinner time that night. While driving the trip to Hartford, they talked about Ann's family. "Alfred is a bit stiff," she laughed, "but, then again, he is an insurance man!"

"I'm sure he is a very nice guy if Ann married him."

"Their kids are great," the proud grandmother gushed. Sally yawned and napped for a while. Soon they pulled up to the Barkley residence just in time for dinner. Sally's grandchildren came running out shouting, "Grandma, grandma, we're so excited you're here!" And they all smothered each other with hugs and kisses. Bart watched with a big smile, yet with a bit of a heavy heart, knowing that he would never have grandchildren of his own.

Sally's daughter had labored over a pot roast with all the fixings that afternoon, so they all sat down to a comfortable meal and caught up. She and her husband had two children, eight-year-old Nathan and his six-year-old sister Lana. Alfred was a husky six-footer and worked as an insurance executive in the Insurance Capital of the World, a nickname for the capital city of Connecticut. His large expressive blue eyes and bushy eyebrows stood out, but overall, he was a handsome man, despite overly protruding ears. They talked of the trip from Florida and the usual delays and craziness while driving through New Jersey and New York. The kids did some reading exercises for their proud grandmother and then headed to bed. The next morning, Alfred went to work while Sally and Bart slept in and enjoyed a late breakfast with Ann and the kids.

"Anyone want to go to the Mark Twain House?" Ann asked, quite certain of the response. Nathan and Lana quickly raised their hands, and Sally shouted, "Yes." The Barkleys had just moved to Hartford from Providence in November so none of them had found the time yet to visit the stately old mansion, which Twain had built in 1874. Bart was still tired from the two-day drive and wouldn't have minded an afternoon of reading. But he was not going to be a party-poop, especially in front of the enthusiastic others. A history buff and a fan of Twain's writing, he would normally have jumped at the opportunity, but just not then. It took Ann less than fifteen minutes to thread her way from her house on Oak Street to Farmington Avenue. And there it was, a large reddish American gothic-style house. They eagerly piled out of the car and walked the length of a long porch to the front door. They were greeted by two young women dressed in the garb of the 1880s. Both wore dresses with high necks, wasp waists, puffed sleeves, and bell-shaped skirts. Sally mentioned the wasp waist, but the kids and Bart had no clue what that meant.

"Oh," she explained, "back then women wore a corset or girdle to help them look very thin at the waist, causing their hips to curve out below."

"Boy, that must have been uncomfortable," Nathan observed.

"I'll say," Lana agreed. "Glad I didn't live back then."

The two young women guides were very polite, but any questions had to be asked in the present time, as if it were actually during the mid-1880s. They explained that Twain had lived in the house with his family from 1874 until 1891. He had brought his family to the Nutmeg State in 1871 to be close to his publisher. And then in 1891 he moved them all to Europe. He had made some poor investments, and Europe offered a less expensive lifestyle and gave him the opportunity to go on a lecture tour there. His most notable failed investment was in a typesetting machine invented by James W. Paige. The Paige Composition Typesetting Machine went belly-up in 1894, leaving Twain heavily in debt.

"This is the famous 'Angel' bed where Mark Twain loves to smoke and write," the young guide told them while speaking as though he were still alive. The bed was incredibly ornate with carved bed posts and figurines. It was also very narrow in size.

"How could he possibly sleep in that bed?" Nathan asked.

"Do you mean how does he sleep in it?" the guide gently corrected him.

"Yes," he replied, a little annoyed.

"Well, the beds in this era are quite small," she said matter-of-factly.

They were able to see the typesetting machine, which devastated Twain financially, a few desks at which he had worked, some watercolor paintings, some of his shirts, Mrs. Twain's nightgowns, and even the last pair of spectacles that he ever wore. The guides noted that Twain writes his best books while living in the house, including *The Adventures of Tom Sawyer*, *The Prince and the Pauper*, *The Adventures of Huckleberry Finn*, and *A Connecticut Yankee in King Arthur's Court.* They went on to relate one of the really interesting things about the great author, in a life full of them, which had to do with the day he was born and when he would die. Late in his life, Twain bragged about coming in on Haley's Comet in 1835, saying he would leave in the same manner. Sure enough, in 1910, Haley's Comet appeared again, and Mark Twain died.

The Barkley family's visit to the grand old house—sans Alfred—was a great success and had taken up the late morning and early afternoon. The five sightseers were tired and hungry. They enjoyed a late lunch in Hartford before returning to their home on the tree-lined Oak Street. Bart and Sally took a nap while Ann and the kids watched some educational TV. The trip to Mark Twain's house dominated the dinner conversation. "What was your favorite part of your visit today?" the interested father asked his two children. Nathan started to answer, but Alfred held his hand up and cut him short. "Let your sister go first this time," he said with a smile.

"Well," Lana responded, "I thought that the girls who walked around with us were kind of special. They were so pretty, and they wore old dresses."

"That's great," Alfred beamed, "It sounds like you all had a wonderful time of it. Now, how about you Nathan?"

"I thought it was really neat that we got to see some of his old stuff, especially his last eyeglasses."

It had been a wonderful day for everyone, except perhaps for Alfred, who was away in his Hartford office doing his insurance job. He said that he wished he could have joined them, and Ann interjected that Alfred took his job as an insurance adjuster very seriously and often put in long hours.

The next morning, a Saturday, gave everyone in the household a chance to sleep a little later than usual. Bart and Ann were fine with that plan. When they gathered for breakfast, Ann was the first to speak.

"Would anyone like to visit the home of Harriet Beecher Stowe?"

Sally's eyes lit up. "Count me in," she said enthusiastically. Nathan and Lana didn't know who she was. Alfred, who fortunately didn't have to work on Saturday, and Bart expressed their willingness to go, and both had read *Uncle Tom's Cabin*. The adults, especially Sally, knew what a significant historical figure Stowe was and that she had been a prolific writer. Sally took the lead and explained to the kids that her most famous book of the more than thirty she had written was, of course, *Uncle Tom's Cabin*, which depicted the impact of slavery, especially on families and children. Embraced by the North, it met with hostility in the South. In what might have been an apocryphal story, it was reported that President Abraham Lincoln had suggested to Stowe upon their meeting, "So you're the little woman who wrote the book that started this great war." The book was a best seller in the United States, Great Britain, Europe, and Asia and was translated into sixty languages. It was also the first American novel to ever feature a black hero.

Ann turned the car onto Forest Street and pulled up to number seventy-three. "Here it is," she announced. The Stowe house was across the street from the Mark Twain residence. "How neat," Nathan exclaimed, "they were neighbors!"

The house itself was a stately five-thousand-square-foot, three-story structure of whitish-grey color with a blue roof. Everyone agreed their favorite room was a large and colorful drawing room with numerous paintings on the wall along with a beautiful grand piano. In the middle of the elegant chamber was a hand-carved wooden table, red-cushioned chairs, and a loveseat. On the table were several dishes and a copy of *Uncle Tom's Cabin*. Throughout the house were at least four copies of the book, all with different covers. Several informational brochures told of this remarkable woman's life. She had lost two of her seven children to alcohol and drug addiction and was one of the first to write about them as a physical disease rather than a moral failing. Another pamphlet described Stowe as the sixth of eleven children born to religious leader Lyman Beecher and his wife, Roxanne Foote Beecher, who died when Harriet was only four years old. On the way home, Sally added one more interesting story about the fascinating woman. "Apparently, she campaigned for women's rights, arguing in 1889 that "the position of a married woman was in many respects precisely similar to that of a negro slave. She could make no contract and hold no property. In the English common law," Sally continued to quote the famous author, "a married woman is nothing at all." In the front seat of the car, sitting next to his wife, Alfred Barkley made an issue of sinking lower in his seat and cringing. Everyone laughed.

It had been another educational but tiring day for the clan, and they all elected to have takeout Chinese food for dinner. They all went to church on Sunday morning. After the service, Bart announced that he wanted to take everyone for brunch at a local diner he had spotted. He had seen My Diner several times on their travels around town over the past few days. "There's nothing better than a diner breakfast," he exclaimed. "What do you say? Besides, let's give Ann a break in the kitchen!" Everyone was very enthusiastic, and after waiting for fifteen minutes, they were presented with eggs and bacon, pancakes, and French toast, coffee for the adults, and juice for the children. The waitress was friendly and managed to get everyone's order right. It was a relaxed and enjoyable time, and they all shared lots of banter and laughter. Feeling full and satisfied after their hearty brunch, they came back to Ann and Alfred's home and lounged around the house in the afternoon. The adults talked while the kids went to play with friends in the backyard. It turned out to be an early night for everyone since Sally and Bart would be leaving to return home early the next morning.

CHAPTER 49

■ Ann had packed them a few things for their drive—muffins for the morning, water, crackers and cheese, turkey sandwiches, fruit, and cookies. Because they were leaving so early, the children and Alfred were still sleeping when they left. They had said their goodbyes the night before. Ann made coffee and gave them disposable cups for their trip. She laughed, "It's so early. I don't want you to fall asleep at the wheel!"

"You have been a wonderful hostess, Ann. Thank you for having me, it has been great fun," Bart gushed. After hugs and kisses, the two travelers were on their way. "As Ben Franklin put it," Bart smiled at Sally, "people, like fish, begin smelling after three days!" She laughed and gave him a good pop on his arm.

They were barely out of Hartford for ten minutes before Bart turned on the radio. Sally was driving the leg at least to New York before turning the wheel over to him. A mellow and velvety voice singing "The Shadow of Your Smile" resounded through the car but not loud enough for her. "Please turn it up Bart, this is my favorite song! "I just love Johnny Mathis. Who is your favorite singer?" she asked.

"Let me think a minute...I guess Frank Sinatra."

"And, what's your favorite song?"

"That would be 'My Way,' the song Paul Anka wrote for him."

"Oh, I really like that one, too," she agreed.

It was time to refuel near Washington and change drivers again. For a quick bite to eat, Bart opted for a cheeseburger and fries while Sally was content with a salad, although Bart chuckled when she snuck a fry or two.

Once on the road again, they spoke more about their likes and dislikes. "This is great," she declared, "what a great way to learn more about each other. OK, how about books, Bart. Do you have a favorite?"

Without hesitating, he responded promptly. "There is no question that my all-time favorite is *The Grapes of Wrath* by Steinbeck."

"How come?"

"It just has stuck with me all these years. The injustice of it all turned me into a justice kind of guy; it just resonated with me. You know it won a Pulitzer?"

"Yes, of course. I read it too and loved it. When I visited Monterey years ago, I also read *Cannery Row* because its setting was so indigenous to the area."

"Not to belabor it," he responded, "but did you also read *Of Mice and Men?*"

"You're not belaboring anything, Bart, I love to talk about books and especially learning more about you. Yes, I did read it, and I loved it."

They continued their banter, and their discussion of books and movies took them all the way to North Carolina. Sally's favorite movie turned out to be "The Sound of Music," while his was "Twelve Angry Men."

They both agreed that neither one of them liked the opera.

"One of my girlfriends actually thinks that she is an intellectual because she is a fan of opera," Sally complained, "and that I'm not because I don't like it!"

"Are you?"

"Am I what?"

"Are you an intellectual?"

"Do you care?"

"No."

"I don't consider myself to be one," she smiled, "although I'm not fully sure that I know exactly what an intellectual is. What do you think it means?"

"Beats me. A highly developed intellect? Frankly, I don't really give a rat's ass!"

"Well, that makes two of us!" And they both shared a hearty laugh about the whole thing.

Sally and Bart kept driving until dinner time on Monday and spent the night in Walterboro, South Carolina, off of I-95. They found a local diner and had a relaxing meal. They each had a glass of wine, and when they returned to the hotel, went for a walk to loosen up their muscles, which were a bit tight from being cooped up in the car all day.

Once back in their room, they turned on the local news and decided to shower so they could get a relatively early start in the morning. They were tired, and the lights were out by nine. The ride home from Walterboro could be done in less than eight hours, so they slept in until eight. Bart smiled as he packed up the car to leave. *Sally is so easy to be around, and we have a lot in common, even a love of diners!* They had a hearty breakfast before hitting the road again at nine fifteen.

Sally was driving, and they were reminiscing about their educational visit to the home of Mark Twain.

"You know, Sal," he began, "Mark Twain is known for a thousand quotes. Want to know my favorite?"

"Of course!" She was exuberant in her response.

"He said that the two most important days in your life are the day you were born and the day you find out why."

"Wow, I don't think I've ever heard that."

"Pretty profound," he acknowledged.

"I'll say. It really makes you think."

"I actually have four days," he said, "and I hope that it won't offend you by telling you them."

"Oh, gosh. You won't," she replied, puzzled by his comment.

"OK, those days are the day I was born, the day I married Ginny, the day Stephanie was born, and the day I met you."

Far from being offended, she reached over and squeezed his hand. "That is so sweet Bart!"

"How about you? What are your two most important days?"

"Well, actually now that I think about it, I have three. One of them is when I was born, the second is when Ann was born, and the third is when I first met you." He smiled at this response, and his face turned red.

"Copycat," he murmured as he took her hand.

They made good time, the traffic was light, and they enjoyed talking about everything under the sun, looking at the sights along the way, and just enjoying each other's company. When they arrived home safely at five thirty that evening, they were travel-weary, but they unpacked and then decided to have a takeout pizza dinner. They snuggled on the couch, and after watching a few mindless TV shows, they decided to hit the sack early. They fell asleep in each other's arms within minutes of their heads hitting their pillows.

CHAPTER 50

■ Bart was doing some errands in downtown Fort Myers the very next day when, without warning, the sun suddenly disappeared behind the clouds, and the skies opened up, depositing a heavy sheet of rain. South Floridians are used to it and no longer marvel at what can appear so quickly as a heavy rain, and in the next minute stop. It was like turning on and off a faucet. He ducked into a nearby coffee shop to avoid being totally drenched and read his paper over a cup of java. Within five minutes, the rain completely stopped, and the sun came out. Go figure, he chuckled.

Stepping back out onto the street, Bart was met with an almost unbearable humidity, as so often happened after a sudden outburst of rain on a hot and already steamy day. Several people were shouting, and he suddenly noticed a scuffle to his left, where it appeared that a man was attempting to steal a woman's purse. By the time he ran up to the fracas, the thief had already punched her twice and had his fist ready to impart a third. Bart arrived just in time to grab the assailant's arm and pull it back. The young woman, although clearly injured by the blows, continued to hold onto her purse as she started to sink to the ground. She turned around to face her rescuer just as the assailant swung wildly at Bart's jaw. He missed with his punch, as the Good Samaritan ducked and countered with a savage uppercut, which found its mark. The man staggered back against the wall for a moment, as Bart stepped forward to finish the job. He knew from a number of skirmishes on the streets of Buffalo and then again at Pitt, that one never backs off if your opponent is in trouble. The uppercut was quickly followed by a karate chop to the bridge of the nose and a violent whip of the back of his hand to the thug's throat. The coup de grace was a thunderous punch to his jaw. He fell against the building and crumpled to the ground. Bystanders were already attending to the woman, who was seated on the ground while still clutching onto her purse. The police and ambulance had been called, and several witnesses to the attempted theft and the ensuing fight gathered around the savior to congratulate him. "Sir, you are a real hero," several of them said. One person asked for his name, which he reluctantly gave. The young woman was clearly banged up. She had a badly swollen cheek, an eye that was turning black, and her nose was bleeding. Her attacker looked to be in worse shape. He remained stretched out on the ground and appeared unconscious. Several teeth had been dislodged and were on the pavement several feet away from his bloody nose and his now purplish and bleeding lips. His breathing was erratic, and he was giving off choking sounds. A trip to the hospital would be in order for him. Several policemen were there when the ambulance arrived. The shaken woman was able to stand up on her own and moved toward the gurney with the help of the two paramedics. When she saw Bart standing there, talking with one of the bystanders, she broke away for a moment and went up to him.

"I don't know who you are, sir," she said through her tears," but I thank you for saving my life. Thank you so, so much." With that she reached out her hand in a sign of gratitude. He took it and gave it a gentle squeeze.

He looked at her with a comforting smile. "Your pretty face is going to be quite sore tomorrow, but I'm glad that you're okay."

As she approached the gurney, she turned one last time. "Thank you again." He was glad that he just happened to be there at the right time. Her assailant was a big man—considerably younger than Bart and about his size. *The coward might have really inflicted some serious damage if he had gotten in that third blow,* he thought to himself. As it was, she was hurt pretty badly. As he was leaving the bustling scene with people still milling around and talking about the incident with others, Bart noticed the two policemen talking with the woman on the gurney, almost as if they knew her. One of them came over to him to take a brief statement. He felt good about himself and that he was able to protect her from that thug. *And he didn't even lay a finger on me,* he chuckled proudly.

During his Buffalo youth, he had learned—sometimes the hard way—how to fight. The first blow was important, if you could land it. And once you had your opponent in trouble, it was necessary to step in right away and finish the job. Bart Steele also had one special thing going for him. He had large knuckles, and they were very hard. To settle major disputes, fistfights were the usual method. But for minor ones, the kids in his neighborhood resorted to knuckle fights. That was when two boys just punched their fists at the other, purposely striking the other's knuckles. In his entire childhood, Bart had never once lost a knuckle fight.

The next morning, he played tennis with his regular group. The greeting was unexpected. "Well, here he comes folks," his best friend Ken Clark let the chant. "A real hero is in our midst."

Bart raised a quizzical eyebrow. Ken noticed and smiled to the group.

"You mean you didn't see it, Bart?"

"See what?"

"Your photo in the paper this morning and an article about how you rescued a damsel in distress?"

He hadn't seen the paper, having slept through the alarm. He hadn't had time for breakfast or to read the newspaper. So, he didn't know what they were talking about.

Ken shoved the newspaper in his face. "It's right here!" Bart read it and smiled. Apparently, someone had snapped his picture along with that of his prone victim, who had been identified as a local tough named Barrett Wright, and the woman he had saved.

"Looks like you really coldcocked the bastard, Bart." Les Crane chimed in. The group was early and had fifteen minutes to take to the courts; they spent that time listening to their friend tell them about his encounter the previous day. Bart enjoyed the attention and told them that he was glad that he was in the right place at the right time. "Man, I really nailed the bastard," he proudly exclaimed.

When he got home, there were already three messages from Sally as well as two more on his cell phone. He called her and explained that he had been playing tennis and catching up with the guys. He told her he was hopping into the shower but that she could certainly come in. When she finally came over, he filled her in on the excitement. "You could have been hurt, Bart."

"But I wasn't," he responded with a huge grin.

They spent Saturday at the same beach where Frank Bender had received some justice. Showering, a good meal, a good movie, and much needed lovemaking that night completed a happy day. They both went to church on Sunday and joined Ken Clark and his wife for brunch afterwards. Bart was reading the Sunday Sports section while Sally was making an apple pie when there was a knock on the door. *Could it be Riley and Livingston on a Sunday,* he wondered. *What the heck could they possibly want now!* He opened the door, but Livingston wasn't there. Instead, Detective Vince Riley was accompanied by a young woman who looked familiar. Her black eye, purple welts, bruised and swollen cheekbone and lips were a dead giveaway. It was the same young woman he had rescued just three days before.

Riley broke the silence. "Hi Bart. My daughter, Laura, has something she wants to say to you." Soon they were all seated in the family room, and Sally brought some lemonade and cookies.

"Mr. Steele," a trembling Laura Riley began, "I am so glad that you were there! I am so glad that you were willing to get involved." She got up from her seat and walked the five feet to his side and hugged him. It brought tears to his eyes and to Sally's as well.

"Laura, you have a wonderful father, and I see that the apple doesn't fall far from the tree!" They all laughed.

"Bart," Vince Riley broke in. "I'm in the business where I so often see that a bystander who could have helped someone, unfortunately chooses to remain a bystander. They allow a crime to be committed or someone to get hurt when their intervention might have prevented it. Laura and I," he continued, "will be eternally grateful that Bart Steele didn't even give it a thought. He stepped in against a very big and bad man and saved her from what could have been a fatal injury."

They talked about the event a bit more and of Laura's condition. The twenty-three-year-old had suffered a cracked cheekbone and contusions around her eye and on her lip. Fortunately, her teeth were not broken or loosened, although she twisted her back when she fell against the wall after her assailant had hit her the second time.

To lighten the mood a little, Vince Riley interjected, "Thank God she didn't have any teeth damaged! I paid big bucks for those!" They all laughed as Laura gave a playful jab at her father's arm.

"But I can't say the same for your victim, Barrett Wright," Detective Riley laughed out loud.

"How is he doing?" Bart asked, "although I couldn't care less."

"Well, you broke three of his teeth, his jaw, the orbital bone around his right eye socket, his nose, and his right cheekbone. Other than that, he's fine! Remind me, Bart," Riley chuckled, "never to tangle with you!"

"When I saw what he did and was doing to your daughter, I kind of lost it. He was a big guy, and I knew I couldn't afford to hold back."

They spent about ten more minutes conversing and finishing their lemonades and cookies, and when Laura and Vince Riley had driven off, Sally embraced Bart for several minutes before speaking. "I'm so proud of you, Bart Steele. You are an amazing and wonderful man!" She kissed him full on the lips without letting go.

"Well, you know what?" he reflected. "Vince Riley is a pretty nice guy."

CHAPTER 51

■ Later that week, about eight-thirty at night, Maryanne Meroni made a routine trip to her pharmacy to pick up a few things. Unfortunately for her, a seedy and evil individual was also there and noticed the petite and pretty young woman. She probably didn't notice him and the small tattoo on his neck, but he was very mindful of her presence. He left the store and headed to the pharmacy parking area, which was unattended and mostly dark with only dim lighting emanating from the building. There were only four cars in the lot, including his own, so he knelt behind an old Hyundai, which he thought might belong to her and put on some gloves. She emerged from the store a few minutes later, totally oblivious to the imminent danger that would soon be unleashed upon her. All was still, and there was no sign of anyone else. Maryanne had just put her key in the door lock when he struck. He hit her hard in the back of her head with a rock, while at the same time placing his other hand around her mouth. As her attacker stuffed the unconscious young woman into the trunk of his car, he applied some duct tape to her mouth and arms and quickly drove off. When he got to his destination—an abandoned farm about three miles away—he pulled over and turned off his headlights. He opened the trunk. She had regained consciousness but was still dazed. Her frightened and panic-stricken eyes showed she recognized the grim event that was in store for her. She was bleeding from the back of her head, but Maryanne attempted to scream for help but all that came from her mouth were muffled sounds as she struggled for her life. He raped her under a tree, and then strangled her to death. Then, he just left her there. The monster wore gloves and a condom to avoid DNA evidence being left. The evil son of Golden Valley, Minnesota, had now claimed his fourth victim.

Back in his car, Billy Ray pored through the contents of Maryanne's purse. He was annoyed that she had only eighteen dollars. *More beer money,* he groused, a little disappointed in his take. In a life full of despicable choices, this wretched action was one of his most contemptible. But he wasn't done yet wreaking havoc with the lives of innocent women.

Billy Ray had a mean streak in him and a definite problem with women. His mother had been such a soft touch for him, probably because she felt guilty about his contentious and short-lived relationship with his father. Whatever it was, he enjoyed exercising power and control over a woman. That was one of the traits of the serial killer that he was. He couldn't exert such power over men because he wasn't strong enough. Billy Ray didn't respect his mother. Why would he respect other women? Clearly, he was a misogynist in the worst sense of the word. He hated women and now enjoyed the thrill of killing them. This time it was a man walking his dog who discovered the body. The police acted under the assumption that the wicked perpetrator was the same person who had ended Holly Shannon's life. Unfortunately, once again, there were no leads. The perpetrator must have worn gloves throughout the entire ordeal, and there were no prints whatsoever. The terrain was dry, which aided the rapist and murderer to escape the scene without leaving any footprints. There was a pharmacy bag left at the scene, leading the officers to the conclusion that she may have been attacked and abducted while attempting to get into her car. Surveillance tapes obtained from the pharmacy outdoor security cameras were grainy and didn't reveal much. The darkness and remoteness of the area where her car had been parked didn't help the forensic experts. They could follow her out of the store but could barely see her at her car nor the shadowy figure that seemed to confront her. The tape was enlarged to its maximum degree, but even Maryanne's face was scarcely visible.

Newspapers worried in print that a serial killer may be on the loose, while the police attempted to ease the public's fright. But bad news travels quickly and successfully, and the Fort Myers community worried out loud. Meanwhile, the cause of this public torment continued his life as a parasite. Billy Ray was more concerned about getting only a combined forty-five dollars from the two crimes than he was about ending the lives of two young, innocent women. The greedy psychopath had no conscience. Bart read about both murders and fumed and seethed over them. He saw the families interviewed on television and empathized as one only can if placed in the same position. The coverage was an instant reminder about his daughter's brutal murder. As if he needed any reminder. Thoughts of her were always with him. Torturing and killing Darrell Martin would not bring her back, but at least he had had the satisfaction of inflicting some justice on the bastard. And that scum Martin had the opportunity to understand a little bit about suffering himself before his captivity had ended so violently. Of course, this would be of little comfort for the Shannon and Meroni families.

With little or no evidence at either scene, it appeared that there would be no justice for them or their daughters. By now, Bart had lost confidence in the justice system. He mourned for them and would have given anything to have the good fortune of encountering the beast, whoever he was.

CHAPTER 52

■ The wonderful Hartford trip behind them now, Bart and Sally took it easy for several days. Bart went back to playing tennis with his regular group, and they continued to play singles together on Friday mornings. Several weeks had passed, and Bart had another successful medical checkup. Life was pretty good. Their relationship escalated to the point of them discussing marriage, although both thought they should wait a little longer before finalizing things.

As for the brutal murders of Holly Shannon and Maryanne Meroni, the police were feverishly trying to piece things together to assuage a nervous and anxious public. The media kept the stories alive, which only served to inflame the growing tension, but the police didn't even receive the usual phone calls and bogus tips that always seem to arise after unsolved murders. Detective Riley was particularly perturbed because he had been among the first law enforcement officers to appear at both crime scenes, and there was just nothing for him to go on. No prints, no evidence, no leads, and no clues about who did those unspeakable crimes against two such young, lovely women who were in just the early stages of their adult lives.

CHAPTER 53

■ It was the middle of July, and Billy Ray Dirks was restless. He didn't bother looking for a job and spent his evenings drinking and trolling for women. He was down to his last thousand, which included the theft of forty-five dollars from his murdered victims. This poor excuse of a man was also feeling sorry for himself.

Many years ago, after he got into a fistfight with his father, they never spoke again. Both parents knew from the time that their son was seven years old that something was amiss. Billy Ray seemed to take joy out of hurting defenseless animals such as small cats and dogs. Pulling wings from grasshoppers, probably something every kid did at least once, was a particular favorite of his. Billy Ray Dirks even loved to hold a small bird in his hand and then crush it. His friends, except for Jimmy Shaw, were all repulsed by the cruel acts. Billy Ray and Jimmy ended up being best friends, and they spent an inordinate amount of time together while growing into their teens. Neither of them had any kind of relationship with their fathers. Both were bright students, as long as they were interested in the subject matter. If not, which was usually the case, the only way they passed the course was due to a forgiving teacher.

Their disrespect for girls was so profound and well-known that no female would even attend the high school senior prom with them. Both boys spent what is supposed to be a special night in the park, smoking weed and drinking beer. Some of their friends went away to college, but that was never a viable option for either one of the two misanthropes. The only reason Billy Ray's mother was able to prevail on him to seek counseling was because Jimmy had already succumbed to his mother's demand. The boys always carried very sharp knives with them, ever since they were kids, and they made sure that everyone knew about it. Once out of high school, they did odd jobs and tinkered around Tony's Auto Body Shop. Those funds, supplemented by regular thefts from their mothers' purses, sustained them. Then Jimmy killed himself late one night. He hanged himself in the Shaw's garage, where he was discovered the next morning by his distraught and confused mother. Billy Ray was not totally shocked because his friend had spoken on several occasions about ending it all. But they had been drunk on beer and high on weed those times, and Billy never really thought that his friend would follow through with those intentions.

After Jimmy was buried that rainy and dreary March morning, his best friend became even more of a recluse. Billy Ray's father, already estranged from his son and angry with his wife for years of coddling him, as he put it, abruptly left the household. Frank Dirks was never heard from again. Mother and son continued to live together in their small house, and Bonnie helped to make ends meet by sewing draperies and quilting. When he felt like it, which wasn't often, Billy Ray did handyman work and occasionally helped out at Tony's Auto Body Shop. It was a great way to learn about cars and how easy it was to hotwire them. He got a great deal from Tony on a 1971 Chevy when he was in his twenties and later on a 1987 model. And it was then that he established his only romantic relationship with Patty Post. The relationship seemed to progress quite well until she really got to know him and his ill temper. It wasn't one single incident that led her to end their romance, but there was a serious one that probably served as the catalyst. They were at a movie theater together one night when a young man sitting directly behind her brushed his foot against her seat again—after Billy Ray had warned him the first time. It seemed to be unintentional, and the boy apologized, but the bully brandished his knife and threatened the boy aloud in the crowded theater. Patty was mortified, especially since she and Billy Ray were double dating with her friends. Patty was very shaken, and when the movie was over, she told Billy Ray that she had a terrible headache and wanted to go home. He wasn't happy, but he did what she asked.

Now, a very fidgety and agitated Billy Ray Dirks was hunched in front of the TV, thumbing through a porn magazine. The misogynist got up and wandered around his small apartment and worked himself into a rage. Tomorrow, he would find something to satisfy it.

July in Southwest Florida was usually a hot and sticky month, and Billy Ray hated the high humidity that accompanied the heat. He thought how comfortable it would be right then in Minnesota, compared to his hellhole of an apartment with the air-conditioning barely able to keep up with the heat index. Low on food, it was time for another run to the food and liquor stores. He needed some beer and cigarettes. He pulled up to the Supermart and was about to jump out of his car when he noticed a BMW pulling in across from him. A very pretty blonde woman looked in the mirror for a moment before exiting her vehicle. *What a stunner,* he thought, although she looked to be older than his previous targets. Just as he was about to follow her into the grocery store, a better idea came to him. Since there was a concrete block in front of his car that would prevent him from moving forward, he eased his stolen Toyota out of its spot. He then maneuvered the vehicle around the parking lot so that he could back it in behind the BMW. *Man, she is beautiful and must be rich,* he thought to himself. Twenty minutes later, she emerged from the store ladened with a bag of groceries. She was oblivious to his eyes tracking her every move as she placed the bag in her trunk and drove off. Following her from a safe distance, the two drove for about ten minutes to a residential area. Lucky for him, it wasn't a gated community. She pulled into her driveway and disappeared into the garage. Once she was out of sight, he continued past it while noting the address and the absence of surveillance cameras. The blonde lived very close to a cul-de-sac, which he circled, all the time looking for signs of neighbors or dogs. He didn't see either.

It was one fifteen in the afternoon. He returned again at ten forty-five that night. He could see her through some flimsy draperies. There was no sign of any neighbors. Billy Ray knew that almost all of the snowbirds from the north would be gone by now and hoped that her immediate neighbors fit into that category. The houses in the area were all built in the typical single-story Florida style, with an open concept kitchen and great room, and two or three bedrooms. Builders throughout Florida realized that new Floridians preferred one-story dwellings because hot air rises, and a single floor can help to cut down on cooling costs. Such a style also made sense during the June-to-November hurricane season, limiting the amount of wind each structure would encounter. There was another reason as well. Older retirees liked not having to navigate any stairs. There were no lights on either side of the blonde's house, but he knew that could be because many Florida residents tended to retire early. The next night he patrolled the area again, but this time he planned his arrival for nine at night. She lived on a short quiet street with only fifteen houses. There was some kind of forest preserve that ran all the way along the other side of the street. As he drove down Palmetto Cove Drive, it was very quiet, and the only lights seemed to be those of an occasional streetlamp. Only three of the homes had any of their lights on. And the closest one to her house was five houses away. He would return the next night, but it wouldn't be for the same reason.

It was misty and dark when Billy Ray left his apartment at ten fifteen. He would be at her place in twenty-five minutes. Traffic was light, and he arrived early at the Palmetto Cove neighborhood at ten thirty-five. He eased his way down the street to avoid any hint of suspicion, and he noticed that the same three homes had their lights on but no others. He retraced his steps a few minutes later, and one of the three was now dark. That dwelling was seven houses away from his target. He returned to the main street before circling back to 22531 Palmetto Cove Drive. The blonde had turned her lights out, leaving the entire street dark except for the three streetlamps, which seemed to be struggling to project more than a dim beam. She had obviously gone to bed, and the timing seemed perfect. He turned off his car lights and parked quietly in the driveway next to her home. He silently shut the front door of his car and walked furtively to the back of her house. The screened lanai was about twenty-five feet from a small pond. The doors on either side of the lanai cage were both locked. It was easy enough to cut through the screen with his knife, however, and he unlocked the latch nearest to his getaway. There was a small swimming pool and a hot tub adjacent to it, and he was careful not to step on anything. Fortunately for him, the moon was out and shone on the lanai floor, making it easy for him to tiptoe over various debris and move to the glass slider. He looked for some sign of an alarm or warning system, but there were no visible telltale red lights. The glass slider didn't present much of a problem for him. All he had to do was make sure that he dislodged it quietly. Sure enough, a slight upward tug moved the slider off its track, and he slipped inside.

There were no sounds inside whatsoever with the exception of the icemaker in the refrigerator. A few cubes were produced and dropped into the bin inside the freezer, and he froze in place from fear of being discovered. Recognizing the source of the noise, he moved slowly toward what he thought would be the master bedroom. His gloves were on, a condom was in his pocket, and he was poised for the next step. He was sweating profusely as he stepped into her bedroom, where he could hear her breathing. He pulled out his trusty weapon. The only other sound was that of his heart pounding.

He fell on her and cupped one hand around her mouth and held the knife to her neck with the other. She woke up in a panic and felt the cool sharp blade against her neck. "If you make any noise whatsoever, I will slit your throat and kill you," he threatened her. "Nod if you understand," he demanded.

She nodded vigorously as she pressed her head deeper into the pillow to avoid the blade piercing her skin. She could smell his hot breath. And with one hand, he pulled off the sheet covering her and tore the nightgown from her body. There was little doubt in her mind what would come next. At that exact point, a car going by the house illuminated just enough light for her to make out a small skull and crossbones tattoo on his neck and just below his left ear. The unexpected light unnerved him for a moment. In her panic, she was still able to remember something her Smith College roommate had told her years before. She took advantage of that nanosecond to thrust her right forefinger down her throat. The result was an instantaneous eruption of vomit, a gush of which splashed all over his face. For a moment, she choked.

"You bitch!" he screamed recoiling away from her. Then the phone rang, and she tried to reach for it. She knocked it off the cradle and heard a familiar voice. "Sally, Sally, is that you? Are you okay?" He heard the sound of what appeared to be a struggle. "I'll be right there," he shouted out loudly.

Billy Ray wiped the vomit off his face and slashed at her. "You bitch, you dirty bitch! I'm going to kill you!" He slashed at her again, and the sharp blade sank into her left cheek right to the bone. She screamed so loudly it spooked him. Hearing a man's voice on the dangling phone shouting epithets added to his panic. Still covered in vomit, he made one last attempt to kill her. He wielded his blade in an attempt to slash her throat, but his slight hesitation gave her just enough time to cover her throat with two hands. The knife almost severed the little finger on her right hand and inflicted a deep wound in her forearm. Again, she wailed in agony, and her attacker worried that the guy on the phone would be there soon. In fact, it was possible that he might live right down the block.

"I am leaving now," he raged, "but I will finish you off, bitch, the next time!" He knew she couldn't identify him in the dark.

She was sobbing and screaming in pain while he raced out of the house. The sound of sirens filled the night air. On his way home, Billy Ray could hardly contain himself. Strangely, he felt humiliated by the experience. He may have killed her or at least maimed her; of that he was certain. But he was feeling sorry for himself. *When this blows over,* he thought, *I will definitely come back and kill her. In fact,* he added sadistically, *she will beg me to kill her.* He was supposed to be in control, and yet, she had turned the tables on him. Such disobedience infuriated him to the point of rage. She wouldn't be so lucky the next time, he promised himself.

CHAPTER 54

■ Both police and an ambulance arrived simultaneously. Bart had called both from his car and got there before them. Sally was in shock and had lost a great deal of blood. The medics applied compresses to help stop the blood flow and called ahead to the hospital to have a blood supply ready. Bart accompanied her in the ambulance to the hospital and was able to see her two hours later. It was almost two in the morning when he was allowed into her room. The entire left side of her face was covered with huge bandages, as was her right hand and forearm. She was heavily sedated and could barely speak. He held her left hand and spoke softly to soothe her.

"The doctors say you will be fine," he said calmly. The peacefulness in the room belied Bart's sense of rage and the ordeal that the poor woman had just suffered. She would be in the hospital for three days, and then it would be home where Ann could fly in and help him look after her.

The day after the vicious attack on Sally, Detective Vince Riley came by to see her in her hospital room. He had previously met Sally, of course, that day when he and his daughter Laura had stopped by to thank Bart for defending her against Barrett Wright. Riley took down everything she told him, including the threats that her attacker had made in a rage before he fled the scene. Bart didn't even have to ask.

"I will assure you of around the clock police protection until we find this thug," Riley promised.

"Thanks so much, Vince," a grateful Bart acknowledged.

Sally mumbled her appreciation as well.

"We will find this bastard, and that is a promise!"

The two men shook hands vigorously as good friends do, and Bart thanked Riley again.

"By the way, Vince, how come I never see Livingston anymore?"

"Well, as you know, he got promoted and is breaking in his new office."

"Give him my best, will you?"

I'm going to find you before Vince does, Bart silently promised the unknown assailant, *and when I do, you will be begging for mercy before I kill you.*

Only Bart and Vince Riley knew that Sally had seen a tattoo on her attacker's neck. The media would never know, nor could it. If Billy Ray heard that the police were looking for a man with a skull and crossbones tattoo below his left ear, all he would have to do is cover it with a band aid. But Sally's assailant felt that he had nothing to worry about. He was frustrated by his failure to rob, rape, and kill her, but she had humiliated him by vomiting right in his face. Initially, when he got home, Billy Ray was hopeful that he did kill her. His knife had found its mark several times, and he could almost hear the blood gushing out of her. Her main wounds were on her face, right hand, and forearm, and her screaming probably helped her to unnerve him. Unless she had received immediate care, however, she would be a goner. But all of Billy Ray's wishes were out the window when he read the newspaper two days later and saw a report on the attack the next night on the evening news. Clearly, she was quite alive, but it was obvious that he had inflicted a great deal of damage on her body, particularly her face.

"Good," he exclaimed when he first saw the photos, "The bitch deserved it!" But he still sought revenge for her retching on him, and he planned retribution. *When all of this cools down, I will go back and finish the job.* His bravado remained unwavering. He knew that the Shannon and Meroni girls could never identify him because they were dead, and he was one hundred percent confident that this West woman couldn't either because it had been so dark.

Billy Ray remembered that moment when the car had gone by, and its lights raced across the room, but it was only for a nanosecond. He was certain that she didn't get a glimpse of his face. So, the police wouldn't know who they were looking for, and he wouldn't have to skulk around in fear of being identified. As the newspaper reported it, she didn't see his face and a police artist didn't even bother making a sketch of the intruder.

CHAPTER 55

■ Three days later, he struck again. Karen Taylor, a diminutive twenty-three-year-old redhead, had the misfortune of being in the same bowling alley with the evil sexist. After rolling a few games, he was having his second beer at the bar when he witnessed what appeared to be a curvaceous redhead telling off her drunken boyfriend. She slapped him across the face, returned her rented bowling shoes, and marched out of the building. The boyfriend started after her, but then abruptly stopped himself at the lobby. It probably wasn't the first fight in their relationship. Luckily for Billy Ray, he had already returned his shoes and didn't have to delay his departure. He found her in the parking lot about eight cars away, bent over at the waist sobbing on the side of the car. Unfortunately for Karen Taylor, no one was around at that moment. He crept up behind her in the soft balmy summer night, and all he had to do was to push hard on the back of her head, and the car did the rest. He quickly carried his unconscious victim to his car, put on his rubber gloves, dropped her into the trunk, and sped away. He arrived at his destination, which was just one hundred yards or so from the same park where he had attacked the Shannon woman. He opened the trunk and caught a right fist in the nose from the redhead. She wasn't going down without a fight. He punched her in the jaw while they both grappled with each other. Her act of defiance, especially by a woman, infuriated him, and he fell back into the trunk with her. She attempted to scream, but fear seemed to take over her vocal cords. He put his hands around her neck and squeezed as hard as he could. The only noises to penetrate the night air were the muffled gurgling sounds of someone trying desperately to breathe. It was finally over, and he looked around to see if there were any eyewitnesses to his latest crime. It was eerily quiet as one would expect in a secluded park at ten thirty-five on a dark night. He looked back in the trunk and noticed that the dead woman's purse was inside. *Good,* he said to himself, *it's not a total loss.*

He dumped the body under a tree, returned to his car, and quickly pored through the contents of her purse. The only thing of value to him was twelve dollars, and that angered him. He had murdered three Florida women and gained a lousy fifty-seven dollars for his efforts. He threw out her purse and everything in it except for the twelve dollars, and without his car lights on, threaded his way out of the park and headed for home.

CHAPTER 56

■ Upon hearing about the latest murder the next day, the Fort Myers-area public went into a frenzy. Women were afraid to go out at night, unless with a number of friends. Clearly, a serial killer who had already killed at least three young women was on the loose, and there were possibly more. Sally West would have been victim number four, had she not found a clever way to stop her attacker. Suddenly, women were instructing each other on how to fend off an attack. Some bought guns, and others went to self-defense classes. The local bars noticed a definite drop in female clientele, especially after nine at night.

Meanwhile, life was really miserable for Chet Wade. He was Karen Taylor's date that night at the bowling alley, and several customers had noticed them arguing. At first, the police thought Chet might have been Karen's attacker, but a lengthy interrogation of the husky young man proved otherwise. Although inebriated, his tears were real and compelling, and both interrogators were certain of his innocence. A successful lie detector test exonerated him. All poor Chet could think of was that she died because of him. He knew that Karen would never have been vulnerable to an attack if he had run after her following their argument. Chet Wade was the most tormented person in Fort Myers. The Taylors might have been a close second. Not so for a certain inhabitant of a dingy and small apartment in Fort Myers. Nobody would suspect Billy Ray, nor had anyone seen his face, so he knew he was safe. After a few days, which just happened to coincide with Sally's release from the hospital, her assailant decided to take a drive by her house. He knew it was probably reckless for him to do so, but arrogance and overconfidence had always led him to do what he wanted. As he turned the corner onto Palmetto Cove Drive, he froze. In front of Sally's house was a police car. *Holy shit,* he said to himself, *she must have around-the-clock protection.*

He casually pulled into the first driveway, turned around, and headed the hell out of there. Revenge might be more difficult and take more time than he first thought. But he was determined to exact it, whatever the time frame.

CHAPTER 57

■ Sally West sat down in her living room with Bart and Vince Riley. The three tried to piece together her whereabouts for a few days before she was attacked. She sat in a robe sipping tea, holding the cup in her left hand. Bandages continued to cover the left side of her face and her right hand and forearm. Sally thought about it long and hard. Detective Riley suspected that her assailant must have seen her at some store in the area and had probably followed her home.

"I was never out by myself at night for at least two weeks or so before then," she asserted.

"He may have seen you during the day, followed you home, and then returned that night or perhaps within the next few nights. Try to remember, Sally," Riley implored. "It's important. We will nail this bastard, I promise. But it will really help to go over your schedule for those days."

"The only place I visited was the Supermart on Terry Drive last Monday and then again on Wednesday."

"Did you notice anyone looking at you in a funny way?"

"No, not really."

"What do you mean, not really?"

"I just meant no. I didn't notice anything unusual."

"Anything happen in the parking lot?" She shook her head. "No."

"My guess is," the detective continued, "that someone either saw you at that store for the first time or perhaps was stalking you from a previous encounter. He probably followed you home and then returned later that night. There were several murders in Virginia a few years ago that followed that script."

"Do you think this guy is a regular at that store?" Bart asked.

"Perhaps, and let's hope so. One thing we might have going for us is he thinks Sally can't recognize him."

"But I saw the tattoo," she reaffirmed. "But he doesn't know that. The night was so dark," she continued, "he probably wouldn't have a problem going back again to the Supermart—that is, if he went there regularly in the first place."

"It's a start," Riley remarked. "The only problem is you will have to wear a disguise if we decide to do it at the Supermart, but Bart will have to be by your side."

"Let's do it," an excited Bart Steele said, "but Sally, only if you are up to it."

Sally West nodded her head vigorously.

"You will have to wear a wig and dark glasses," their detective friend cautioned them. "And Bart," he said firmly, while looking him squarely in the eyes, "you must promise me not to take things into your own hands."

"I promise, Vince."

Two weeks after their discussion with Vince Riley, the bandages came off. Bart told Sally how pretty she still looked. Sally dissolved in tears and almost collapsed in his arms. Her plastic surgeon, Ralph Peters, told her he'd had to sew forty-seven stitches in and on her left cheek and that he had additional plans for more surgery for her to "touch things up."

"After a while, you will hardly notice them," he assured her. But this was now, and she thought she looked like something out of a horror movie.

"You are alive, hon, and we should both be grateful for that. It may take some time," Bart attempted to assuage her, "but this will all work out and just like Dr. Peters said."

She wasn't so sure. "Bart, let's go out and get a wig," she said bravely. "It's time we catch this bastard. Besides," she added with a wry smile, "I've always wanted to be a brunette!" It was hard for Sally to look in the mirror. The grim sight steeled her resolve to catch the evil bastard.

What a trouper, he thought.

They went to a wig salon, and after trying on several, she found one she liked along with some big sunglasses to hide what he had done to her face. A long-sleeved blouse would conceal her forearm wound.

"I've always wanted to go to bed with a brunette," he chuckled on the way home, "and I think tonight's the night!"

"Don't be so sure," she replied while tickling his ribs.

263

They decided to make a run to the Supermart every day for the first week, at about eleven in the morning and two in the afternoon. If they didn't catch a glimpse of him, they would switch the times but continue their daily vigil. Bart feared that eventually her attacker would return to Sally's house, but he didn't share that concern with her. He didn't have to. Anxiety and an uneasiness about a possible reenactment of that horrible night gripped her every day. They told Vince that they were ready to implement the plan. Vince cautioned him again. "Bart, don't do anything yourself. Get his license plate if you can, and let me do the rest!"

CHAPTER 58

■ It was a muggy Tuesday morning later in the month when the couple made their first joint visit to the Supermart. Bart stayed close to Sally while they picked out a few items. Her dark glasses did a pretty good job of covering both sides of her face. There was no sign of her assailant, so they paid for their groceries and went home. They followed the same pattern that afternoon and each morning and afternoon for the rest of the week. Once on Friday morning, Sally thought she might have seen her assailant and nudged Bart, but to no avail. The man did have a tattoo on his neck but on the right side, and it was a sword rather than skull and crossbones. She quivered in fear at the moment she thought the man was her attacker, and she didn't really compose herself until they reached home. At eleven fifteen the following morning, they faithfully trudged into the Supermart again. Bart was looking over some potato chips when he felt a sharp jab in his ribs.

"There he is," she whispered. He was careful to turn around slowly and look casually at a man about ten feet away. Sure enough, he had a skull and crossbones tattoo on his neck below his left ear. Bart wanted to attack him right then and there. Sally sensed that anger, grabbed his arm, and walked to the other end of the aisle.

"We must do what Vince asked," she admonished him. "You just can't go up and attack him!"

"But Sal..."

"But Sal nothing. I'm the one he attacked, and we're going to do it Vince's way. Besides, I don't want to have to visit you in prison. And, he might have a knife or a gun. Who knows?"

Bart got the message and knew she was right. But walking away from this man was the most difficult thing he had ever done. He promised himself it wouldn't happen again.

They waited outside for Billy Ray in the sweltering sun, and they knew they had to be ready to get his license plate number. Little did they know how useless that information would be. Bart had a pad and a pen with him, which he started carrying on the first day they went to the Supermart earlier that week.

After about ten minutes, they saw the lowlife heading towards his car, which fortunately was only about ten cars from theirs and in the same aisle. He seemed totally oblivious to what was happening around him. Having memorized the plate number, Bart jumped into the car, quickly wrote it down, and pulled up near Billy Ray's Toyota. Immediately, Sally sensed what was happening. "No, Bart, we're not going to follow him!"

"Sal, we have to see where he lives. What if the plates or even the car were stolen? Where would we be then?

"Well, be careful," she implored, "he gives me the willies. Promise me that you will call Vince."

"I promise, but we can't let this opportunity slip by. We may never see him again. Do you understand, Sally? This may be our only chance."

"Okay, Bart, we will just see where he lives and then go home, right?"

"Absolutely, I wouldn't do anything to jeopardize your safety. As soon as we get home, I promise I will call Vince."

She was still filled with trepidation as they followed their quarry, taking great care to follow him at a safe distance. Billy Ray finally pulled onto Montrose Street and then drove another one hundred yards or so to an apartment building. The street was peppered with apartment buildings lined with trees. They paid very close attention to which one it was. Sally wrote down the address as they drove by the entrance and saw him disappear behind the front door. Bart had noticed the man was of average height, probably about five feet nine, and wore a Fu-Manchu-style mustache that gave him a sinister look. He had an obvious paunch and probably weighed one hundred and sixty pounds or so. *When we meet,* Bart thought, *he should be easy to overpower.*

Much to her relief, Bart turned the corner and headed for home. As soon as they pulled into her garage she said, "Let's call Vince."

A police car sat there in front of her house. At first, when Sally was released from the hospital, Bart tried almost everything to persuade her to live at his place. But she felt so much more comfortable in her own home, despite the attack, and was eager to renew her life with her own clothes and other comfortable possessions at her beck and call. The decision was made easier when Vince offered police protection around the clock, and when Bart moved in with her.

Once they were inside her house, Bart had no sooner sat back in her soft sofa when she began to badger him.

"Let's call Vince right now."

"How about after dinner, Sally?"

"Either now, or I will call him myself!" She was animated and adamant.

"Okay, okay," he relented. "Let me just talk with him man to man."

She slipped into the kitchen but hovered near the door to be sure that she heard the conversation. He was unaware of her presence.

"How's it going, Vince? Okay, thanks, and Sally is doing fine. We wanted to report to you that we saw the little bastard at the Supermart just now, but we weren't quick enough to get his license number."

"Are you sure that he was the one?" the detective asked.

"Sally was sure. He had the small tattoo under his left ear."

"Well, that's a good start, Bart. Now we know two things."

"The first one I understand, Vince, but what's the other?"

"One is, of course, that we know he does go to your super-market, and he will probably return again. The second—equally important—fact is that he is comfortable being seen in public and doesn't suspect that any of his victims would identify him. In other words," Riley opined, "he is overconfident, just like we want him to be."

Sally stepped out of the kitchen and appeared very agitated.

"Next time we see the bastard, Vince, I promise you we will get his license plate number." Bart lied. He clearly had lied about not having the license number or Dirks' apartment address.

"Good Bart, we will need it to catch him. Have a good one, and do give my best to Sally. Glad that she's doing well."

Sally wasn't doing well at all at that point, standing directly in front of Bart, hands akimbo with a very angry look on her face. "Bart Steele, you lied to Vince. How could you? Especially on something this important. How could you?"

He had never seen her so ill-tempered, so upset.

"Sally, hear me out!"

"Don't you 'Sally' me," she replied icily.

"Please listen to me. I know what I'm doing. There is a very good reason why I didn't completely level with Vince."

"I doubt it, mister," she fumed while sitting across from him in a chair. "I can't wait to hear it," she said sarcastically. Her legs were crossed, and one was pumping up and down vigorously.

"First of all, let's look at what the police have on him. There is absolutely no evidence from his four attacks, assuming that he is the one who killed those three women, other than you who saw a tiny tattoo on his neck. The police have no forensic evidence whatsoever—no fingerprints, no DNA, no nothing. They can't arrest him based on you seeing a tattoo."

Leaning forward towards her, he took a deep breath and continued. "Even if they did, his attorney would say that it was too dark for you to see your attacker's face, but somehow you managed to see a tattoo? Do you see where I'm going here, Sal?"

"I'm starting to, Bart."

"If I give Vince this guy's license plate number, what will that accomplish? He probably stole the car and the plates, and the police could hold him maybe for a few days. When he was released, he would simply move to another state and continue his killing spree."

"I guess you're right," she said dejectedly.

"Then we would never catch him. Ever! Vince is a great law enforcement officer, I'm sure of that, and he is our friend, and he desperately wants this guy off the streets and behind bars. But he has nothing on him."

Sally moved out of her chair and sitting next to him on the sofa, took his hand in hers.

"I'm sorry, Bart. You're probably right, but what can we do about it?"

"I have a plan, but you're not going to like it."

"Try me."

"I want to stake out his apartment and see where he goes at night. If he visits a bar, I might go in and sit next to him and develop a friendship or something."

She shook her head back and forth vigorously. "No freaking way," she insisted. "He almost killed me, and I sure as hell don't want him to kill you!"

"He won't."

"Why, because you're a macho tough guy?" she exclaimed with a hint of a smile.

"No, silly. Have you seen him, and have you seen me?"

"Yes, I know you are bigger, and I know that you are a tough guy...for an older man."

"C'mon," he grimaced, "give me a break."

"Bart, he traffics in guns and knives, and you know what they say about bringing a knife to a gunfight."

"I will either befriend him or surprise him. One way or another, I will get a confession out of him."

"Well, you'll have to record it."

"Whatever it takes, hon, whatever it takes. Let me explain something to you again."

"Yes professor!"

"No, seriously," he responded to her attempted humor. And then he repeated the story about how the murderer of his daughter had walked free.

"You know that I sat in court in total disbelief," he said sadly, "because the system failed both her and me. The jury felt, after hearing from his sleazebag defense lawyers, that there was a reasonable doubt. And the bastard gave me a wink as he exited the courtroom. I will never forget it."

"I will never forget you telling me that, Bart. But did you ever find out what happened to him?"

"No," he lied. "Apparently he moved out of state and is still probably killing innocent young women."

She squeezed his hand tighter with her unbandaged left hand and could feel his anguish. "Sal," he said earnestly, "that is why we have to do this my way. Just as soon as he sees a police car looking for him to ask questions, he will leave the area. And," he declared with a solemn look on his face, "we will never have peace. We will always wonder if or when he is coming back."

She reluctantly nodded her head in agreement. "But, Bart, please let me always know what you're doing, and please be careful. He may be smaller than you, but he is dangerous, and you know he carries a knife and probably a gun with him."

"I promise you, Sally, that I will be very careful." He took her in his arms, and they held onto each other for quite a while.

The one thing that especially concerned Bart was the time-table. How long would Billy Ray choose to remain in the Fort Myers area? He could leave at any time and come back again later. No one would be the wiser. Sally and Bart could spend their remaining years always looking over their shoulders and wondering if he would strike again. Until Bart acted to rid this menace from society, they would live the rest of their lives under the Sword of Damocles. So, he knew that time was not his friend and that he had to move pretty quickly. The very next night he put on his jeans and work boots and told Sally of his plan.

"I'm going over to watch his apartment for an hour or two and see if he goes somewhere."

"I'll follow him if he does, but I will be very careful," he assured her.

"I still don't like it Bart, but I understand the rationale. Please," she beseeched him, "be very, very careful."

They kissed each other goodbye, and he was on his way. It gave him more than a degree of comfort to see a police car still sitting in front of her residence. He pulled out of Palmetto Cove Drive and onto the main road. It would be about twenty-five minutes before he reached his destination. His Toyota turned onto Montrose Street at seven twenty-five that night, and he looked for a dark area away from the streetlights but near enough the entrance to be able to see him if he left the building. The parking spot was perfect for his purposes, and he glided in and turned off the ignition. Now, it would just be a matter of waiting. He didn't see any trace of the grey Toyota but it could have been parked further up the street or even around the corner. Afraid to lose his own strategic parking spot, he hadn't scoured Montrose Street for a glimpse of the car. At nine thirty, a dark-colored Ford pick-up truck pulled up in front of 730 Montrose to let someone out. It was him! He waved to his driver and disappeared. Bart was tempted to follow the truck but decided against it. This time as he drove past the entrance to the building, his eyes were fixed on finding a certain grey Toyota. Sure enough, there it was about twenty cars in front of him on the other side of the street. Something inside of Bart wanted to damage the punk's vehicle in some way or at least flatten a tire, but those were juvenile thoughts. Such adolescent acts would only serve to warn his foe that maybe someone was after him. That would be the last thing Bart would want; he didn't want to tip him off. He must catch this scum on the sly when his antenna was not up. That would not be easy to accomplish. He waited for another fifteen minutes to see if Billy Ray would leave again. But he did not.

Driving home, Bart made the decision to return to Montrose Street the very next night. Sally heard the garage door open and was there to meet him at the kitchen door. They sat down in the kitchen, and, over coffee, discussed his activities that evening.

"I'm going again tomorrow, hon. It will be a Friday night, and I'll bet he'll go to some bar. I'll sidle up to him, sit down, and we will become best friends!"

"Bart, please tell me that you'll be careful. You're scaring me. While I agree with you on some things," she vacillated, "I still think we should call Vince."

"We can't, Sally. Even if Vince agrees with my plan, and I'll bet that deep down he would, he has to play it by the book. He is a lawman," Bart explained, "and he has to follow the law. Unfortunately, if they do, they'll never put this guy away."

"I know you're right, Bart, but I'm scared."

He reached over to give her a reassuring hug. "Hey, I've dealt with much tougher guys than this dude!"

"Maybe," she cautioned, "but they weren't armed."

If only she knew, he thought to himself. *If only she knew.*

CHAPTER 59

■ Friday morning arrived, and it was another steamy one in Southwest Florida. But then again, it always is in July. It was an especially long day for Bart Steele because his intuition told him that tonight would be the night. He did some chores around the house and ran an errand to the hardware store. Sally wanted to get something at the Supermart, but he nixed it. What if something went wrong, and, somehow, the bastard recognized her? It wasn't worth the risk, and Bart got the item for her on his way back home.

They had dinner in, and he waited impatiently until the bewitching hour of nine o'clock. He put on his jeans, work boots, and a black, long-sleeved shirt and kissed Sally goodbye. She hugged him tightly for a minute before letting go.

He arrived at Montrose Street at nine twenty and drove almost the length of it before spotting the grey Toyota. Greatly relieved, he turned around and worked his way back towards the entrance to the apartment building. He found a spot under a tree and would not be easily visible. Bart only had to wait for about fifteen minutes until the subject of his surveillance emerged from the building. There were no cars driving on the street, so he had to be especially circumspect in following his adversary. They both drove for about ten minutes before the bastard pulled off the main road and into a strip mall. Billy Ray pulled in front of a closed barbershop just a few doors down from a liquor store and stopped. Bart casually parked in a spot four spaces away without attracting any attention. As his hated foe was in the store, Bart crept up to the Toyota and knelt beside the rear left tire. He unscrewed the valve stem cover and could barely hear the air coming out of it as he pressed the metal pin inward. It seemed interminable as he continued the pressure while keeping his eyes fixed on the store. It was over within minutes, and Billy Ray was at the checkout paying for his liquor.

Bart had chosen the back left tire for a reason. He wanted to be sure that the flat tire would be visible as the driver opened his front door. As his prey walked to his car carrying a bottle of booze, Bart was careful to remain hidden behind the front passenger's side. "Oh shit, sonofabitch!!" were the words that pierced the silent night air. "Of all the fucking times for this to happen." The infuriated driver opened the trunk to get the jack and lug nut wrench and tossed in the bottle. He was in the process of loosening the tire lug nuts when a figure appeared at his side.

"Need a hand, fella?"

Without looking up, Billy Ray said, "Yeah. Thanks, I appreciate it."

"Well, how about a foot instead?" With that said, Bart unleashed a tremendous kick with his right foot. The heavy and solid work boot caught Billy Ray on the side of his jaw and sent him tumbling on his back to the ground. Bart stepped forward to finish the job. But his adversary, dazed but not unconscious, grabbed his tire wrench and whacked him on the outside of his knee. As he bellowed and bent over in pain, Billy Ray followed that up with a blow to the face, which Bart was able to deflect with his left elbow. Now, Billy Ray had the upper hand and stood up and moved forward to take advantage of it. He lashed out with a knife and found Bart's ribs but lost control of the blade, which fell to the pavement.

In serious pain from the attack, Bart had been driven up against the Toyota. He took another shot to the ribs and crumpled to the ground. Billy Ray wasted no time in climbing on top of him, forcing the wrench against Bart's throat. With both hands, the murderer tried to exert enough force to asphyxiate him. Their faces were close enough that Bart could smell Billy Ray's foul breath. He was choking and almost out of options. Bart's left side was aching and throbbing, and he had little movement from his left elbow all the way to his hand. Only the strength in his right had prevented the killer from crushing his larynx. He was in great pain and feeling dizzy. But with one last great effort, Bart thrust his forehead quickly forward in a head butt that struck his bitter enemy on the bridge of his nose. Screaming in pain, Billy Ray lost his grip on the wrench.

They both were now on their knees. Billy Ray picked up the knife and slashed Bart above the ribs and on his forearm.

Instinctively, as a defensive measure, Bart drove his fingers toward the knife-wielder's eyes and found them. Billy Ray grunted loudly with pain as he was blinded in both eyes. Bart moved forward quickly and followed up with a solid karate chop to the bridge of the nose and then a vicious chop with the back of his hand to Billy Ray's windpipe. In severe pain, unable to see, and choking, Billy Ray dropped to his knees.

"Who are you, man? What did I ever do to you?" His words were barely audible.

"I am your worst fucking nightmare, that's who I am," Bart spat out the words. "Who are you?"

When Billy Ray waited too long to answer, Bart punched him in his right cheekbone and heard it crack.

"Billy Ray Dirks," he gasped. At last, the bastard had a name. He was still on his knees and hunched over. Bart leveled his right shoulder at him and sent him down onto his back like a sack of potatoes. Straddling him with his knees pinning down both of Billy Ray's arms, Bart finally had his foe defenseless. He would have to move quickly. His eyes focused for a moment on the liquor store, and he could see the clerk on the telephone, probably calling the police. "Billy Ray, I need some answers from you, and I need them now. And if I don't like them, it isn't going to be good for you. Understand?"

His helpless adversary lay bleeding, but he nodded his head.

"Did you kill those women?"

"What women?"

Bart grabbed his nose and yanked it. And then, he picked up the knife that Billy Ray had dropped and brandished it in front of his eyes. Billy Ray was still having difficulty seeing, but he could make out the knife that was flashing in the moonlight.

"I'm, I'm, I'm not sure what you mean," he stuttered.

Bart cut him on the cheek.

"Does this help you remember? I will ask you one more time, Billy Ray. Whether you leave here in a body bag or an ambulance depends on your answer."

"Yes, okay, I killed them."

"Holly Shannon, Maryanne Meroni, and Karen Taylor?"

The murderer nodded. "Yes."

"Did you attack and try to rape and kill Sally West?"

"I'm, I'm not sure. I'm just not sure."

Bart cut him on his other cheek. "Do you remember now?"

He could now hear police sirens in the night air, and they didn't seem to be very far away from the death struggle. Bart knew that he was running out of time.

"Yes...I did, and I'm sorry about all of them." Tears formed in the killer's eyes, but Bart wasn't buying the possible histrionics. He sensed that this sadistic killer had done his handiwork before his gut told him so, and he acted on it. "Now, Billy Ray, one last question. Where are you from?"

"Golden Valley, Minnesota."

"Did you kill anyone there, too?"

"I, ah, I ah..."

Bart sliced the knife across his forehead. Billy Ray struggled to move but was helpless.

"Remember now?"

"Okay, yes, I killed a couple years ago."

"What were their names, Billy Ray?"

"Ah, I think it was Patty Post and Peter McFadin."

"You've ruined a lot of lives, haven't you, you piece of shit?"

The sirens were getting much closer.

"Tell you what I'm going to do, Billy Ray. Garbage like you doesn't deserve to live. You find a lawyer to badger some poor witness, and you go free, and then you kill again. Well, not this time."

Billy Ray's eyes, swollen and bloodshot, finally opened wide and exuded the unmistakable look of fear. Bart recognized it, and the feeling of power almost overwhelmed him. But he was tired and aching and more enervated than he could ever remember.

"Are you going to kill me?" Bart's drained, bleeding, and exhausted victim gasped.

"Yes, I am Billy Ray, and I'm going to show you the same degree of mercy you showed them." That response elicited a look of terror and hopelessness. Totally out of energy, helpless, and resigned to his fate, Billy Ray lay there quietly and awaited his punishment. As the police cars entered the strip mall, Bart plunged the knife into Billy Ray's heart, and having totally spent himself, fell almost on top of him.

Police Officer Jake Lewis was the first one to reach the scene. "Geez," he uttered, "this is a really bloody scene, and both guys seem to be dead." His partner, Officer Julie Hart, took Bart's pulse and yelled, "Hey, Sarge, this one is still alive!"

It didn't take medical personnel or a law enforcement officer to see that one of the two was very dead. Newly arrived, Sergeant Holt took a good look at the carnage and grimaced. "Wow, that's about as much blood as I've ever seen," he remarked. He assured Bart that help was on the way. An ambulance pulled up, and Bart was gingerly placed on a gurney.

"Hey," someone shouted, "I know that guy!" It was Detective Vince Riley, and he hopped into the emergency vehicle along with Bart and the paramedic. The paramedic, a young woman appearing to be in her thirties, was very efficient. She gave her patient oxygen and applied compresses to his forearm and chest area.

"This guy has lost a lot of blood, but I think he'll be okay."

Vince Riley immediately called Sally West and instructed her to meet them at the hospital. "He is going to be alright," he assured her. "Sally," he said again, "he will be okay. Let the police officer in front of your house take you there. I'm calling him right now."

At first, Bart went into intensive care. He had lost at least two or three pints. But a man his size has about twelve pints in his body, so losing three was not a life-threatening proposition.

It certainly wasn't good, but the loss wouldn't kill him. The laceration in his forearm required twenty-seven stitches, and the wound above his left ribs needed another thirty-three. Billy Ray had narrowly missed an artery near Bart's heart by only centimeters, which meant that Bart came within a little more than an inch of having an artery severed. If it had been, Bart would most likely have bled out and not even having an ambulance would have helped. His other injuries were not severe although traumatic—bruises to his left knee and elbow, where he had been hit with the tire wrench. He was lucky to be alive.

It was almost one in the morning before the doctors' work was completed and Sally and Vince Riley were allowed to see the patient. The detective had no clue what had transpired earlier or why. But Sally was sure that she did. While she and Vince had been waiting in the waiting lounge area, it all came pouring out. At first, Vince was angry and felt betrayed by both of them, but he came to understand the rationale for Bart's action plan once Sally explained it all to him.

Once in his ICU room, Sally rushed to Bart's side and held tightly onto his hand. She was initially shocked at the extent of his injuries but somewhat relieved when he gave her a weary smile.

"I'm sorry, Vince," were the first words out of Bart's mouth. "If I didn't do it my way, I knew that we would never be free of Billy Ray Dirks. By the way, that's his name."

"Well, that *was* his name," Riley corrected him with a slight wisp of a smile. "Do you feel like talking, or should we come back tomorrow?"

"I'm fine now, Vince, but why don't you and Sally get some sleep? I'll see you tomorrow." It took him less than a minute to fall into a deep sleep.

CHAPTER 60

■ "Good morning, Mr. Steele," was the nurse's greeting the next morning. She took his vital signs and administered a few pain and other medications. "How are you feeling today?"

"Feeling fine," he returned her smile, "though a little sore."

"I would imagine you are after the beating your body took."

"You should have seen the other guy," he replied with a wink.

"I heard," she acknowledged. "Someone will be here very shortly with your breakfast. Try and eat what you can to build up your strength."

It was almost ten that morning when Sally and Vince gave his door a little knock and peered inside. Bart was sitting up as best he could, but his knee and elbow throbbed. He also felt like an elephant was sitting on his chest. Detective Riley gave them a little time alone and went to the cafeteria for a cup of coffee. "I told him all about your plan, Bart. What in God's name were you thinking?"

"I was thinking about us, Sal," he responded more tartly than he should have. "I'm sorry, darling, I was just so worried about you. Are you okay?"

"I'm fine, Sal, I really am. He was even worse than we first thought. He deserved to die. I saw a chance, and I took it. Maybe

285

I was a little foolish and a bit overconfident," he conceded, "but I didn't know for sure that I would ever get another one."

"He almost killed you!"

"Yes, but he didn't."

She stroked his hand with her good one and began to sob. "I don't know what I would have done if I had lost you. I almost died when Vince called me last night," she whispered.

"I'm so sorry, Sal. I didn't want to worry you."

"What if they charge you with murder, Bart?"

"They won't."

"But it was premeditated."

"Only you and I know that. He tried to kill me, and I defended myself."

"But will that be enough?" She looked very worried.

"Of course. Self-defense is always a good defense."

At that point, Detective Riley peeked his head in the door after a gentle knock. "Feeling up to talking a bit?" he asked.

"Now is as good a time as any, Vince."

"Tell me what happened," his law enforcement friend said as he sat down in the bedside chair. "I'm going to be recording our conversation, so please start at the beginning and don't leave anything out. I will tell you when."

At that point, Sally slipped out of the room and allowed the men to talk alone.

"I'm sorry that I didn't tell you beforehand, Vince, but the information would have compromised you and put you in a pickle. That bastard had to die and a lawman like you couldn't do it."

"Sally explained that to me. Initially, I was really pissed at you, Bart, but I understand your reasoning. Mind you, I don't agree with it," he smiled, "but I understand it."

"It was the only way, Vince."

"Yeah, and you almost died. He came ever so close to killing you!"

That all said, Bart began the taped tale. "One other thing," the detective interrupted, "did you go to Billy Ray's apartment with the intent to kill him?"

"Heck no, Vince," he shaded the truth. "I just wanted to see where he hung out and what he did."

"Well, that's a relief," the detective sighed.

"But, Vince, here is the bottom line. Billy Ray admitted to me that he killed the Shannon, Meroni, and Taylor women, and that it was him who attacked Sally."

"Admitted to you or was coerced by you?"

"He actually bragged about it when he had me in a real bad position on my back. My head butt saved my life. The bastard even told me that he had killed a couple in Minnesota some years ago."

"Did he give you names?"

"Yes, but I'm not certain of them. I think it was Patty Post and Peter or something McFadin."

"Wow!" Vince Riley exclaimed. "You obtained a treasure trove of information and at the same time took a very bad guy off the streets." With that said, Detective Riley turned off the tape machine. "Vince, I have to ask you something. Is it possible that I could face a murder charge? Sally is concerned."

Detective Riley sat back and had a good laugh.

"No, seriously, Vince. She's really worried."

"Bart, there isn't a jury in North America, much less Fort Myers, that would find you guilty of murdering a scumbag like Billy Ray Dirks. Especially when the only weapons used in the fight belonged to him. So, no, you will not be charged with murder. Besides," he added, "you helped us solve two murders in Minnesota, three in Florida, and an attempted rape."

"I hope so, Vince. I hope so."

"Bart, I should probably start worrying about my job. You don't want it, do you?" They both had a long, hearty laugh.

"Vince, would you mind sending Sally in. I have some explaining to do."

She was there in a minute.

"Sal," he began somewhat sheepishly, "there are some things that I need to tell you."

"Not now, Bart, you lost so much blood, you almost died."

"No, I need to get this off my chest now."

She knew him well enough to know that he meant business. They were holding hands when he continued, and she held on tightly.

"When I'm finished telling you all this, Sally, you may not want to have anything to do with me."

Things were getting ominous now, and she was feeling very uneasy. She fidgeted in her chair and wondered where this was going.

"I have killed four people, including Billy Ray," he blurted out his confession, "but they were very bad people."

Sally West released his hand and withdrew it from the bed. She stood up and began pacing. "I know this is hard for you to hear, and it's difficult for me to tell you as well." He sensed her shock and a little hostility as well. "Hear me out, Sal," he pleaded, "and then you can leave me if you wish."

She nodded her head and was silent, but the tears were a giveaway.

Bart took a deep breath and began. "When Stephanie was murdered, my world came to an end. I couldn't eat, I couldn't sleep, and I didn't want to live. I was so distraught, and I knew that I could never go on with my life as long as there was no justice for her."

Although fidgeting nervously, her eyes showed some signs of empathy.

"When the guilty bastard Darrell Martin was found not guilty by the jury, I was beside myself. And then Sal," he began to cry,

289

"the bastard rubbed it in by winking and smiling at me on the way out of the courtroom. From that moment on, I knew I had to track him down and kill him. It was the only possible way to avenge her."

Sally was sobbing softly now but still hadn't reached back for his hand. But she continued listening.

"I finally found the lowlife at a bar and did to him what the justice system and the jury should have done." He paused for a moment and took a sip of water. "I'm not proud of what I did, but Stephanie got some justice."

"You said you killed two other people," she reminded him.

"Yes, I'm going to tell you about the others. Shortly after that incident, I was reading the paper about the death of Casey Moore, an innocent and affable black teenager." He looked at her for some kind of recognition, but there was none. "I was still feeling considerable pain over Stephanie and read about this poor kid being gunned down by his girlfriend's father."

"You know, Bart, I kind of remember. That was the case where the father was exonerated because the defense lawyer basically discredited the prosecution's witnesses. Yes, I do remember," she went on, "but the father died soon after, and bribery money was found on his body." Then, she looked right through him. "It was you, wasn't it?" Her eyes were opened wide.

"Yes, but it's not what it looks or sounds like. I didn't really kill him."

"Oh, okay. So, he just killed himself?" she said judgmentally and somewhat sarcastically.

"C'mon, Sal. When I later confronted him about it, he attacked me with a knife. We had a life-and-death struggle outside of a bar and tumbled over the bottom step. His own knife went into him, but he was breathing when I left him. And, Sal, I called it in to 911 to get an ambulance right away."

"That makes it okay then?" she mocked him.

"The Casey Moore family got redemption, and Mark Hollister got his just reward," he said somewhat triumphantly in an effort to mollify her.

"Bart, you are really pushing it," she chastised him, "but tell me about the fourth."

"Do you remember the Frank Bender case? It was very recent."

"You know I do," she nodded her head affirmatively. "He obviously murdered his wife. Everybody knew that," she said convincingly. "Did you?"

"Yes. Again, the system didn't work, and Kathy Bender's family, the Henrys, were left to grieve."

"And so that justified you killing him?"

"Yes and no," he replied.

"What the hell does that mean, Bart?" She was clearly agitated as she admonished him.

"Yes, he had it coming, and no, God didn't grant me the right to kill him."

"Well, at least we agree on that!"

"Do you want to know how I did it?"

"Of course not!" she exclaimed. "Well, maybe..."

And then he explained how Frank Bender spent the last few moments of his life.

"Have you told Vince?"

"No, not yet."

"You know that you'll have to tell him."

"Yes, I know," he said dejectedly.

"And they will send you to prison." She was teary but in control.

"Tell me something I don't know, Sal."

"I can't tell you how disappointed I am in you Bart Steele. You have totally jeopardized our life together. I don't know if I can live with a murderer." She spoke in a staccato cadence. "What makes you different from Billy Ray?"

"If you don't know the answer to that, Sally," it was his turn to admonish her, "then we don't have anything else to talk about."

She was hurt by his abruptness and turned away. Brushing her tears aside, she got up and brusquely left the room. *Well, that went well,* he castigated himself.

Having seen Sally leave his room with tears running down her cheeks, Vince Riley appeared at his bedside with a puzzled look on his face.

"I told her the whole enchilada, Vince, and she is furious with me. I've destroyed one important friendship, so I might as well destroy another."

"Bart, you're not making sense. Talk to me."

"I will soon, and you won't like it any better than Sally did."

"What's up with you? Too many meds?"

"I wish it were that, Vince. What I told you earlier was the truth, but it wasn't the entire truth," he confessed.

Bart clearly had his detective friend's interest. Vince could detect the change in his demeanor; the expression on Vince's face had turned solemn.

"What's the matter, Bart, it can't be that bad."

"Unfortunately, it is, my friend," he responded dejectedly. "There is more to tell, Vince."

CHAPTER 61

■ Vince Riley stared out of the window for a moment and then inched in closer to Bart.

"Oh boy! Bart, you're not making this easy. Perhaps I won't record this part," the detective announced.

"Vince, you were right about me all along."

The detective raised a quizzical eyebrow.

"I killed Darrell Martin," Bart confessed. "I was so distraught when he walked free despite murdering my Stephanie. And then," he continued as his voice started to crack, and the tears began running down his cheeks, "the bastard winked and smiled at me on his way out of the courtroom. Can you imagine, Vince? He actually winked at me! I completely lost it and charged him, but a burly bailiff or police officer, I forget which, stopped me. And I'll never forget what he said: 'I know how you feel, Mr. Steele, but you can't do it this way.' That's what gave me the idea for revenge."

"I know, Bart, I know."

"You mean you know that I killed him?" Bart was astonished.

"Yeah, it was obvious to me that you had."

"We weren't so friendly back then, but how come you didn't go after me?"

"For one thing, Bart, we had no proof. For another, I put myself in your shoes. My Laura means everything to me, and I just knew that I would have done the same thing. As a law enforcement officer," he went on, "that is hearsay, and I would appreciate you never telling anyone about this conversation."

"Thanks, my friend. I really appreciate your candor and, of course, I would never say a word to anyone."

"Thanks."

"But, Vince, that is only part of it." Once again, the detective raised his eyebrows.

"I felt good about avenging her murder," the confessor continued, "but I guess I should have felt contrition. I didn't. And then I read about Casey Moore's murder. By then, I had a cancer diagnosis and was told I had maybe six good months to live. That combined with losing my only daughter turned me into an avenger. What did I have to lose, Vince? The cancer death sentence made me think that I could do something positive, helpful before I left this earth."

"So, it was you who killed Mark Hollister?"

"Yes, but not the way you think, Vince."

"If you're feeling well enough to continue, Bart, I am eager to listen."

"I called Mark Hollister and falsely told him that I had witnessed him killing Casey Moore. I threatened to tell the police if he didn't come up with ten thousand dollars. When he agreed to pay me off, I knew that he was guilty. But I knew that in the courtroom that day."

"You attended the Hollister trial? You were there?"

"Yes, I was there, and I saw Hollister wink at his friends right after he was acquitted. It was the same wink that Darrell used."

"Then what?" Vince Riley prompted him.

"Hollister showed up at Hogan's, which was the drop off point. I was only going to rough him up, leave him unconscious with the ten thousand scattered around. But he came armed with a knife and tried to kill me. He slashed at me but missed. I was able to overpower him. As we were grappling over the back steps of Hogan's, he fell, and his knife went deep into his stomach. Suddenly," Bart continued, "there were lights and noises all around me, and I just tossed the money on him and ran. But Vince," he insisted, "Mark Hollister was still breathing when I left him, and he was the one who attacked me!"

"Did you call for an ambulance or 911?"

"Yes, but I didn't leave my name. I used a burner phone."

"I must admit," Detective Riley said, "that I didn't figure that you were in on that one."

"Vince, I'm not done yet." The detective leaned forward.

"And then I read about Virgil Stassen walking free after killing Kelly Richards because he confessed before his lawyer arrived."

"That's the law, Bart."

"I know, I know, Vince. But it was so obvious that he had killed her. When I saw him in the restroom that day after I saw a movie, I just saw red. I wanted to kill him for the Richards family, but I just couldn't do it. He was the perfect target just standing at the urinal next to me, just doing his business. I shoved his head into the wall hard and dragged him over to the toilet stall and smacked him around."

"Well, you really did do a number on him, Bart. He still has trouble hearing out of one of his ears."

"I feel guilty at times about it, Vince, but then I think about Kelly Richards and her family, and the feeling passes. I also didn't tell Sally about it."

"So, Bart, I'm feeling like my Catholic priest today, listening to your confession. But you are not surprising me. I figured that the Stassen attack was probably you."

"Well, I have one last story for you."

"Go ahead and shoot. Let me have it."

"The Frank Bender drowning was on me."

"I thought it was Bart. All along, I thought it was you."

"How come?"

"The photo placed you there, and I thought it was more vigilante work on your part."

"Again, Vince, I'm not trying to excuse what I did, but he was so obviously guilty of killing his wife."

"But that wasn't for you to decide, Bart."

"I know, but it was so unfair. Her family suffered just like I suffered."

"So how exactly did it go down, Bart?"

"I saw him on the beach that day, and he wandered way out in the water to jump waves. I casually walked out towards him but was careful not to attract any attention. I was at least fifty feet or so to one side and at least twenty feet behind him. I stayed under water until I was really close, and then I put a head lock on him and sat down in the water."

"How did you get out without being noticed?"

"I swam underwater for at least eighty feet before I came up. No one ever noticed me, and I casually walked back to the shoreline and on the beach."

"Bart, I have to ask you this. I understand what drove you to be an avenger or vigilante of sorts, but are you now done with it? Are you done with this life? Can I, as a law enforcement officer, know that from now on you will leave these things to us and the justice system?"

"I was just going to get to that, Vince. I know what drove me to be an avenger, but that part is over now. Perhaps it was the grim reality of it all with Billy Ray, or maybe something else. I don't know. But I am done with it. I also recognize, Vince, that you are going to have to arrest me. Sally will take it hard, but I stepped way over the line. I'm very sorry about it and, most of all, I'm sorry about deceiving you. You are a true friend. But I suspect," he added disconsolately, "that I have lost both of you."

"Bart, I'm not going to tell you that this isn't serious, but your friendships with Sally and me are not at stake here."

"Thanks, Vince, but I'm afraid that Sally's is."

"Let me talk with her, and then I'll send her back in. Clearly, she is free to make up her own mind," he continued, "but I will do what I can."

"Vince," he said as the detective was at the door, "thanks, thanks so much."

Bart Steele had his lunch at his bedside and quasi-read the newspaper. He couldn't concentrate. Vince had been gone for at least thirty to forty minutes. Then, suddenly there was Sally, walking towards him. Her eyes were all puffy and red; obviously, she had been crying.

"I'm sorry, Bart. I'm so sorry." She was clearly a bit shaken as she sat on the edge of his bed and clutched his hand with her good one.

"So am I, Sal, and I wish it hadn't come to this."

"Vince told me that you carried things too far but that you only wanted justice. I can understand about Stephanie, and then I was assaulted—and all those other families. I understand."

"I did take it too far. It was like I couldn't help myself. Part of me was in the Shannon, Meroni, Taylor, and Moore families. Part of me was in the Henry family. When you lose your daughter," with tears running down his cheeks, "you have lost a part of yourself forever."

299

"I know, I know," she tried to soothe him.

"I guess I screwed up my life," he said morosely, "but I just tried to right a few wrongs. My victims were bad people, but I had no right to do what I did to them."

"Bart, I'm not happy about what you did, but I understand why you did it. Vince helped me get there," she explained, "and I'm so grateful that he did."

"Sal, that means the world to me."

As she laid her head on his chest, she whispered, "I'm with you wherever it goes, whatever happens." She looked up and saw that the detective had joined them. Sally got up to leave, but Vince motioned her to stay put.

"I've been thinking," he began. "Here's what we have: Bart killed a very nasty man in Billy Ray but was really defending himself in the process. Because he encountered the monster before he could kill again, we now know that he was the one who murdered Holly Shannon, Maryanne Meroni, and Karen Taylor. The parents of Patty Post and Peter McFadin in Golden Valley, Minnesota, also know that their children were killed by him. Without Bart, all of those parents would have no closure. If it hadn't been for Bart, the Henry family would always carry the special pain of knowing that her killer went free. If not for Bart," he went on while looking at Sally, "you would always be looking behind you, fearful that your attacker was lurking behind the next door or bush."

"Thanks, Vince, but I know that I was very wrong to take matters into my own hands."

"You were, Bart, in the eyes of the law, but not in the sad eyes of all those grieving families. You were probably viewed as a godsend to them."

"But, but, what about our conversation where I confessed to you that I had killed two people and two others had died in fights with me?"

"What conversation, Bart? I remember you mumbling some things to me, but you were almost delirious from your pain meds. I couldn't really understand anything you said." Sally's eyes lit up like a Christmas tree, and she began crying again. Bart soon followed.

"How can we ever thank you, Vince?"

"You just did."

"Oh, by the way," Vince added while standing in the doorway with a grin, "I want to be the best man at your wedding!"

ACKNOWLEDGEMENTS

■ We live in a marvelously connected time when there are so many unprecedented and valuable resources available through the internet to any writer. I am indebted to many of them, especially Wikipedia, the Biography and History Channels, Criminal Defense News (Axelrod and Associates), *The National Law Review, The Guardian, The American Prospect, The Week, Crime,* ERA and Women's History.

My gratitude is further extended to a number of individuals who read the manuscript and offered constructive advice and encouragement. They include Clark Bell, Don Gilmore, Jim Vaules, Tony Romanovich, Bob Oswald, Bill Simpson and Ed Smoragiewicz.

Very special thanks to Kiki Keating for her determination in finding the right publisher; to Janice Beetle and Jaime Morton of the KikiNetwork team for their ideas to improve the manuscript; and to Amy Herzog and Tessa Avila at Why Not Books, for accepting this project and bringing it to publication.

I am especially indebted to my wife, Michele, for typing the manuscript (and its many edits and versions), and for her excellent editing skills and valuable suggestions. This has definitely been a team effort.

ABOUT THE AUTHOR

■ Tim Norbeck worked in healthcare for 53 years and was, most recently, the CEO of a national healthcare-related foundation. He is recognized for having significant expertise on many diverse issues impacting America's healthcare system. During his career, Tim enjoyed the opportunity to speak on behalf of physicians in all 50 states. He was president of The Physicians Foundation and led the organization as CEO from 2006 until his retirement in 2020. His numerous writings, articles and speeches have appeared in a variety of industry-related and other publications including periodic blogs for Forbes.com and Vital Speeches.

Tim began writing novels near his retirement and his first, *Two Minutes*, was published in 2018. His third novel, *Almost Heaven*, will be published in late 2022.

A Buffalo, New York, native who also spent more than 30 years in Connecticut as the state medical society's CEO, Tim is an avid tennis player and history aficionado. He lives with his wife, Michele, and rescue dog, Trouper, in Bonita Springs, Florida.

Made in United States
Orlando, FL
11 June 2022

18708369R00188